The Bachelor of the Albany

Marmion Wilard Savage

Savage, Marmion W.

THE

BACHELOR OF THE ALBANY.

BY THE
AUTHOR OF "THE FALCON FAMILY."

———

"The most ordinary cause of a single life is liberty, especially in certain self-pleasing and humorous minds, which are so sensible of every restraint, as they will go near to think their girdles and garters to be bonds and shackles.—BACON's *Essay on Marriage and Single Life.*

———

NEW YORK:
HARPER & BROTHERS, PUBLISHERS,
82 CLIFF STREET.
1848.

DEDICATION.

My dear Lady Morgan,

I am induced, both by your friendship and your genius, to present you with this "airy nothing." The criticism of great talents is always gentle, and an offering dictated by sentiments of affection is safe from scrutiny into its intrinsic value. You will not slight even this trifle, but accept it graciously for the sake of

THE AUTHOR.

28th September, 1847.

CONTENTS.

CHAPTER XIII.

CHAPTER XIV.

CHAPTER XV.

CHAPTER XVI.

THE BACHELOR OF THE ALBANY.

CHAPTER I.

> The sense to value riches, with the art
> T' enjoy them, and the virtue to impart,
> Not meanly, nor ambitiously pursued,
> Not sunk by sloth, nor raised by servitude;
> To balance fortune by a just expense,
> Join with economy, magnificence;
> With splendor charity, with plenty health:
> O, teach us, Bathurst! yet unspoil'd by wealth!
> That secret rare, between th' extremes to move,
> Of mad good-nature, and of mean self-love.
>
> POPE's *Epistles.*

Spread, Narrowsmith and Co.—Picture of a fine Family—The Reverend Mr.
Owlet—Character of Mr. Spread—The Model House in Abercromby
Square—The Spreadlings—The celebrated Mrs. Martin—Revolutions of
Mrs. Spread's Nursery—Miss Stanley, the Churchwoman—Miss Picker-
ing, the Jobber.

Not very many years back, there existed, at Liverpool, the opulent mercantile firm of Spread, Narrowsmith, and Company. No
account of their transactions or enterprises is necessary, as with
their commercial history, the sailings and returns of their argosies,
we have nothing to do.

It is not in the estate of poverty alone that men become acquainted with " strange bed-fellows." There never sat two men, on opposite sides of the same desk, of characters so utterly at variance

as Mr. Spread and his partner. Antonio was not more unlike Shylock. The former realized your ideal—indeed, almost the dramatic conception of a British merchant, familiar to playwrights, and cheered by the galleries: generous, enlightened, independent, upright in all his dealings, as unostentatious as he was bounteous in his charities. The other had the acquisitive propensities, without the liberal spirit of commerce; a man of sordid principles, and who acted up to them; miserly and pitiful, hard and grasping as a vice, a man to squeeze a pippin, or skin a flint, who to save one sixpence would do a shabby action, and to make another would do something shabbier still. To this respectable personage was united, in unholy wedlock, a woman, with whom he was as fitly yoked as ever a husband was to a wife. Mrs. Narrowsmith was just the consort for a Harpagon or a Gripus; she saved candles'-ends, pinched her servants, wrangled about kitchen-stuff, dyed her gowns, turned her petticoats, darned her carpets, outdid Ovid's Metamorphoses with an old coat or a tarnished curtain, and never allowed a fire in her house (except the nominal one for culinary uses) from the first breath of May till the first gale of November. But enough of the Narrowsmiths for the present. We shall meet them again, and oftener than it is agreeable to meet people like them.

It is not to be supposed that between such a family and the amiable and worthy Spreads there subsisted any cordial intimacy. The thing was out of the question. Independently of the strange and objectionable people who composed such society as the Narrowsmiths cultivated, the bare sight of Mrs. Narrowsmith would make Mrs. Spread and her daughters shudder; in warm weather Mr. Spread used pleasantly to wish himself in his partner's kitchen; a dinner in Rodney-street was the heaviest penalty that could have been inflicted upon the comfortable people of Abercromby Square, and the next punishment—in point of severity—was the necessity of returning the entertainment. This excruciating interchange of civilities seldom, however, took place more than once a-year; the wonder was how the Narrowsmiths ever made up their minds to give their annual bad dinner, and it was no less surprising how the Spreads survived to return it with a good one.

Family pictures are generally dull affairs, but we must give a sketch of the Spreads, and it will be altogether the artist's fault if it is not a pleasing one, for they were both physically and morally a "fine family," and all over the world, although Byron said it with a sneer, such a family is a "fine thing."

"*Places aux dames!*" In the foreground stands the tall, comely figure of the mother of the family; her cheek still blooms, though her summer is nearly over; her form tends to luxuriance, her features are radiant with intelligence and benignity. Her hair is fair and abundant, her eye mild and gray, her voice soft and distinct, her mien dignified, her deportment quiet. She looks as if she loved books, music, pictures, flowers. Her tastes are obviously healthy and elegant; her mind pure and strong; her heart full of all the womanly affections, one of those rare prizes in the matrimonial lottery not always drawn by men who deserve them as well as Mr. Spread did.

The eldest daughter, Augusta, was very nearly the fac-simile of what her mother had been in her girlhood. The same height, the same style of figure, saving the matronly exuberances; her hair perhaps a shade darker; but she had her mother's firm and graceful deportment exactly, and as to their voices, it was next to impossible, notwithstanding the disparity of years, to distinguish them asunder. Elizabeth, the second, was both shorter and plumper. Her hair was nearly black; her voice a tone or two deeper than her sister's, and perhaps just a little husky, but not disagreeably so; her cheek was pale, unless when exercise, gayety, or other excitement flushed it. One quality she had, for which some blamed, and some commended her: she was remarkably still and silent; few beyond her own family knew the extent of her information or the worth of her character. Of a religious family, she was the member who made religious subjects most her study and her care; but the milk-white hind, the type of Catholicity, was more her favorite than the panther, the emblem of Church-of-Englandism. Elizabeth was on her way to Rome, and had just performed half the journey, for she had reached—Oxford!

And here we must let the reader into a little piece of secret history, that is to say, it was a secret to all the world except the Spreads themselves, and one individual more. Elizabeth was affianced to a young clergyman of the name of Owlet, a fellow—and an odd fellow—of Baliol, and a minor canon of Salisbury. Owlet was a man of much learning, eccentric habits, and Puseyitical opinions. He doted on the dark ages, indeed was so fond of obscurity that he was hardly ever seen or known to be abroad except in the twilight. He was particularly bent upon reviving the Mystery Plays and Moralities, and had quarreled with his dean for objecting to the dramatic representation of the story of Balaam in his cathedral. With Mr. Spread's strong sense of the ridiculous, he could not but smile at the absurdities of his contemplated son-in-law; but, with all those absurdities, Owlet had gained the affections of his daughter, and as he had also made a conquest of a tractarian peeress, who had a snug living in her gift, and had promised to bestow it upon him, Mr. Spread saw no reason for opposing a union on which the hearts of the principal parties were resolutely bent. The reverend gentleman was to be inducted into his benefice in a few months, and it was settled that the wedding should take place immediately afterward.

Mr. Spread was one of the freshest and handsomest men of fifty in England. His complexion was florid, his nose aquiline, his chin double, nay, triple; a perpetual pleasantry seemed to be playing about his mouth, and he had that kind of an eye that seems to be always looking out for somebody to do a service to, or something to say a gay or good-natured thing of. In person, he was of considerable volume, but the protuberance was not *a parte ante*, as in the aldermanic and episcopal conformations; he carried his head erect, and at the same time somewhat advanced, so that his figure had a slight resemblance to a crescent, with the convexity behind, and this perhaps was the reason that he began to carry a cane long before his limbs were conscious of any diminution of their vigor and elasticity. The manners of Mr. Spread were a little formal, slightly Grandisonian and Sir Rogerish. For a moment you thought him pompous, but directly he smiled or talked, the amenity of his eye or the hilarity of his voice entirely removed the impression. He dressed well, with a tendency to the fashions gone by, rather than to the modes of the day. For instance, he always appeared in a white cravat, and never wore a frock-coat, or carried his watch in his waistcoat pocket. To these few personal details we have only to add that he was short-sighted, and wore a ponderous double eye-glass, resolvable into a pair of spectacles, and pendent from his neck by a gold chain of corresponding massiveness.

Mr. Spread was a model of a man of business; activity without bustle, dispatch without hurry, form without punctilio, order without rigidness, dexterity without craft, vigilance without suspicion. Business inundated without overwhelming him, and care neither corroded his mind nor sat on his brow. It was wonderful with what perfect serenity and ease he managed the multiplicity of affairs, private and public, in which he either was involved of necessity, or spontaneously engaged himself. He felt as every man ought to feel, that he had duties outside his counting-house, and obligations to society, as well as to his wife and children. He never shrunk from any of the responsibilities of life; he was a magistrate, a juror, an elector, and at one time had, at a great personal inconvenience, even consented to go into parliament, because the constituency of a large manufacturing town insisted upon having him to represent them, and his refusal to gratify their wishes would have endangered the success of the liberal interest.   Then, if a relation or an old school-fellow desired to name him his executor, or was anxious that, after his decease, Mr. Spread should be the legal guardian, as well as the hereditary friend of his children, to refuse to act in either capacity would have been utterly foreign to his character.   Nor was this all; he was (perhaps Mrs. Spread had helped to make him so) a lover of literature and art, for ever ready to aid with his purse, and, what was to him still more valuable, his time, in the establishment or direction of any society or institution calculated to advance science, or diffuse exalted tastes and sterling information through the country.   Of giving his countenance to benevolent undertakings, he was more chary; he hated the false philanthropy that creates distress with one hand while it relieves it with the other; he objected to paying Paul out of the robbery of Peter; held that there was no more difficult problem than to help the poor without sowing the seeds of pauperism; but of all things what he most deprecated in disposing of the funds at our command for charitable uses, was their investment in sentimental speculations or romantic schemes, to make bad Christians of Gipsies or Jews, confer the blessings of episcopacy upon the South Sea islanders, or discover the lost tribes of Israel in the tents of the Calmuc Tartars.   He thought that there was ignorance and irreligion enough at our own doors to employ both our purses and our piety; and that the home department of England and Ireland ought to be tolerably well administered, both in civil and ecclesiastical affairs, before it could be our duty to interfere either in the secular or the spiritual concerns of Madagascar or Tahiti.

There was but one son, and his name was Philip; he reminded some people of his father, some more of his mother.   He was of an ardent and volatile temperament—studious by fits and starts; now a paroxysm of study, now a collapse into utter inactivity.   He took up a subject, pursued it keenly for a week, then dropped it forever. He had read a good deal, inconsecutively and superficially.   Sometimes his rage was for science, French mathematics, German metaphysics; botany to-day, geology to-morrow.   There was not a little of juvenile coxcombry about him; he had a knack of picking up languages, and was a little too fond of parading his acquaintance with foreign tongues, when plain English would have served his turn. The excuse for him was, that he was very young, and certainly one ought not to be hard upon the faults of youth, when they lean to the side of letters, as those of Philip did; besides, he inherited his father's softness of disposition, and sterling worth. Everybody was fond of him; and he was particularly a favorite with women. Your very shrewd women would certainly smile at his unseasonable displays of learning, and your fastidious women would ridicule his little provincial *gaucheries*; but he was a general favorite notwithstanding, and unfortunately he was only too susceptible of the tender impressions made by the fair sex. His life was a series of little desultory attachments, or flirtations, for he was as *volage* in love as he was in literature, and changed his beauties as often as his books.

The house of the Spreads was a model house: not a model of splendor and luxury, but of respectability and comfort. It was the freshest, warmest, brightest, airiest, cleanliest, snuggest house that ever you set your foot in. The defects of its light were those of the climate; and if its atmosphere was not always the purest, its corruptions were chargeable upon the general atmosphere of Liverpool. It was obvious at a glance that good sense and correct taste were the regulating principles of all the household arrangements. You could have inferred the mind in the drawing-room from the order in the kitchen; and argued, from the cook or the housemaid, up to Mrs. Spread herself. There is nothing more characteristic of the residences of people of true refinement than what may be called harmony of style; offices in the ratio of the house; servants enough, and no more; liveries, equipages, plate, furniture, decorations, all in keeping with each other, and adjusted to the proprietor's rank and fortune. The Spreads understood this perfectly; they were free from the two vulgarities of wealth—superfluity and display; a quiet elegance and a liberal economy distinguished their establishment in all its departments. Then those departments never came into collision; there was no confusion of jurisdictions, or clash of offices; there was a place for every thing, and every thing was in its place. The butler did not groom the horses, nor did the groom open the wine; the cook never made the beds, the housemaids never dressed the dinner; the kitchen did not intrude into the hall, and the nursery was never known to invade the parlor.

The mention of the nursery reminds us that a notice of the junior branches of the family has very improperly been omitted. There is nothing small to the eye of philosophy, and that of history

ought not to be more disdainful.   There were Spreadlings as well
as Spreads; by no means insignificant members of the household,
and the more to be respected because they did not "come in after
dinner."   There was an octonarian, named Theodore ; and the two
minims of the fair sex—Katherine, a demure, little hussy ; and
Maria, who was more a tom-boy ; both promised to be pretty, and
as they were brought up in rigid habits of veracity, the reader will
be so kind as to presume that they kept their word.   They were now
undergoing, in common with their small brother, all the educational
processes of the age, under the energetic direction of the celebrated
Mrs. Martin, author of a work on the "Godmothers of England," a
lady eminent for her skill in mastering young mistresses and gov-
ernessing young masters.   It need hardly be stated that, in a family
like the Spreads, the instructress and ruler of their children occupied no degrading situation.   So far was Mrs. Spread from requiring her either to make or to mend the clothes of her pupils, that she
would infinitely sooner have performed these, or any other menial
offices herself, than imposed them on Mrs. Martin, who, indeed,
was not a lady who would have brooked a treatment derogatory to
her state and dignity.

Mrs. Spread's nursery had passed, as greater states do, under a succession of administrations: there had been "all the talents" and "all
the follies ;" alternately a Queen Log and a Queen Stork.   There
had been one or two " shave beggars," ladies who undertook to teach
before they had been taught themselves, and to learn to rule at the
cost of their pupils and their parents.   But the most remarkable
governments were those of Miss Stanley and Miss Pickering.   The
former thought of nothing but the church and the church-catechism;
it was church, church, church, from Monday to Sunday, and from
Sunday back again to Monday.   She corrected her pupils with the
collects and punished them with the Psalms.   She was so thorough
a churchwoman that she would have upset a kingdom, not to say a
nursery, to maintain even a church-mouse.   At length Mrs. Spread
had good reason to suspect that, out of respect for the ordinances
of the church, Miss Stanley must have been privately married, for
she became as ladies wish to be who love their lords, when they
have lords to love; and in the fullness of time (but not in Abercromby Square) was this examplary churchwoman in a condition
to be churched herself.   Whether she was or not is another question.

Miss Pickering had a great many good points about her ; active,
useful, clever, a great deal too clever—that was her weak side ; she

jobbed a little in books and stationery, and was convicted of peculation in the children's wardrobe. After she had been cashiered for these malfeasances, it turned out that she was the daughter of an Irish gentleman who had, in his time, been treasurer of his county, which accounted, to Mr. Spread's satisfaction, for the proficiency of his progeny in the art and mystery of jobbing.

CHAPTER II.

O rus, quando ego te aspiciam ?   Quandoque licebit,
Nunc veterum libris, nunc somno, et inertibus horis,
Ducere solicitæ jucunda oblivia vitæ ?   HORACE.

Dissolution of the Firm—Mr. Spread's Motives—Passion for Rural Life—Mr.
Spread's Parliamentary Habits—A Domestic Parliament—Who constituted
the Upper House—Portrait of Mrs. Martin—Breakfast Talk on Bees—
Philip Spread upon Insect-Geometry—Triumph of the Country Party—
Regrets of the Mother of the Family.

ABOUT the period when this story commences, a measure was in
agitation of no less importance than the dissolution of the mercantile
firm mentioned in the last chapter.   The desire for this change
originated with Mr. Spread.   In the first place, he had realized an
ample income, with what he considered a sufficient provision for his
wife and children.   He was no millionaire, nor was it his ambition
to be so ; satisfied to live and move in the temperate zone of life,
equally removed from the frigid and the torrid, the extremes of
poverty and affluence.   Money thus having always been, with him,
an object only desirable with a view to its rational expenditure, not
intrinsically entitled to his homage and devotion, why was he to
protract his commercial life beyond the period when (his moderate
aim having been successful) his tastes prompted, and his duty per-
mitted him, to withdraw from the pursuits of trade ?   Other considerations, possibly, also influenced him.   The character of his
partner was so utterly uncongenial with his own as to lead to frequent differences, if not collisions, between them, more frequent
than Mr. Spread could reconcile either with his notions of the
efficiency of a mercantile company, or with his personal repose,
which essentially depended upon his being in peace and harmony
with every one about him.   Besides, a passion for rural life had for
several years been springing up, by small degrees, in the several
members of his family.   Civilization has two contrary movements ;
its first impulse is out of the woods townward, turning swains into
citizens and burghers ; its second direction is back to the woods and
fields, changing the citizen into the swain again.   For a considerable

time the rural propensities of the merchant's household, checked by
the necessities of their position, discovered themselves only in a
little speculative chat at dinner, or a day-dreamy dialogue at breakfast.   Whether or not the tall Augusta and the plump Elizabeth,
after retreating to their pillows, prattled *more puellarum* about
myrtles and roses of their own planting—whether or not they built
picturesque cottages in the air, and stocked ideal green-houses with
flowers of all hues from the luxuriant nurseries of fancy, is of course
only known to the sylphs of their bed-chamber, or the fays that
sentineled their bower.   The sentiment, however, was of old growth,
and when the time came for indulging, or at least expressing it freely,
it seemed (as is often observed in the progress of *public* opinion) to
start into life a full-grown feeling, past debate, and ripe for legislation.

What, indeed, is there to attach any man to a place like Liverpool, after he has retired from the docks, and bid a long farewell to
the counting-house?   When a merchant has completed his career
in a large manufacturing or commercial town, he ought to leave it at
his earliest convenience, for a town of that description is one of the
most incommodious places in the world for a man to saunter about
in, with his hands in his pockets, let them be replenished never so
well.   As long as you move in any of the great thoroughfares of life,
at the same rate with other people, you proceed smoothly and
agreeably enough; but diminish your speed, and you experience a
shock directly; stand still, and the next instant you are jostled and
perhaps flung into the mire.   It is one of those laws that are common to intellectual and physical movement.   It will neither do to
bustle on fashionable promenades or lounge in the resorts of business.

We have mentioned that Mr. Spread sat in parliament at one
period, the representative of a borough constituency in Lancashire.
He occupied the seat only so long as he felt it to be his public duty
to retain it; it materially interfered with his private affairs, and he
could ill brook the long separation from his family which the con-
scientious discharge of his senatorial functions involved.   In fact he
was essentially a family-man, who was never at home in clubs, and
could not domesticate himself in hotels or lodgings.   While he continued, however, in the House of Commons, there was no more
assiduous or zealous member in that miscellaneous assembly; and
when he withdrew from it, he had become so attached to its forms
and usages, that he carried some of them away with him into retirement, and adopted the playful practice in his family, when the case
was one that allowed of it, of considering his wife and children as a

little senate, formally putting the question to them, and deciding it in one way or the other by a majority of votes; sometimes, in minor matters, even taking the suffrages of the little estates of the nursery, which (not, perhaps, without a satiric touch intended for the Chamber of Peers) he designated the Upper House.

An instance of this pleasant usage, which occurred in relation to the change of life which Mr. Spread contemplated making, as soon as his commercial career should terminate, affords a fair opportunity for introducing the reader into the bosom of this worthy family.

They were assembled one morning in full Witenagemote, with their good looks and their good appetites; the breakfast-table laughing with china and silver, the side-board covered with manly fare, and a glorious fire bouncing and blazing on the hearth, for it was the decline and fall of the year; and at the hour of nine on a November morning in England, the sun in all his glory is not to be compared to sea-coal.

Mrs. Martin was sitting there in her wonted place of honor, as stately and important as if she was the *mater-familias* herself.   Mr. Spread paid her profound respect, not unmixed with gallant attentions, at which Mrs. Spread would now and then affect to be very much piqued indeed.   Mrs. Martin was a woman to command respect, and not too old, let me tell you, to inspire sentiments, also, of a gayer description.   She was not handsome, but handsome enough; middle-aged and middle-sized, a pair of vigilant black eyes, the very eyes for a school-room, a voluble delivery, an animated and peremptory manner, altogether a woman admirably qualified for the office she held, except, perhaps, that she was a little too fond of theory and system-building.   She was attired in dark-green silk; a small lace cap, which neither concealed nor was intended to conceal her black hair, enhanced the dignity of her aspect; the red cashmere shawl over her shoulders was a present from Mrs. Spread, and had cost more guineas than governesses in other houses receive for a year's stipend.

Mr. Spread, having amply discussed some Scotch haddock, and reviewed several marmalades, without dipping into them (no uncommon practice with reviewers of other things), desired his son to hand him the honey, quoting at the same time (for he was wont to be classical at breakfast) a line from the Georgics of Virgil, on the subject of the bee's confectionery.

"It is odd," said Phllip, "that Milton should have omitted honey among the dishes which Eve serves up to the angel Raphael, at the first *fête champetre* of which we have any record."

"Milton bore the bees a grudge," said Mr. Spread, "on account of their monarchical form of government."

"I suspect," said Mrs. Spread, "it was rather because the monarchy goes in the *female line*."

"Milton was a misogynist," said Philip.

"What's that?" inquired his father, affecting ignorance, "What's a misogynist?"

"A woman-hater, sir."

"Then why not say woman-hater, Philip?"

It was a slight tap, but Philip colored, and made no reply, having no good reply to make.

"I wonder have the French bees a Salic law?" said Elizabeth. It was her first remark that morning, and her father patted her cheek and called her his "loquacious little Bessie?"

The bee was a favorite subject of Mrs. Martin's, and she now expatiated upon it with her usual fluency, holding up the bee-hive as a model school for all the virtues; and thinking, perhaps, what a capital queen-bee she would have made herself. She would certainly have made the drones stir themselves; whether or not she could sting, too, upon fit occasion, probably Theodore knew better than any one else.

Philip listened rather impatiently to Mrs. Martin, as he was anxious to hold forth himself. He considered the bee as an architect and a geometer, an insect Jones, or a winged Apollonius. "As soon," he added, with considerable pomposity, "as soon as we have bees of our own, I shall prepare a paper for the British Association on the mathematics of entomology."

"That's the fourth paper, Philip, love," said his mother, "that you have pledged yourself to prepare for the British Association: *nous verrons*."

Mrs. Martin would now have willingly gone into the subject of indecision of character, but Mr. Spread anticipated her, by saying—

"I doubt very much, Phil, if this house, or any house in Liverpool, exactly answers the conditions which Virgil considers indispensable to an apiary."

"Of course, I mean," said Philip, "when we have got our *maison de campagne*. That's a settled point, you know, sir."

"Is it, indeed?" said the amiable father, doing his best to look mysterious and doubtful.

"Settled, papa," said Augusta and Elizabeth, simultaneously, each laying her hand on one of his shoulders, while she spoke.

A charming picture it would have made—that fine, benevolent gentleman, the worthiest of all the sons of British commerce, seated at his generous breakfast, radiant with pleasantry and goodness, between these two lovely and beloved daughters, cherished by their affection, and exulting in their beauty.

"Somewhat precipitate legislation, girls," he replied, trying to look cold as William Pitt, while he glowed with the ardor of Charles James Fox—"Precipitate legislation," he repeated, for it was his habit to reiterate his words, when he was particularly tickled by any fancy, or when any phrase that he employed pleased him.

"The law of the land," cried Philip.

"Don't leave us, Mrs. Martin." The hour had come for the resumption of that lady's scholastic duties, and she had risen to retire, surrounded by her vassals, with the dignity of a princess royal. "You are one of the states of the realm—ay, and I dare say upon this occasion those little sluts of the shire—and you, too, Master Theodore, will expect to be allowed to vote."

"The villa, the villa!" cried the representatives of the nursery, with one accord.

"A trio of facetious urchins," said Mr. Spread; "what, if *la reine s'avisera?* I should like to hear what the queen says."

"I suppose I ought to act the patriot queen," said Mrs. Spread, gravely, "and identify myself with the feeling of my people."

"*Vive la reine!*" cried the whole little senate, and in a few minutes its several members were dispersed in boudoirs, studies, and school-rooms, over the whole house. The faintest audible sigh escaped from the charming mother, in the midst of the acclamations of her children; and while she contemplated their enthusiastic faces with maternal rapture, a slight shade of feeling, related to regret, for an instant eclipsed her countenance. In the bustle of rising from the breakfast-table, neither was the sigh noted nor the eclipse observed, save by the quick ear and vigilant eye of conjugal affection. Her husband knew, with the divination of love, what was passing through her mind.

She was thinking of the many happy days she had passed in Liverpool, the place where she had first known and so long enjoyed the complicated and unutterable happiness of a wife and a mother. She did not disapprove of the change of residence that was now formally resolved on, but she could not quit, without a pang, the house that was hallowed by so many sweet remembrances; it seemed almost ingratitude to talk with levity of leaving Abercromby Square.

B

"We have been very happy here," she said, with her hand locked in her husband's.

"We have—we have been happy—very happy, my love," he replied, with deep feeling.

A tear stood in Mrs. Spread's eye; another gushed to that of her husband; it was drop answering drop; that lucid language, which, as the Attic historian so beautifully expresses it, is "common to sorrow and to joy."

The Spreads were, indeed, a happy family—happy in the pleasures of memory, happy in the pleasures of hope and imagination, also; but happier still in hopes not to be disappointed, and imaginings destined to be realized.

CHAPTER III.

I have often thought those noble pairs and examples of friendship not so truly histories of what had been, as fictions of what should be ; but I now perceive nothing in them but possibilities, nor any thing in the heroic examples which methinks I could not perform within the narrow compass of myself.   *Religio Medici.*

Friendships of Mr. Spread—Mr. Barker, the Bachelor of the Albany—His Intellectual Character—His Three Hatreds—Whether Mr. Barker had a Heart or not—Approach of Christmas—Preparations for it in Liverpool—Old Mrs. Briscoe—The Smyly Girls—Mr. St. Leger—Mr. Spread called to London—What the Junior Spreads thought of Mr. Barker—Speculations on his Coming—Philip Spread's Inconstancy, and Sudden Devotion to Astronomy.

THERE are men in the world, and not unamiable men either, who have no friends.   They attach themselves to their wives, their children, to a nephew, perhaps, or a niece ; but, out of the domestic circle, they have nobody to take the moiety of a care off their shoulders, or double the enjoyment of an hour's sunshine. Mr. Spread was so far from being one of those isolated men, that, on the contrary, he rejoiced in a plurality of friendships, and plumed himself on being an Achilles with more than one Patroclus, to buckle on his armor for the fight, or to relax with after the engagements of business, and the conflicts of the world. But if there was one friend in the troop who was more decidedly an *alter ego* than the rest, it was a certain Mr. Barker, a man of much worth and more eccentricity, who was now growing gray in a small set of chambers in the Albany, where he led the life of a bachelor and a cynic, attended by a single servant, frequenting society chiefly to pick quarrels with it, and never extending his visits or progresses five miles beyond Piccadilly, except when his friend, Mr. Spread, prevailed upon him to pass a Christmas or an Easter at Liverpool. Mr. Barker was one of the privileged men of the sphere he moved in.   He was eccentric by license, and his tongue had a charter. Possessing an income of some twelve or fifteen hundred a-year, he

plumed himself upon escaping the trammels and responsibilities of
life. He had few intimate friends, and Mr. Spread was at the top
of the short list. Barker would have had more friendships if he
had been more tolerant and less crotchety; but he rarely curbed his
humor, and when he was in his perverse vein spared nobody that
crossed his path. He had a dry, sharp logic for the people he
chose to reason with, but when he despised an opponent, he disem-
barrassed himself of him, or tried to do so, with the first sophism
that came to his hand. Of all the forms of opposition he loved contradiction most, and his great delight was to involve his adversary in
the syllogistic difficulty called a dilemma. Barker rejoiced in paradox, and had some odd opinion or another upon most subjects, but in
a pugnacious mood he would attack his own most favorite tenets, if
any body else presumed to maintain them. He hated three things
intensely—music, the country, and a lap-dog. Music was, perhaps,
what he most abhorred. He called the piano an instrument of tor-
ture, and thought Edward the First the best of kings, because he
persecuted the Welsh harpers.

Next to Mr. Barker in Spread's affections stood Mark Upton, an
eminent solicitor and a member of parliament. But Upton and
Barker were no very great friends. Barker said that Upton had no
mind, and Upton used to say that Barker had no heart. Spread
was more disposed to concur in the former judgment than the latter. He never heard his friend of the Albany accused of heartless-
ness without repelling the charge warmly.

"He has a heart, and a sound one, only he has the folly to be
ashamed of it. I love Barker. He is upright and downright, speaks
his sentiments flatly and roundly; he hates his enemies, and tells
them so; he loves his friends, and says nothing about it."

It was now verging to the season which, in Catholic Oxford, is
called the Feast of the Nativity, but by Protestant England is still
named Christmas—the season of pudding and pantomimes, mince-
pies and maudlin sentiment, blue noses and red books. Now
nurseries were growing licentious, and the masters and mistresses
of seminaries—the He-rods and the She-rods of British infancy—
preparing to turn their innocents loose and wild upon the world.
Now were malicious bachelors purchasing small drums and tiny
trumpets, to present to the children of unfortunate married men.
Now young ladies were busily exchanging polyglots and pin-cush-
ions, beautiful books and books of beauty, Olney Hymns and Cha-
pone's Letters, with cases and boxes of twenty kinds. Now land-
lords were beginning to get praised in provincial papers for lowering

rents that ought never to have been so high; and laboring men were about to be compensated for a year of hunger, with a single day of roast beef and plum pudding. Folly, in white waistcoat, was now quoting old songs, and dreaming of new monasteries, as if it was a whit less difficult to turn a modern Christmas into an ancient Yule, than to change a lump of sea-coal into a log of pine. Sensible people, on the contrary, content to live in their own times, and not so ravished as Mr. Owlet with the ages of darkness, or the things thereof, were buttoning their coats, without a sigh for the doublets of their fathers; going to and fro upon rail-roads, with a decided preference of speed and security to robbery and romance; nay, they were dispatching or meditating hospitable messages to their friends, and preparing for the festivities of the season, without a thought of a boar's head, or a notion on the subject of medieval gastronomy.

The Spreads, among others, were now beginning to discuss the hospitable plans which the approaching anniversary suggested: who were to be invited for the helydays—what were to be the amusements—what the cheer—what mighty pies—what ample rounds—what cheeses of Gloucester—what hams of Yorkshire—what turkeys of Norfolk. Many relations had they, more friends, and a still larger host of acquaintances. But at Christmas it was their wont to ask those only who had no firesides of their own, round which to assemble at that gracious season; the waifs and strays of society, the solitary bachelor, the lone maiden lady, the child who had no parents, or whose parents were too remote to allow of his return to their hearts and homes, at the time when "Home! home!" is the universal cry through the schools of England. There was old Mrs. Briscoe, whom it was, indeed, very good in any body to invite, for she had certain oddities, which made her an exceedingly troublesome visitor, particularly in the night season. There were Adelaide and Laura Smyly, clever, handsome, laughing girls, with no fortunes but their high spirits and good looks—orphans, twins, so exceedingly like each other, that people were always calling Adelaide Laura, and Laura Adelaide; and Mr. Philip Spread was unable to fall in love with one without falling in love with the other also. Then there was Mr. St. Leger, a young Irishman in Mr. Spread's counting-house, who had never any great fancy for a trip in the depth of winter to the coast of Kerry, where his father lived.

As to Mr. Owlet, his presence was a matter of course, when he was not engaged more piously elsewhere, composing a tract, restoring a church, hunting for relics, founding a monastery, or reviving some enlightened usage, or frolicsome institution of the twelfth and thirteenth centuries. Mr. Barker, too, was always welcome, but then it was not always an easy matter to prevail upon Mr. Barker to come. As to Mark Upton, he was always up to his eyes and ears in professional or parliamentary business; always preparing bills or composing blue-books. Nobody ever thought of asking him to merry-makings. He was the sort of man who would discuss the evidence before the Andover committee in a box at the opera, Grisi performing *Norma;* or go into the question of the broad and narrow guage in a gondola, or on the pass of the Grimsel.

Upon the present occasion all the personages mentioned, except Upton, were to be invited. Mrs. Spread was to write to old Mrs. Briscoe; Miss Spread undertook the dispatch to the Smyly girls, who were either in London or Hampshire; and Mr. Spread undertook to invite St. Leger, and write to Barker, whose crotchety notions of propriety would have made him highly indignant, had the most welcome communication imaginable been made through a female medium, when there existed a gentleman, who might have been made the instrument of conveying it. A circumstance, however, occurred, which varied these arrangements to a certain extent. Mr. Spread was suddenly called to London, by an important matter of business requiring his immediate personal attention; there was no occasion, therefore, to write to Barker—Mr. Spread would meet him in town, and bring him back with him for the holydays.

" *Must* you go yourself—*can't* you send Mr. St. Leger?" said Mrs. Spread, in those soft, earnest, conjugal tones of hers—thinking of the time of the year, of rail-way accidents, of all things possible and impossible, and always unhappy at an hour's separation from her husband. Her hand was on his shoulder as she spoke. She knew in her heart of hearts that he was just as reluctant to leave his family, even for a single day, as they were to be left by him; yet she added,

" You *know* you *need* not go *yourself*."

"I *must,* love," was his laconic answer.

Mr. Spread, though never ruffled by his affairs, underwent an instant change, directly his mind was occupied by any matter of business. The alteration was chiefly in his eye: it lost its social sparkle, and took a considerate and official expression. There was evidently no help for it; that look said so even more distinctly than the peremptory words which it accompanied. There was nothing to be done but to pack his portmanteau, cover him with kisses, load him with commissions (trust women for that), insist upon his return in three days at farthest, and order the carriage to take him to the rail-way station. His last words, as the train began to move, were—"I'll bring Barker back with me." Then a storm of "Good-by, papas," rose from the platform, and followed, and still followed him, until the engine rushed into the tunnel, like a fire-eyed dragon into his cave.

The young Spreads (it may easily be supposed) were by no means so fond of Mr. Barker as their father was; he scolded the girls, looked cross when they laughed, criticised their dress, snubbed them when they talked of pictures or books, rated them for crossing their letters, and put them on half allowance of kisses, they were so afraid of giving vent to their usual tenderness in the presence of so austere a character. Philip, too, stood in great awe of him; Barker checked his fopperies, interfered with his self-display, and detected his ignorance of books which he quoted without having taken the preliminary trouble of reading them. Nothing escaped Barker, not even the way he tied his cravat, or arranged his hair, which was generally, indeed, after the worst European models—Young France and Young Germany.

But if Barker was bland and clement any where, it was with the Spreads. Spread possessed an influence resulting from an ancient friendship; but Mrs. Spread, under the guise of almost timorous respect, exercised a still greater ascendency over him. Although Barker had never had an establishment of his own, and shuddered at the thought of having one, no man knew better what a well-regulated house was, no man was more uncomfortable where things were at sixes and sevens, or retained a more vindictive recollection of the annoyances occasioned by the misrule of children and maladministration of a household.

"Do you think he will come to us, mamma?" said Elizabeth, as they sat round the fire after Mr. Spread's departure, chatting of their social arrangements.

"I think he will, and I hope he will," said Mrs. Spread, with emphasis on the word "hope." "Of all your papa's friends, I think he loves Mr. Barker best."

"You may hang up your harp, Augusta by the waters of Mersey," said Philip.

"I wish Mr. Barker was married," said one of the little girls.

"More extraordinary things have happened," said Mrs. Spread.

"You see, Augusta, you have a chance," said Philip. There was an old joke in the family about Augusta making a conquest of Mr. Barker.

"That would be a prize, indeed," said Augusta; "but I am not so ambitious. What think you of Laura Smyly for him?"

"Philip says no to that," says Mrs. Spread, smiling.

"How can you say so, mother," remonstrated Philip, looking much piqued, "when you know I am in love with Miss Marable—or at all events with Bessie Bomford?"

There was a general laugh at this *naïve* declaration of the fickle Philip; who, to escape the ridicule he had so justly earned, strode over to the window, and affected to take a sudden interest in the heavens. It was a tolerably clear evening for Liverpool, and some half dozen stars and fragments of constellations were just dimly visible in the murky firmament. He showed them Orion, and informed them that it was Cassiopœia's chair, pointed out the part of the sky where the new planet was not to be seen, assured his sisters that from his own researches he suspected there was still another planet beyond that again, and grew so eloquent on the precession of the equinoxes that little Katherine, who thought he said *procession*, inquired if it were as fine as the lord mayor's show.

CHAPTER IV.

Why, do you see, sir, they say I am fantastical; why, true, I know it, and I pursue my humor still, in spite of this censorious age. 'Slight, as a man should do nothing but what a sort of stale judgments about this town will approve in him, he were a sweet ass. For mine own part, so I please my own appetite, I am careless of what the fusty world speaks of me. Puh!   *Every Man out of his Humor.*

Mr. Spread in London—The Albany—The Bachelor's Chambers—His Breakfast—His Library—The Bachelor appears—His Person, Dress, and Address—His Convivial Correspondence, and Comments thereon—Peeps into London Houses—The Animals' Friends' Society—Barker offered the Vicepresidency, and declines it—His Scheme of Life—His odd Opinions on Winds—Spread's Cowardice—Barker and Spread Paralleled.

THE business which Mr. Spread had in London was connected with the termination of his mercantile career. Lawyers were to be employed, deeds were to be executed or canceled, suits instituted, obligations discharged, debts called in, accounts balanced, and so forth. Much as he delighted in Barker's society, and great as was his eagerness to meet him, he deferred his visit to the Albany until he had first seen his friend Upton and his other professional advisers, and put his affairs in a way to a speedy and satisfactory issue. Then he might have been seen, one bright, frosty forenoon, proceeding from his lodgings in Suffolk-street, along Pall Mall, up St. James's-street, and thence to his friend's chambers, healthy in mind and body, handsome and well-dressed, his decent corpulence attired in an ample blue body-coat, with gilt buttons, his waiscoat buff, his trowsers gray, his boots brilliant, compelled to exercise his ponderous eye-glass, but losing little that was to be seen with its assistance, whether a political friend dropping down to Brooke's, a caricature of Lord Brougham in a shop-window, or, peradventure, a pretty woman on her wicked way to expend her husband's dear-earned cash in shawls and ribbons at Swan and Edgar's.

You know the Albany—the haunt of bachelors, or of married men who try to lead bachelors' lives — the dread of suspicious wives, the retreat of superannuated fops, the hospital for incurable

B*

oddities, a cluster of solitudes for social hermits, the home of home-
less gentlemen, the diner-out and the diner-in, the place for the
fashionable thrifty, the luxurious lonely, and the modish morose,
the votaries of melancholy, and lovers of mutton-chops. He know-
eth not western London who is a stranger to the narrow arcade of
chambers that forms a sort of private thoroughfare between Piccadilly and Burlington Gardens, guarded at each extremity by a fierce
porter, or man-mastiff, whose duty it is to receive letters, cards, and
parcels, and repulse intrusive wives, disagreeable fathers, and im-
portunate tradesmen. Here it is that Mr. Barker had long established his residence, or, as Mr. Spread called it, his tub. It was a
small, but complete suite of rooms, sufficient for the Cynic himself,
and Reynolds, his man, and arranged and furnished with a precision
and taste rigidly baccalaurean.

When Spread arrived, his admission was impeded for a few moments by the wary and almost repulsive demeanor of Reynolds,
who (being a new appointment) was not yet acquainted with the
faces of his master's friends, and consequently insisted upon proper
verifications before he allowed any visitor (no matter how distinguished his appearance) to enter the penetralia. Upon this occasion, the cautious valet required Mr. Spread's card, and, upon receiving that document, proceeded to lay it before the bachelor, who
(not being an early riser) had not yet left his dressing-room. When
Reynolds returned, it was plain, from his gracious and respectful
manner, that he had registered Mr. Spread forever at the top of
his master's list of friends. With the most sedulous attention, he
ushered the worthy merchant, from the little ante-chamber where
he had left him standing, into an inner-room, where the bachelor's
breakfast was prepared, and a good fire blazed and chirped on the
hearth.

Spread had time to observe the accurate organization of the
apartment before Barker made his appearance. Every thing was
substantial and comfortable ; nothing ambitious or superfluous. The
only article that might, perhaps, have been impeached of sensuality
was a chair, constructed and cushioned after a plan of Barker's own,
and placed (as Spread well knew) at a particular angle, in a particular position, so as to enable its occupant to enjoy the fire at the distance he liked best, and at the same time make use of a table on the
left and a book-stand, containing about a hundred volumes, which
stood upon the right-hand side. About the position of this chair,
with respect to those three objects, the fire, the book-stand, and the
table, Barker was rigorous in the extreme ; and the slightest de-

rangement of this established order of things (the topography of the chamber) ruffled his serenity for hours. Reynolds was the only servant who had ever shown that strict attention to these minute but important regulations, which was indispensable to the bachelor's comfort.

The breakfast was a good one without being that of a Sybarite. It was evidently, too, an intellectual as well as an animal repast. There was the egg and the newspaper; a plate of shrimps, and a heap of notes and letters on a small salver; muffins, marmalade, coffee, rolls, and a small volume in French binding, which Spread took up, and found was a volume of the Provincial Letters, a book which was a favorite of Barker's, because it abounded with that sharp sarcastic logic which he loved to indulge in himself. The contents of the book-stand, indeed, were of themselves a key to the humor and intellectual habits of the bachelor. There were old Montaigne, Rabelais, Quevedo, Molière, Cervantes, Voltaire, Sterne, Swift, Fielding, Pope, Dryden, Paul Courier, Burton's Anatomy of Melancholy, Grimm's Memoirs, Walpole's Letters, Chaucer, Shakspeare, Massinger, Jonson; very few modern books, except Mr. Twiss's Life of Lord Eldon, Lord Campbell's Lives of the Chancellors, and one or two odd volumes of Carlyle and Dickens (evidently none of Barker's pets).

The lowest shelf was assigned to the folios. A splendid edition of Lucian, bound in vellum, and a good copy of Bayle's Dictionary were the most remarkable.

While Spread was glancing over this small library, several growls were audible from an adjoining room, and Reynolds was continually passing and repassing, doing a number of petty things, with the air of a man who carried a monarchy upon his shoulders; at length he seemed to be near the close of his duties as gentleman of the bed-chamber, and, approaching Mr. Spread, intimated to him, in a low, deferential tone, that he might expect to see Mr. Barker in a few seconds.

Reynolds then cast a last anxious look at the table, made a slight change in the position of the volume of Pascal, which Spread had displaced by about half a quarter of an inch, and retired to some distance to wait the great event of the morning. Almost the next moment, a small door, between the fire-place and the window, opened, and the Bachelor of the Albany issued forth.

Imagine a small, well-made man, with a smart, compact figure, excessively erect, his action somewhat martial, his eye gray, cold, peevish, critical, and contemptuous; a mouth small and sarcastic, a

nose long and vulpine; complexion a pale dry red: hair stiff and
silvery, and evidently under the severest discipline to which brush
and comb could subject it, with a view to its impartial distribution
on each side of a head, which was carried so high, and with such an
air, that it was clear that the organs of firmness, combativeness, and
self-esteem, were superbly developed. With the exception of a
plain, but rich *robe-de-chambre*, his morning toilet was complete;
trowsers of shepherd's plaid, seemingly made by a military tailor,
and tightly strapped down over a pair of manifest Hoby's; a double-
breasted cashmere waistcoat, of what mercers call the shawl pat-
tern; the shirt-collar severely starched, and a little too exalted above
a cravat of dark-blue silk, carefully folded, and tied with a simple,
but an exact knot.

The meeting was cordial; Barker unusually bland and propitious,
Spread actually overflowing with friendship. The bachelor inquired
less dryly than usual as to the health of the merchant's family, and
then applied himself systematically to his breakfast, still chatting
with his visitor about private affairs and public—the marriage of his
daughter, the state of the funds, the frost, the corn-laws, and the
Maynooth Grant. At length Spread, observing that Barker took no
notice of the pile of notes at his side, begged that he would make no
stranger of him, but read his letters.

"They will keep very well," said the bachelor, with a peevish
glance at the heap,

"I feel like a man of business," said Spread; "I can do nothing
myself until I have read my letters."

"But I'm not a man of business," said Barker, dryly.

"I fancy," said Spread, "that the greater number of the notes,
there, judging from their sizes and shapes, are addressed to you
more as a man of pleasure: I should not have thought there were so
many people in town."

"The town's always full enough of disagreeable people," growled
Barker. He finished his egg, and added, "I am more of a man of
pleasure, Spread, certainly, than a man of business; but take that
batch of notes, open them *seriatim*, and then read aloud; they are a
fair sample of the civilities dayly inflicted on me, and you will see
how much my happiness is promoted by my correspondents on note-
paper."

A more agreeable occupation could not have been suggested to
Spread. Accordingly, he drew the pile toward him, and opening
the first that came to his hand, commenced reading—

"Mr. and Mrs. Crowder—"

"Enough," muttered Barker; "I never go to aggregate meetings. The Crowders invite a party of four-and-twenty to a table not large enough for sixteen. Read the next."

"Sir Thomas and Lady Broderick—dinner—"

"A bad dinner, and worse company. Do you know, Spread, I wish it were the custom for dinner-giving people to inclose their bill of fare and a list of their guests." Barker's mode of speaking when he made such observations as these was a low, voluble grunt.

"Now, here's something nice," said Spread, holding up a note on light-blue paper; "let us see."

"Mrs. Penrose—a *conversazione*. You won't refuse Mrs. Penrose. I suppose she will have the *élite* of the literary world?"

"I was fool enough to go to one of her *conversaziones* last year, and I had the honor of being presented to Uncle Bunkle, Peter Parley, and Charlotte Elizabeth. The star of the evening was announced as a second cousin of Mr. Pinnock."

"Will you dine with the Robinsons?"

"Robinsons! what Robinsons?"

"Archdeacon and Mrs. Robinson."

"Oh! I recollect—I dined with them once, two or three years ago; the party consisted of two mutes, three dumb-belles, and a Quaker. Mine was the only tongue in the room, except one in a turkey. The conversation was carried on by nods and signs. The husbands winked at their wives, and the wives kicked their husbands under the table."

Spread laughed and broke the last seal.

"Pratts."

"D—n the Pratts—that's an invitation to Reynolds, not to me."

"How so?" inquired Spread.

"They want Reynolds's services to attend at dinner."

Now Spread was well acquainted with the Pratts, and knew them to be utterly incapable of the meanness imputed to them. He was just going, in his zeal for justice, to remonstrate with his morose friend, when the bell of the outer door rung, and Reynolds came in to receive his master's pleasure as to the persons who were to be honored with, or be refused, an audience.

"Should it be Mr. Smith, sir—"

"I'll see Mr. Smith—you know him—a tall man?"

"Yes, sir," said the valet.

And it was Mr. Smith. Barker proceeded to the ante-chamber to receive him, and presently Spread heard the bachelor speaking in his gruffest manner, obviously much exasperated by something that his visitor had either done or said.   Then doors were opened abruptly and shut violently, after which succession of noises Barker returned in a sultry chafe, and it was some time before Spread could divine the cause of his agitation.

" Animals' friends—stupidity of servants—asses—rascals—animals' friends—vagabonds—vice-president—me—imagine—"

Spread looked as if he would like some more lucid explanation of what had occurred.

" Scoundrel! not the Mr. Smith I wanted to see, agent to a confounded society, called the Animals' Friends."

" Wanted you to subscribe ?"

" Wanted me to accept the office of vice-president.   Imagine, vice-president of the Animals' Friends !"

" A very responsible office !" said Spread, with mock solemnity. " They are going to send a deputation to the pope, to interest his holiness to put down bull-baiting in Spain.   You would be the second personage in the embassy." *

Barker was greatly moved by this little annoyance, which, however, he had brought upon himself, by the loose description he had given of Mr. Smith to Reynolds.   Indeed, it was generally by trifles of this nature that his temper was ruffled.   He was a man to bear the serious ills of life as becomes a philosopher to bear them.   To be sure, he was not often tried so severely, for he had no relations, or none that he knew of, to plague him, either by living or dying— in many cases it is questionable which is the most perplexing course for relations to take—no duties to discharge, or neglect, save those which sat very lightly upon him (as they do upon most men), that is to say, his duties to his country and his species ; no ambition to be thwarted, no love to be crossed, no expectations to be disappointed. He took large, and what he considered sufficient, securities against the freaks of fortune, by refusing to entangle himself in the responsibilities of life ; laughed, and with reason, at those who mingled the cup for themselves, and then complained of its bitterness ; who made their own bed, and would not lie down patiently on it—those, for instance, who married, and bemoaned the expensiveness of a wife and children ; who solicited public trusts, and complained either of public criticism or public ingratitude ; who thrust themselves into

* It appears from the newspapers that the respectable society in question has actually taken the ludicrous step alluded to by Mr. Spread.   No doubt they found it easy enough to fill the dignified situation declined by the bachelor.

parliament, and objected to committees and late hours; or who registered their franchises, and thought it a hardship to record their votes. It was the glory of Mr. Barker that he had neither wife nor child, neither a house, an office, nor a vote; he was dependent on nobody, and nobody was dependent on him; it was impossible to be more unattached than he was—impossible to have fewer ties, without entirely forsaking the haunts of men.

Barker retired moodily to exchange his *robe-de-chambre* for the blue frock, which was his invariable morning costume. He buttoned it sharply to his chin, gave his hat a somewhat belligerent cock, drew on a pair of white doe-skin gloves, and proceeded to walk with Spread in the direction of the Reform Club. The wind was from the northeast. Spread was withered and unhappy; Barker said he never felt so comfortable. He took the part of the northeast, spoke of the south with contempt, and expressed himself disrespectfully of zephyrs. At the corner of Pall Mall they separated, Spread having first consented to take a chop with the bachelor in his chamber at seven. He had intended to communicate to his friend that morning his plans for the future, particularly his intentions to settle in the country, but it was too hazardous to venture on such a ticklish subject while Barker was in a humor to fancy a northeaster.

They had been noticed walking down St. James's-street by two members of the House of Commons, who were well acquainted with them both.

"Observe Barker and Spread," said one; "two characters more dissimilar do not exist."

"Barker is the most *angular* man I ever encountered," said the other.

"Angular!" exclaimed the first: "he is so full of angles that to understand him is as difficult as taking a trigonometrical survey. Spread, on the contrary, has not a single corner in his mind; it is one of the roomiest minds I ever knew, yet there is not a nook in it for a single crotchet, not stabling for one hobby. He was a great loss to the House.

CHAPTER V.

Come, come, thou art as hot a Jack in thy mood as any in Italy; as soon moved to be moody, and as soon moody to be moved. Thou wilt quarrel with a man for cracking nuts, having no other reason but because thou hast hazel eyes. Thou hast quarreled with a man for coughing in the street, because he has wakened thy dog that hath lain asleep in the sun. *Romeo and Juliet.*

Round Tables and Square Ones—Claret and Sherry—Mr. Barker is excited and pugnacious—Holds up a Mirror to Mr. Spread—Dancing in Fetters—Barker agrees to spend the Christmas at Liverpool—Energetic Aphorism of Mr. Spread—The Northeast Wind—Mr. Spread discloses to the Bachelor his rural Plans—The Bachelor's Wrath—Observations on Contentment and a Homily on Social Obligations.

THE chop was over—the dry sherry remained upon the small square table. Barker liked a square table. Spread preferred a round one.

"You don't drink sherry?" said the bachelor.

"Not after dinner," said Spread.

"Reynolds, claret!—a magnum of thirty-four."

"I love a bounteous glass," said Spread, as Reynolds set a glass before him which might hold about half a pint.

"A *magnum* bottle requires a *maximum* glass," said Barker.

"Particularly," added Spread, "when the wine is the *optimum.*"

As he spoke he filled the goblet to the brim with the rosy liquor. Barker filled a smaller glass with the Amontillado.

"That's a great wine," said Spread, having made his first libation. He loved good wine, as good men have ever done, and as good men will ever do, without disparagement to Father Mathew.

"I stick pretty much to sherry," said Barker.

"You are wrong—sherry is an unsocial wine. Drink claret, Barker—claret is the wine to pour into the wounds of life—it is your dry sherry that isolates you in the world—that keeps you a bachelor."

"Its best recommendation," said Barker.

"It won't do, Barker," said Spread, warming; "I tell you it won't do."

"You see it *does*," replied the bachelor, dryly; "sooner than have your cares and responsibilites upon my back, I would be vicar to Atlas, and carry the globe on my shoulders."

"My cares, as you call them, have neither broken my constitution nor impaired my spirits. I am a gayer fellow than you, Barker—I am at least *as* healthy—*as*—"

"I'll tell you what you are, Spread;" and Barker threw back his head, put his arms a-kimbo, and standing up, planted himself with his back to the fire, controversial as a game-cock. It was his usual attitude when he was going to defend a paradox of his own, or attack the opinions of another, and was in his declamatory vein. "I'll tell you what you are, Spread—you are a merchant, liable to all the hazards of commerce, the vicissitudes of public credit, the caprice of the elements, the frauds or the misfortunes of all the houses connected with you over all the world. You were a member of parliament but the other day, the victim of Mr. Plumptre, at the mercy of Peter Borthwick; at this hour you are a voter for Heaven knows how many boroughs and counties; at the next election, the protectionist squires will worry you like a fox; I only hope Lord George may not be in at your death. I won't count your guardianships and trusteeships; I believe you are legally responsible for half the widows and orphans in Lancashire. Pray is there an association of any description of which you are not, at least, honorary secretary, or a joint-stock company in which you have not shares? Not one, I believe in my conscience; but this is not all, nor the worst of it: you are a married men; you have—how many children have you?—no matter—and as to god-children, I presume, with your passion for responsibilities, you are sponsor for some round dozens of Lancashire witches and Liverpool scamps."

Spread enjoyed his friend's humor, and never interrupted its career. But when Barker came to a halt, he replied, that if he had his yoke to bear, like other men, as yet he had not found it an oppressive one.

"But why bear any yoke," demanded Barker, returning to his seat, "heavy or light, when a man can avoid all yokes, as I do, 'safe out of Fortune's shot?' If *you* can dance in fetters, let me tell you, Spread, it's a rare talent; it's no accomplishment of mine, and therefore I don't go to the ball."

"You'll go to the ball sooner or later, Barker," replied Spread,

replenishing his glass—"every body does—no ball, no supper—no
enjoyment of life, without taking one's fair share of the business and
cares of it; we'll meet at the ball yet, depend upon it—and who
knows, Barker, but I may live to see you, some merry morning,
tripping it *in vinculo matrimonii*." *in the forest of mass offen*

"When I become a man of business, a slave of the lamp," said
Barker, about to help himself to more Amontillado, "I shall probably become a slave of the ring too—not till then."

"One glass of this," said the jovial Spread, pushing the jug of
claret toward his saturnine friend.

Barker was complaisant enough to comply. Spread filled at the
same time, and thought it a propitious moment to remind Barker of
his standing engagement to keep the Christmas with him at Liverpool. Whether it was the influence of the generous liquor, or
his attachment to Spread, the bachelor made but little opposition.

"We shall be a small party," said the hospitable merchant; "but
we shall be a gay one."

"We differ in many things," said Barker, taking a second glass
of the old Bordeaux, "but we agree in some things. We both love
an old wine, an old book, and an old friend."

"We do," said Spread," repeating the words, "old wine, old
books, and old friends; all good, all excellent; the old friend the
best of the three; but to fight the battle of life a man must have
something more, Barker."

"An old wife, I suppose," said Barker, gruffly.

"I meant a young one," said Spread.

"I am content with the old friend," said the bachelor.

"Just one word upon that point, my dear Barker," said the honest merchant, earnestly, and rising from the table as he said it. "I
have friends, and I prize them; no man prizes friendship more. I
know—as Montaigne says, that 'the arms of friendship are long
enough to reach and join hands from one end of the world to the
other;' but you will live to acknowledge the truth of what I am
about to say, and it is the fruit of twenty years' experience—*One
love is worth a thousand friendships.*"

Barker smiled cynically, and Spread, having thus vigorously
summed up the argument, retired; not before he had made considerable impression on the magnum of claret; without, however, passing the frontier of temperance, an indiscretion he had never in his
life been guilty of. The northeaster was still blowing, parching the
earth, and chilling the very souls of men. Spread could not help

thinking, as he buttoned himself up to his throat, of Barker's perverse fancy for the rascalliest wind that blows.   Boreas is a ruffian
and a bully, but the northeast is a rascal.   Æolus has not such a
vicious, ill-conditioned blast in his puffy bags.   It withers like an
evil eye; it blights like a parent's curse; unkinder than ingratitude;
more biting than forgotten benefits.   It comes with sickness on its
wings, and rejoices only the doctor and the sexton.   When Charon
hoists a sail, it is the northeast that swells it; it purveys for Famine
and caters for Pestilence.   From the savage realms of the Czar it
comes with desolating sweep, laden with moans from Siberian mines,
and sounding like echoes of the knout; but not a fragrant breath
brings it from all the rosaries of Persia, so destitute is it of grace
and charity.   While it reigns, no fire heats, no raiment comforts, no
walls protect—cold without bracing, scorching without warmth.   It
deflowers the earth, and it wans the sky.   The ghastliest of hues
overspreads the face of things, and collapsing Nature seems expiring of cholera.

Still Spread had not imparted to his friend what he was so anxious to reveal to him—his projected withdrawal from the Rialto and
sequestration in rural life.   In truth Spread was a little afraid of
Barker, and his courage required some screwing up, before he could
venture to broach a subject which he foresaw would lead to an unusual exhibition of moroseness.   The first part of the communication, however, was calculated rather to gratify than irritate the ascetic bachelor.   But there was no staving off the inevitable questions.

"What will you do?—how will you dispose of the time you will
have on your hands?—go into parliament again?—continue in Liverpool?"

"Into parliament! no, no—no intention of it; but it is not probable I shall continue in Liverpool.   We are thinking—"

"Of settling in London, of course."   As if there was no alterna-
tive, over the whole terraqueous globe—no spot habitable but London.

"Not exactly," in a dastardly tone.

"Why, where else, Spread—where else?"

"We are thinking of settling—in the country."

"You can't be serious!" with surprise and vexation.

"Yes, I am," delivered doggedly.

"You don't mean to tell me you are deliberately thinking of a
country life?" repeated Barker, rising from his chair and rising in
tone simultaneously.

Spread adhered to his declaration manfully enough. Barker was instantly in his game-cock attitude, with his back to the fire, and bristling with pugnacity.

"I'll tell you my mind, Spread, frankly, as I always do. The idea of a man like you, who has passed fifty years of his life in Liverpool, between the docks and the counting-house—the idea of such a man turning squire, farmer, shepherd, is the most absurd, ridiculous, preposterous, nonsensical thing I ever heard of!"

"Go on," said Spread, resignedly.

Barker did go on.

"What qualifications have you for a country gentleman? What do you know of farming, of plowing, or harrowing, of planting, pruning, fencing, sowing, or reaping? You have read Virgil—perhaps Theocritus: I don't think you have read a line of Varro, or Columella. There's the sum total of your qualifications to join the agricultural interest. What's a rake?—what's mangel-wurzel?—what's pottage?"

"Rhyme for cottage," replied Spread, disposed to be vexed, but keeping his temper.

"Don't do it, Spread—don't go cottaging and pottaging it at this time of your life: it's absurd enough for a farce. I'll call you Menalcas."

"I anticipate it," said the merchant, with a mock air of resignation, as if the threatened penalty was of the heaviest nature; "but you have been running away with the story, as usual," he added, in his natural tone. "One can live in the country without being either squire or farmer."

"To live in the country," cried Barker, "a man ought to be either a farmer, a fox-hunter, a poet, or a satyr. Are you one of the four?"

"Not one; at the same time—"

"A cottage!" interrupted Barker, with visions before his eyes of eglantine and earwigs.

"You won't hear me," said Spread, with good-humored impatience.

"I always gave you credit," persisted Barker, "for knowing what a comfortable house was as well as any man in England."

"And therefore you conclude that I am going to cottage it, as you call it. I never said a word about a cottage."

When Barker was in the wrong he never admitted it; but his practice was to shift the ground a little. Besides, he had been internally asking himself the question, What is it to me where the Spreads live—Liverpool or London, town or country?

"Have you fixed on a locality?" he now inquired, suddenly assuming a tone of indifference: "have you a house in your eye?"

"As to locality," said Spread, "my present idea is to take a villa at Norwood."

"Norwood!—nonsense!—why Norwood?"

"Or Richmond," continued Spread, having reasons of his own for not insisting on the locality which he named first. "In fact nothing is settled as yet. I am afraid we shall not find it easy to get a place to suit us; we are not very easy to please."

"Why should you?" demanded Barker. "Nobody is, or ought to be, in houses, or in any thing else, who has true taste, and a fortune to enable him to indulge it. Far from being a virtue, what is vulgarly called contentment is, in nine cases out of ten, a vice, sir, and a shabby one."

Here the bachelor was clearly in the right. Let those to whose happy lot fall the choicest grapes of the cluster—those on which the sun has gazed longest and hottest—the full, dark, rich ones, such as are pressed into the cups of kings and fill the goblets of dukes and archdukes—squeeze them to the last sweet drop, squeeze them and drain them utterly: there are twenty green and sour on the bunch for one such ruddy darling of the summer.

But we must enjoy the sweets of life without vainly expecting to avoid its bitters. It is easy to talk of shaking off care, and evading duties and obligations; the thing is possible, no doubt, for a certain time and to a certain extent; the best proof is that Mr. Barker contrived to live to the age of forty on the no-responsibility principle, as if he was no part of the great machine, as careless and uncared-for as the jolly miller in the song. But life is life; humanity is humanity; to be in the world and not of the world is systematically practicable only in the apostolic sense. Life is made up of relations, affinities, dependencies, connections, ties, and obligations: they are as numerous as the wiles of women; as involved as the schemes of diplomacy; as thick, and in the long run as inevitable, as the traps and pitfalls on the bridge of Mirza. To try to escape them is to try to elude a universal law, and, like every such endeavor, is sure to terminate in failure, if not in punishment. The attempt is selfish, and selfishness may succeed for a while, but never eventually or entirely triumphs. Barker and Spread scarcely ever met without a battle upon this point. Spread was always urging his friend to change his mode of life, leave the Albany, enter the world, take a wife, and "give hostages to fortune."

This was a phrase that always provoked Barker. "I call it tempting fortune," he used always to reply, on which Mr. Spread never failed to rejoin that it was one thing to tempt fortune and another to trust Providence, to which Barker would reply with a growl, and change the subject.

CHAPTER VI.

Bear me, oh! bear me, to sequester'd scenes,
The bowering mazes, and surrounding greens,
To Thames's banks, which fragrant breezes fill,
Or, where the Muses sport on Cooper's Hill.
Windsor Forest.

———

Mr. Spread in search of a House—Conflicting Tastes in Houses—Arguments for and against Norwood—Mrs. Harry Farquhar—Mr. Barker accompanies Spread House-hunting—The Poetry of Auctioneering—Remarks on the Names and Sites of Villas—Mr. Spread finds a House to suit the Narrowsmiths, but no House to suit Himself—The House-hunters' Return to Town—Dine at the Piazza, Covent Garden—The Four Novelists—Their interesting Conversation—How Mr. Spread found by Accident what he had failed to discover by laborious Investigation.

No—it was not a very easy matter to find the kind of thing the Spreads wanted. A great many wishes were to be gratified, a great many fancies indulged, a great many requisites combined. As to cottages, they were out of the question; they detested cottages just as much as Mr. Barker did. What they all agreed in coveting was a good, handsome country-house. The first point to be settled was the locality; here tastes varied considerably: Augusta's was pastoral, Philip's aquatic, Elizabeth's alpine, the mother's was chiefly horticultural, Mrs. Martin's academic and sylvan; Mr. Spread's own taste so vaguely and abstractedly rural, that he was almost equally divided between the forest faction, the garden interest, the marine department, and the mountain party. If he had any private feeling it was in favor of sheltered walks and sunny terraces, for exercise, health, and conversation. Then the junior branches had their inclinations too: Mysie was for an island, Katherine only insisted on a grotto, Theodore was probably most anxious about an orchard, and a paddock for a pony. Now, it was no easy matter to unite all these desiderata, even with the aid of the supplement of the "Times," and the guidance of George Robins. A place equally haunted by Naiads, Oreads, Dryads, and Nereids was difficult to

discover; and then Flora must reign, too; and Bacchus and Ceres
were not to be excluded.   There were votes for North Wales,
votes for South, suffrages for Cumberland, voices for the Isle of
Wight, voices for Scotland—nay, at one moment, there was a feeling manifested in favor of the lakes of Killarney, and it was no anti-
Irish prejudice on the part of any member of the family that prevented them from crossing the Channel in quest of a settlement.

  Norwood had fair pretensions.   Mrs. Spread had a married sister, Mrs. Harry Farquhar, who resided there, and that was an argument for Norwood, not incapable of being answered, but still of
considerable weight, pressed as it was by a lady who was wont to
carry her points, and carry them with a high hand into the bargain.
Mrs. Farquhar was a singular woman, very different from her sister,
smart, clever, daring, masculine, a termagant wife, a capricious
mother, an ardent friend, and a bitter enemy.   Her good points,
however, outweighed her bad ones—at least they did so in the esti-
mation of the Spreads; she was partial to them, in turn, and working heaven and earth to have them near her; there was no other
spot, she vowed, in all England to suit them, and she was actually
in treaty for a house, which she took upon herself to say was just
the house for them.   But there were conflicting considerations:
Mrs. Farquhar was too restless and meddling a spirit to make a very
desirable neighbor, even to her own sister, and, besides, there was so
much ill-blood between her and Mr. Barker, that Mr. Spread had
cause to apprehend that he could not fix himself in that lady's vicin-
ity without sacrificing the society of his oldest and dearest friend.
We have seen that, in his late conversation with Barker, Spread drew
in his horns the moment he had inadvertently mentioned Norwood,
and then talked of Richmond as the situation not unlikely to be ultimately selected for his séjour.   He could not have named a place
more likely than the latter to mitigate the rancor of his friend's ani-
mosity to the country.   The facility of access from town, by land and
by water, its decided suburban character, its populousness, its noto-
riety, with the attraction of the Star and Garter, were all such strong
recommendations in the bachelor's eyes that he prevailed upon Mr.
Spread, before he had been a week in town, to decide upon Richmond or its immediate neighborhood, without consulting with his
family any more upon the subject.   Indeed, there was no great occasion to do so, for Richmond united all the conditions insisted on
by the several members of the Spread confederation to a greater degree than Norwood.   There was even an island for Mysie, and a
grotto, at Twickenham, for the young lady with cavernous propensi-

ties. . The question having been thus far advanced, Mr. Spread began to make inquiries about villas on the banks of the Thames; he took notes of several places advertised in the *Times*, and obtained from the auctioneers and house-agents the names of sundry villas, or of people who had villas to dispose of. There was the Ash-groves, Bushy-parks, and Meadow-banks, River-views, Priories, and Dove-cots, a Tusculum, a Sans Souci, and a Vallombrosa. How Barker ridiculed and abused the very names of the places; how he did run down the hills, cut up the groves, and trample the meadows under his feet! However, he was so bent upon keeping Mr. Spread to his engagement to locate himself somewhere about Richmond that he consented, with much less difficulty than his friend had anticipated, to go down with him, one marvelously warm and sunny day, to survey the district, though he positively objected at that late period of the year to taking an early dinner at the Star and Garter. Mr. Spread was of opinion—like a sensible man—that winter is the proper time to form a judgment of a country-house, and he thought, further, that he could make no more acceptable Christmas gift to his wife and children than the villa, upon which their hearts were set. As to the early dinner, he gave up the point at once, and agreed, with Barker, to dine at the usual hour at the Piazza Coffee House, in Covent Garden.

The tour of inspection was amusing enough; it supplied Spread with many subjects for pleasantry, and Barker with equally numerous occasions for a growl. Both gentlemen had abundant occasion to remark the singular fertility of imagination possessed by the auctioneers; what was a castle in print, dwindled to a cottage in reality; gorgeous woods shrunk into paltry shrubberies; stately mansions into citizen's boxes; lawns into paddocks; mountains into hillocks; parks and chases into wretched inclosures, where a herd of field-mice could with difficulty find sufficient range or pasture. They were also led to notice the admirable talent for nomenclature exhibited by the owners of suburban villas; how happily places without a bush were designated groves; and houses staring you in the face, on the sides of public thoroughfares, christened hermitages; they saw lodges, where they would not have lodged for a considerable bribe, and retreats which they were glad to retreat *from;* Vallombrosa was a sun-and-dust-trap on the top of a hill, and the villas with Roman names were the Cockneyist abodes in all the environs of London. Another field of observation was opened by the singular ingenuity with which the builders of numerous houses had selected the sites, so as to give them the full benefit of every bleak wind that

C

blows, and spare them the greatest possible amount of light and warmth. In this respect, Tusculum was as near perfection as a house could be. The shelter from the south was complete, the exposure to the northeast incomparable, it seemed as if the advice of the astronomer-royal must have been taken, or it never could have been placed with such extreme precision, so as to have the *minimum* of the sun's favor in the circle of the year.

" The very place for the Narrowsmiths," said Mr. Spread.

" I had no idea," said Barker, "there was any thing to be had *so perfect in its way.*"

" Let us return to town," said the merchant, in despair. They did so, and owed to a fortunate incident in the evening, while they sat sipping their wine, what they had failed to discover in the morning, with all their pains and peregrinations.

At a table not far from them, in the Piazza Coffee House, sat four gentlemen, whose conversation soon proved that they were all literary men, novelists of greater or less repute. They were, in fact (though neither Mr. Spread nor Mr. Barker knew them personally), P. R. G. Lowestoffe, a voluminous writer of romances; Mr. Warner, great in the line of didactic fiction; Mr. Grimm, author of the " Horrors of Houndsditch," " Mysteries of Bristol," and several other works belonging to the slouched-hat and dark-lantern school; and last, if not least, Lord Francis Shearcraft, who had recently found out a particularly expeditious method of composition, in which he was about equally indebted to the assistance of his bookseller and his cutler. Had the year been younger by some months, these four personages would have gone down to Blackwall, and dined at Lovegrove's, but now they were content to make themselves comfortable in Covent Garden : the banquet being at the cost of Warner, who had lost a bet to Lowestoffe, having rashly wagered that the latter would not produce three novels, of three volumes each, in the space of four calendar months. At a dinner under such circumstances, the conversation fell naturally upon the art of novel-writing in general, and Barker and Spread (being weary after their fruitless expedition, and more inclined to listen than-talk) were both diverted and edified by the dialogue which they could not avoid overhearing. That they could be in any manner practically concerned in it, never, of course, for an instant entered their heads.

" The fact is," said Lowestoffe, justly elated at the victory he had won, " I have got a wonderful knack of novel-writing; I have no doubt I could have given four in the same time, if it had been worth my while.   For some years back I have regularly written four or five at least in the twelvemonth.   My plan is to have one going on at my library table, another at a standing-desk, I throw off a third while I sit sipping my wine after dinner, and a fourth—faith, I can't tell how I manage to produce the fourth—but I do it—it's incredible —but I do it."

" You must find it very difficult," said Warner, who wrote at the slow rate of a novel a-season, " to keep your characters distinct, and the threads of the stories from getting entangled."

" Faith, the threads *do* get entangled a little now and then; but as to the characters, the only difficulty I find is to keep the hair of my heroines of the same color throughout.   I sometimes make a slip there, I confess.   Belinda, in my last historical romance, has fair hair in the first volume, auburn in the second, and jet-black in the third.   The reviewers never detected it."

" And if they had," said Grimm, " your defense would have been simple enough—that Belinda, of course, used some of the hair-dyes and atrapilatories in vogue."

Lowestoffe and the others laughed.

" Still," said Warner, " I can't help thinking, that to create and sustain interesting characters is not so easy a task as Lowestoffe appears to suppose."

" I have a theory of my own on the subject of characters," replied Lowestoffe.   " A novel is, or ought to be, a picture of life; now do we commonly meet with interesting characters in life ?   Why, then, should people expect to find them in novels ?   I write upon what I call the picture-of-life principle ; and I apply it to incidents as well as to characters.   Perhaps you may have remarked, that my novels do not aim at abounding in what are commonly called interesting characters, or entertaining events."

" I certainly have remarked that they don't contain them," said Warner, maliciously ; and Lord Francis and Mr. Grimm said they had made the same observation.

" The *feuilleton* system would suit you admirably ;" said Grimm; " you could supply all the journals in London."

" I am actually engaged at this moment," said Lowestoffe, " to write a romance in the *Mark Lane Express.*"

" Who is to be the villain ?" asked Warner, " Cobden, or Lord George Bentinck ?"

" Nobody like me," said Grimm, " for villains."

" That *is* your line," said Lowestoffe ; " you are, unquestionably, very great in it."

" You have a diabolical imagination, Grimm," said Lord Francis.

" All habit," said the author of the " Mysteries of Bristol." " I ruminate so much on abandoned characters and revolting subjects. Every dilapidated house is to me the scene of some hideous assassination, or still more appalling crime. London, to my eye, teems with conspirators and murderers. I would undertake, in twelve months, to make the parks of this city so horrible, that the inhabitants would resort, for an evening's walk, to Goodman's Fields in preference."

" Very kind to the citizens of London," said Warner.

" Why, in the cellars of this very house," continued Grimm, grow-'ng excited.

" Hush, Grimm—don't ruin the Piazza," said Lord Francis.

" I'll tell you an extremely curious fact," said Grimm, " in illustration of the power of fiction. In my 'Horrors of Houndsditch,' there is one scene laid at a villa near Richmond; I called it the Rosary; there is a brutal murder—indeed, two murders; and then there is a double apparition; all sheer invention, of course. But it turns out that there is actually a villa of the same name, in the same locality; and what do you think has occurred within the last week? Why, the family that occupied it has thrown it up—their servants deserted them in a body—the place is for sale at this moment, the nicest villa residence in England."

" Take a note of that, Spread," said the bachelor, *sotto voce.*

" I know it well," said Lord Francis; " it belongs to the best of all worthy fellows, my friend Dr. Bedford, dean of some place in Ireland : he has resided in that villa for the last ten years."

" Take the Rosary, Spread," said Barker.

Mr. Spread took his friend's advice, and the haunted villa the next day. It was indeed a gem; and it may as well be stated at once, that the Spreads never received, during their tenancy, the slightest molestation from Mr. Grimm's apparitions.

The news of the taking of the Rosary was not long in reaching Norwood, and the ears of the eccentric and vixenish Mrs. Harry Farquhar, who penetrated with a glance into the share Mr. Barker had in the defeat of her arrangements. The bachelor of the Albany will, sooner or later, get a blowing-up, depend upon it.

CHAPTER VII.

Cheer your heart;
Be you not troubled with the time, which drives
'O'er your content these strong necessities;
But let determined things to destiny
Hold unbewail'd their way.

Antony and Cleopatra.

The Tropics of Life—Mr. Barker starts for Liverpool—Rail-way Reading—
Mutual Scrutiny of Faces—Litigious Behavior of the Bachelor—His Char-
acter of Lord Brougham and of Sir Robert Peel—Interesting discovery of
a London Student—Barker attacks the Squires—The Company changes—
Old Mrs. Briscoe and her fat Maid—A Nephew in search of an Uncle—
Conduct of the Nephew—Mr. Barker overhears an alarming Conversation
—How he got involved with Mrs. Briscoe and two other Petticoats—And
in what an amiable Character he arrived at Mr. Spread's.

THERE are certainly turning points in the lives of men, when
things, after going on smoothly or roughly, happily or the contrary,
begin to alter either for worse or better; and it would seem that
these tropical moments generally occur at the precise times when
men are least expecting the tide to change, and most assured of the
stability of their fortunes. At such a crisis, Mr. Barker, with all
his confidence in his no-responsibility system (a confidence hitherto
justified by its almost uninterrupted success), is now arriving rapidly;
and, in truth, since it seems to be an elementary moral law, that
the course of love (at once the original and conservative principle of
society) shall never long run smooth, it would be equally unjust and
contradictory that the stream of a bachelor's destiny (a course essentially anti-social) should flow unhindered and unruffled to the close.

The train started. Every place was occupied, and each traveler
provided himself with one or two daily or weekly newspapers.
There were two *Chronicles,* two copies of the *Times,* the same of
the *Daily News,* one Mrs. Gamp, and no Mrs. Harris. Barker had
the *Examiner,* because it was witty and caustic; and the *Spectator,*
because it was clever and crotchety. The proceedings commenced
with a general reading of the journals. Three gentlemen attempted,

simultaneously, to peruse three of the vast morning papers, spread
to the full extent of the broad sheet.   This was not very easy to do,
so two of them soon gave it up; the third was more persevering and
combative, and continued to travel through his *Times*, from the advertisements of revolted lap-dogs down to the printer's name.   Each
man having satisfied himself with his own papers, proceeded to borrow those of his neighbors, until the system of reciprocity was fully
carried out, except in the case of Barker, who borrowed nobody's
property, and arrayed his visage in such terrors, that only one of his
companions ventured to propose commercial relations with him.
The reading concluded, a general mutual scrutiny of faces commenced; A looked at B as if he despised him thoroughly; B reconnoitered C as if he had suspected him of belonging to the swell-
mob; C evidently considered A an impertinent intruder; and as to
Mr. Barker, he glanced about him as if nobody had a right to be there
but himself.   Indeed he was exceedingly litigious all day, snapping
at some, snarling at others, scowling and growling, mumbling and
grumbling, taking people up and putting people down, asking blunt
questions, giving sharp answers, sometimes right, sometimes wrong,
and treading upon every body's corns.   When, at length, there began
to be some conversation, one of the party, a subdued, hen-pecked
looking man, with a white face and a black coat, in all probability a
perpetual curate, told a lamentable tale of the upsetting of a boat on
the river, which he said he had witnessed with his own eyes, as if it
was usual to witness boating accidents, or occurrences of any kind
with the eyes of other people.

"There were two men," he said, "in the boat—one was providentially saved."

"And the other, sir," interrupted Barker, sharply, "the other, I
suppose, was *providentially drowned*."

The perpetual curate looked aghast.

"Don't you think," pursued Barker, with acrimony, "that Providence had as much to do with the drowning of the one as with the
rescue of the other?"

The curate was meditating a reply, when a paragraph in *Punch*
made the rest of the company laugh, upon which Mr. Barker said,
"he should like to know what *Punch* would do without the fountains
in Trafalgar Square, the Duke of Wellington's statue, or Lord Brougham's nose?"

"I entirely concur with you, sir," said a presumptuous student of
one of the London colleges, who never omitted an occasion for displaying his ignorance in the most high-flown language he could find,

"at least as far as relates to the august Brougham—don't you agree with me, that Brougham is a tremendous statesman? He is certainly, in my opinion, the loftiest, most towering, and I will go so far as to say the most gigantic intellect that ever illumined and enlightened Europe; indeed, I might say the terraqueous globe."

A look of intense scorn was the only notice that Barker took of this burst of eloquence; but in reply to one of the other travelers, he dashed off a virulent sketch of the "august Brougham," concluding by pronouncing him a man of brilliant incapacity, vast and various misinformation, and prodigious moral requirements.

"Well, sir, I hope you will allow that Sir Robert Peel is a great man," interposed the perpetual curate, who always thought the prime-minister a demi-god, whether he was Whig or Tory.

"I am told," muttered Barker, "that Sir Robert is a great eater of beef-steaks and toasted cheese."

"He is a confounded apostate, at all events," said a gentleman with a white hat, a green coat, and top-boots, agricultural all over; "but that is neither a wonder nor a crime in these days."

"His apostasies, sir," said Barker, "are the most creditable passages of his life. He rats opportunely and ably, when he sets about it; he abandons his party manfully, and flies from his colors like a hero."

"I made a curious observation the other day," said the London collegian, "R.P. stands both for Robert Peel and rotten potato."

This luminous remark turned the conversation upon free trade.

"The rotten potato will ripen the corn question," said a disciple of Cobden.

"Yes," said the collegian, "we shall be indebted for the most tremendous political improvement of the nineteenth century to a microscopic fungus in the invisible tissues of a tuber."

"Heaven help the agricultural interest!" cried the squire; "what will become of us, with the enormous burdens upon land—"

"Name them," cried Barker.

The squire was dumb.

"The greatest burdens upon the land of this country, that I know of," pursued Barker, "are your georgical dukes and bucolical marquises."

"Their pockets will soon be light enough," said the squire, stepping out of the carriage, the train having now arrived at the Rugby station.

"Easier to lighten their pockets than enlighten their heads," said Barker, taking a parting-shot at him.

During the next stage or two, Mr. Barker behaved tolerably well, for he slept the greater part of the time. When he awoke, he found the party constructed anew, and now it was that his troubles for the day commenced. His *vis-à-vis* was a raw youth, of eighteen or twenty, with a round rosy face, and a simple, good-humored physiognomy; he was immersed in an immense rough coat, like a bear's skin, with enormous mother-of-pearl buttons, and a dozen pockets of all sizes and in all positions. In fact, he looked something like a brown bear, or a great water-dog, sitting on its hind legs; and he kept his neighbors in constant alarm, by sometimes pulling out a cigar-case, as if he meant to commence smoking, sometimes producing a three-barreled pocket-pistol, and examining the priming, sometimes displaying a wonderful knife with a hundred blades, and, every now and then, giving a blast with a hunting-horn, which he had bought, he informed an elderly lady beside him, at a shop in High Holborn, adding that it was a great bargain, and that if she ever wanted a thing of the kind, he would recommend her to go to the same place. The old lady was as nice an old lady as benevolent features, white cambric, and shining black silk could make her. She seemed, indeed, the incarnation of philanthropy, for she was always warning somebody not to do something or another, imploring the guards to take care of themselves, or administering drops and lozenges to a plump, lazy maid, who seemed neither to attend to her mistress nor to be expected to do so, although her sidelong looks and coquettish cough showed that she was very well disposed to a flirtation with the owner of the wonderful knife. The middle seat, at the right hand of Mr. Barker and opposite the plump maid (whose name appeared to be Letty), was now occupied by a cool, sedate man, who might have been somebody or nobody, a landed man or a funded man, an honest fellow or a swindler, from all that you could gather, either from his physiognomy or his costume. The seat beyond this ambiguous individual, on the same side, could only be said to have been half filled; its tenant was a slight, pale, retiring little girl, with features not in keeping with her dress, for while the former disposed one to believe her of the class that is born to affluence and ease, the latter as obviously suggested that her lot was indigence and labor. A plain straw bonnet, a gray plaid shawl, a frock of dark-blue stuff, and gloves, through which, in more places than one, her fair fingers peeped; such was her simple, almost poor attire. The impudent fat maid evidently regarded her with supreme scorn, as much as to say, "Marry come up, the likes of her in a coach." And, indeed, this was almost the only notice the little girl received during the journey, except occasionally from the officious old lady herself, who seemed possessed by a spirit of nursing and care-taking, which in a professional nurse-tender would have been perfectly miraculous.

As nobody troubled themselves to conjecture who the neglected thing in the corner was, why should *we* speculate on the subject? She looked like a poor girl, found guilty of the crime of poverty, and sentenced to shirt-making for life, a seven-years term, at most, of necessity and needlework. Perhaps it was otherwise. Nobody now cared, and least of all the Bachelor of the Albany, who had quite enough to do to repel the fidgety old lady's benevolent attentions, and to defend himself against the young man opposite to him, who was armed with such a variety of offensive weapons.

" Have a care, sir. I hope your pistol is not loaded," he at length broke out in a surly tone, with a look still surlier, at the formidable simpleton in the enormous rough coat, who, in exhibiting the pistol to the plump maid, had repeatedly pointed it right at Mr. Barker's head. The old lady had already, in her capacity of protectress-general, cautioned the youth twenty times against shooting *himself*, which was the least part of the danger to be apprehended. None of these remonstrances, however, proving successful, the cool man took a different course; he expressed a curiosity to examine the pistol, and the moment it was placed in his hands, he extended it out of the window, and a couple of sharp reports instantly proved that two of the barrels had been loaded. The innocent youth, far from taking offense, laughed loud, said it was funny, and called the cool man a devilish sensible fellow, a compliment which that gentleman could not have returned with the slightest respect for truth.

Barker being now comparatively at his ease, subsided into his corner; the old lady, wearied with her exertions, began to doze; and the sedate man, the fat soubrette, and the hero of the three-barreled pistol fell into chat on their several destinations; the soubrette leading the way by stating the name of her mistress to be Briscoe, and that she was going to spend the Christmas at the house of a certain Mr. Spread at Liverpool. Barker, overhearing this from behind his newspaper, formed a pleasing notion of the party he was on his way to join; and his satisfaction must have been considerably enhanced when Letty unfolded the Christmas presents which Mrs. Briscoe was taking down to the little Spreads, one of which was a complete zoological garden in a wooden box, with roaring lions, growling bears, grunting pigs, chattering monkeys, and all the noises of the animal kingdom. The bachelor instantly de-

termined not to disclose the fact of his being bound to Mr. Spread's
likewise, to avoid being involved in attentions to the old lady, looking after luggage, engaging carriages, and all that sort of thing,
which nobody liked less than he did, and which, it was clear, was
the business of the plump Letty, if her office was not a downright
sinecure.

But Mr. Barker was destined that day to overhear a conversation
which touched him nearer than the revelation of Mrs. Briscoe's
maid.   The simple youth in the rough coat and the sedate gentleman began to be very cordial and communicative, the latter evincing
a desire to know all about the former, and the former not a bit backward to gratify his thirst for information.   Barker did not care one
farthing to hear what passed between them, but we can not always
abstract our minds from what people are saying and doing at our
elbows, particularly in a coach.

The bachelor was first struck by hearing, as he thought, his own
name pronounced—at least it sounded like Barker—it might have
been Parker—he was certain it was either the one or the other,
and it was pronounced by the young man as if he had been telling
the other his cognomen.   Then there followed what was obviously
an historiette of the stripling's life and adventures, the substance of
which was, that he was a son of somebody or other who had died
in the West Indies; that he had been left some small property,
which was growing less and less every day (probably owing to the
proprietor's tastes for pistols, knives, and hunting-horns), and that
he had not, to his knowledge, a single relation living on either side
of the house, except an uncle—(here Barker listened attentively)
his father's brother—(Barker's attention became still more engaged) who resided somewhere in England, *where*, he had not yet
been able to discover, but he was making every exertion to find
him out, or "hunt him up," as he elegantly expressed it—a phrase
which he aptly accompanied with a blast of his horn, as if he
imagined his uncle a hare or a fox, and was giving him chase on the
instant.

The blast ran through the bachelor like the thrust of a cold
rapier; could he have been seen behind his newspaper, the form
of his visage would have been observed to have undergone a comical
elongation during the personal narrative of the unmannered youth
with the horn.   Barker—Parker—Parker—Barker.   The words
"hunt him up," too, lingered in his ears very disagreeably.   In
fact, he felt some sudden mysterious sympathy with the unfortunate
gentleman, whoever he was, who, little dreaming of what was in

reserve for him, was doomed to be "hunted up" by so interesting a claimant to the honor of his relationship. What a relief it was, when, as the train approached the next station, the nephew in search of an uncle informed his companions that he was under the necessity of depriving them of his attractive society. He took leave in the most troublesome and obstreperous manner possible, elbowing every body, then insisting on shaking their hands, then kicking their shins, then begging their pardons, then pressing his cigars on the gentlemen (Mr. Barker particularly), and looking very much disposed to kiss the fat lady's maid, who looked equally well inclined to submit to his impudence. At length, after nearly crushing the quiet little girl in the corner into a mummy, and poking out the old lady's eye with the mouth-piece of the hunting-horn, he jumped out of the carriage, with a whoop like a Cherokee Indian, and, after committing twenty more outrages, while looking after his luggage, clambered, alternately shouting and winding his horn, on the top of an omnibus, which stood hard by waiting for passengers.

"He's an innocent poor fellow," said the sedate gentleman, looking at Barker, as the train again moved forward. "I hope he will not be long before he discovers his uncle. He wants somebody to advise and direct him."

Barker made no reply; but his face showed that he felt in the liveliest manner all the horror of holding the situation of natural adviser and director to such a young man as he had just been delivered from.

"His course would be," continued the other, "to advertise in the *Times*. I knew people of the name of Parker, in Leeds, formerly."

"Is Parker his name?" cried the bachelor, eagerly.

"Well, then, I'm not certain," said the other; "if it was not Parker, it was Barker."

Barker spoke no more. The truth was, that he had a brother, and a brother, too, who had died in the West Indies. He had never heard of this brother having been married, or having had children; and he had always been under the impression that he had lived and died single and childless, like himself. Now, for the first time, had the idea been suggested to his mind that it was possible—just possible—not at all probable, that his brother might have been married, and have had a son, without his privity to either transaction. A pleasant thing it would be—would it not?—should such turn out to be the real state of the case. To a man of his temperament and principles, the shadow of a doubt upon such a point was vexatious.

The thought that such a consanguinity was even *in posse*, filled him with gall and wormwood; and the worst of it was, that a nephew in such circumstances was almost the same as a son. So the world would regard it. Look sharp, Mr. Barker; have a care, good Bachelor of the Albany. Your no-responsibility principle seems slightly in danger just at this moment. A nephew is abroad in search of an uncle!

But his troubles for the day were not yet over. He had determined (a little selfishly) not to entangle himself with Mrs. Briscoe; but Fate, who smiles at human resolves, had made up her mind not only to involve him with the old lady and her maid, but likewise with a third individual of the same sex, more interesting, and eventually more embarrassing, than either, by many degrees. A slight accident which occurred when the train had arrived within a hundred yards of the terminus rendered it impossible to bring it up alongside the platform. The night was dark and wet, the number of passengers unusually great, the quantity of luggage enormous, the bustle prodigious, the uproar and confusion like the Tower of Babel. The women were at their wits' ends, particularly those who, like Mrs. Briscoe and her attendant, were unprovided with a male escort. The porters ran off with trunks and boxes; the pickpockets on duty made away with as many bags and umbrellas as they could whip up in the hubbub, and the omnibuses, coaches, and cabs started away in rapid succession, to all manner of streets and squares, lanes and alleys, wherever they were ordered by the traveler or the thief. Almost the very last passengers in a condition to move were Mrs. Briscoe and Mr. Barker; for the fat maid was utterly useless at a pinch, and Mr. Barker's bag and portmanteau were so long forthcoming, that at last he began to conclude them lost or stolen, and to storm at the rail-way police, the rail-way directors, and finally at rail-ways themselves and rail-ways generally. At length the portmanteau was produced, and was instantly shouldered, along with Mrs. Briscoe's bulkier chattels, and carried off by the last-remaining porter, who was directed by the women to engage a coach, and by Mr. Barker to secure a fly. At the same moment a bag came tumbling down the ladder. It fell at the maid's feet, and she was going to take it up, when Mr. Barker interposed gruffly and said he would carry it himself. He did so, and was very much annoyed by the women following him, and particularly by Letty, who repeatedly offered her assistance. When they reached the stand for the carriages, Barker was quite out of breath, and very well pleased to throw down his load.

" Thank ye, sir," said the fat maid.

" I feel very much obliged, very much, indeed, by your kind attention, sir," added the old lady, courtesying most graciously.   Mr.
Barker started, bowed, and winced at the compliments paid to his
unintentional civility—for, in truth, he had been officiating as porter
to Mrs. Briscoe !   Savage with himself for his precipitancy, he ran
back to the train, and was just in the act of recovering his property,
when a young female presented herself timidly to his notice, and in
a modest, hesitating manner begged he would have the kindness to
direct her to Rodney-street.   Dim as the light was, Barker at once
recognized the quiet little girl, who had sat all day in the corner of
the carriage, unspoken to and speaking to nobody.   It was impossible to answer her morosely.   What remains may be briefly told.
There being but one coach for all, the Bachelor of the Albany arrived that night in Abercromby Square in the amiable but novel
character of escort to old Mrs. Briscoe and the lazy, fat Letty, having also extended his gallant attentions to the little girl whom nobody
cared for ; given her a seat in the carriage (much to Letty's annoyance), and dropped her at the house in Rodney-street, where she
begged to be set down.

" My dear," said Mrs. Spread to her husband, soon after the
arrival, " did you ever see any body so altered and improved as
Mr. Barker ?—only think of his insisting on carrying Mrs. Briscoe's
sac-de-nuit !"

CHAPTER VIII.

Praise the gods, and make triumphant fires.—Coriolanus.

———

A Winter's Night in Mrs. Spread's Drawing-room—How it was furnished—
Picture of Mrs. Spread reading—Mr. Barker and Mr. Spread make them-
selves comfortable, and wrangle at their Ease—The President's Message
—Mr. Barker quarrels with Pico, the Lap-dog—The Critic on the Hearth
—A Whist Party extraordinary, and an Invitation to a Miser's House-
warming.

It was a delicious winter's evening, not on the actual banks of the
Mersey (for the banks of the river at no season are particularly
charming), but in Mrs. Spread's drawing-room. Indeed, it is only
in such places that the evenings in winter *are* delicious, unless you
are an astronomer in quest of a new planet, a meteorologist observant
of Auroras, or an experimentalist with the rain-guage. But in snug
rooms, by the side of "triumphant fires," couched on sofas, or
squatting on stools, a meadowy carpet under your feet, books in profusion, the walls mirrored and pictured, the windows closely curtained, the eye comforted with warm colors, and the ear gladdened
with social sounds, the most superb evening in June is nothing to
one in December, always assuming the heart to be in the right
place, the mind to be tranquil, and enough in the exchequer to wind
up the year's accounts to your own credit and your creditors' satisfaction. Never hearken to those who talk of money having nothing
to do with happiness; it has a great deal to do with it, a great deal
indeed. People certainly may be very rich and very uncomfortable
—the Narrowsmiths were signal instances—but to combine the lot of
poverty with the state of enjoyment, is as difficult a problem as to
square the circle or ascertain the longitude at sea. The world is
an oyster, to be opened with cold iron, if there is no other way; but
use a silver knife if you can get one.

The apartment in question was half drawing-room, half library,
and spacious enough for both purposes. It was quietly rich and
sensibly luxurious. There were chairs of all forms, with arms and

without arms, with long legs and short legs, with high backs and low
backs, straight backs and crooked backs, French chairs for fairies,
American chairs for fidgets, elbow-chairs for old gossips, and prie-
dieus for young ones.   Among the rest was a Gothic chair of black
oak, descended from the days of the Plantagenets, which, being as
incommodious as it was ancient, was never occupied, save by Mr.
Owlet, who thought it the most delicious chair in the house.   The
tables were also numerous, some of marble, for bronzes and alabas-
ters; some of ebony, for nicknacks; a nest of spiders, for embroidery or chess; an oblong table for vagrant books and slipshod literature of all kinds, annuals, quarterlies, monthlies, and weeklies; and
a round table at which the Spread girls alternately made the best
tea in England, and the best coffee out of France.   If the room had
a fault, it was the labyrinth of tables, couches, chairs, stools, screens,
and musical instruments, that made it occasionally as difficult a
thoroughfare as Fleet-street.   You sometimes desired to have the
Riot Act read to disperse a little monster meeting of stools, and now
and then wished a devotion-chair at the deuce.   But there was always a space kept tolerably clear in the front of the fire, a little
arena in which you could expatiate freely without oversetting a
screen or knocking your shin against the claw of the table.   This
little open ground, overlaid with a rug as thick as a jungle (a rug
in which Pico, the Italian greyhound, and a kitten belonging to the
children, which on great festivals was admitted into the drawing-
room by special license, were invisible, when they chose to lie
down, all but the tips of their ears), was flanked by two sofas, while,
fronting the fire, which truly deserved the epithet in the motto, it
was bounded by two, and sometimes three chairs, capacious and
profound enough for the portliest doctor of the drowsiest hall in Oxford.   The sofa on the right was the throne of the mother of the
family; there she wrote her letters, received her visitors, conversed
with her friends, and chatted with her children.   There she read a
great deal, travels, memoirs, history, reviews, now and then a novel;
but she never did needlework, lay or ecclesiastical—never so much
as hemmed a handkerchief for her husband, or embroidered a fald-
stool for an Oxonian chapel.   She left all that to her daughter
Augusta, who was the most industrious embroiderer in Needledom.
There was nothing comelier or handsomer in all motherhood than
Mrs. Spread, as she sat, with a small table beside her, supporting a candle lamp, upon that rosy, cosy sofa, a narrow bandlet of
pearls crowning her serene temples, and the redundant folds of her
dark velvet dress sweeping the carpet in a vast circle, that kept all

but the privileged at a deferential distance from her person. She
was glancing that evening over the pages of a little volume refulgent
in red and gold; it was the new Christmas book of the author of the
Pickwick Papers," which Mr. Spread had brought down with him
from London.

Mrs. Briscoe and Mr. Barker are arrived. The former is immersed in eider-down on the sofa opposite to Mrs. Spread, chatting
with Augusta about coughs and colds (in which she is profoundly
learned), and exceedingly anxious about the uvulas and tracheas of
Lancashire.

Mr. Barker is already engaged in a political argument with his
old friend, in which he is taking up a position he never took before
in his life, merely because Spread has taken the opposite ground.
They are seated in colloquial propinquity on two of the doctoral
chairs facing the fire; the one serene, but animated; the other in
wonderful good-humor, considering the events of the day, but still
pugnacious enough in all conscience. Behind the doctoral chairs,
upon a circular ottoman, are the two Smylys, half afraid of Barker,
whom they never saw before; but they still laugh merrily enough
at intervals, whatever it is that Philip Spread and Mr. St. Leger
are saying to amuse them. Philip is always confounding one girl
with the other, and no wonder, for they are as like as two pins, "particularly Laura," as Mr. St. Leger has just facetiously observed.
Mrs. Martin has not yet descended from the higher regions of the
mansion, where she has been consigning her frocked and trowsered
subjects to the charge of the maid, who in her turn will consign
them to Morpheus. But not a step backward will boy or girl go, until the zoological garden in the box has been visited and revisited—
the bear made to growl, the pig to grunt, the ass to bray, and the lion
to roar. On other occasions, the rod would restrain this untimely
zeal in the study of natural history, but it is the Saturnalia of the
Christian world, and the ivy and mistletoe have superseded the
birch. Seated on a stool at her mother's feet is the silent Elizabeth
(for it is Augusta's turn to minister at the tea-table) reading a letter, and chagrined at its contents. It has come from her tractarian
swain, to explain and excuse his absence; he has obstinate men to
deal with; he meets with new difficulties dayly; fears that the re-
suscitation of the ecclesiastical drama must be postponed to another
year, and has his thoughts evidently more engaged with Balaam
and his ass than with Elizabeth and her love.

Elizabeth having read the dispatch of her unfaithful shepherd,
and tried to convince herself that he was better employed at Salis-

bury, advancing the cause of theatricals and truth, than at Liverpool
paying the hackneyed attentions of an intended, put the letter into
her mother's hands—there was nothing, indeed, in any love-letter
of Owlet's that might not have been read in the High-street of Oxford—and, gliding across the room, seated herself beside her sister,
who wanted her support, in consequence of the enlargement of the
family circle.   Presently, Miss Spread, with the tinkling of a spoon
upon a salver (her father called it the President's Message), announced the completion of her arrangements, when—

"Gollrrrlr—gnlrrr—gnlrr—"

This was not a remark in the Welsh tongue, for there was no
native of the principality in the room, nor any one acquainted with
its language, not even Mrs. Martin, who was so great a linguist:
it was the peevish observation of Pico, the little greyhound, in reply
to an unintentional notice which Mr. Barker, with his foot in rising,
took of his sensitive tail, as he lay snug on the rug before the fire.
Mr. Barker started, looked very cross, and muttered something
about wild beasts in a drawing-room, which Pico seemed almost to
comprehend, for he uttered another—

"Gollrrr—gnllrr—"

and suddenly retreated, with his fierce little black eye fixed on the
equally irritated bachelor, under the ample covert of Mrs. Spread's
velvet, where he still continued to snarl.   Mrs. Spread rebuked and
threatened to chastise Pico, but the ottoman tittered audibly; the
Smyly girls being unable to control their mirth at the skirmish between the two Barkers.

"Let us go to the tea-table," said Mr. Spread, opportunely, taking
his friend by the arm.   "Come, St. Leger.   Mrs. Briscoe, let me
conduct you.   Come, Philip—chairs for the Miss Smylys.   We are
invited to the 'storied urn.' "

"And not without 'the animated bust,' sir," said the young Irishman, gallantly.   He was handing a chair to Adelaide Smyly as he
spoke, and the compliment might have been designed for her; or it
might have been meant for the president of the tea-table; for both
had superb figures (the charms in which the women of England surpass the world), and St. Leger, though nothing of an artist, had an
eye for the line of beauty.

Mrs. Spread never went to the tea-table; she rarely stirred from
her place beside the fire; she called herself a fire-worshiper, and
her husband used to say she was a lóco-foco.

Barker was excessively amusing, without having the slightest intention to divert the company.   The Spread girls thanked him for

the assistance he had given their papa in his researches after the villa on the Thames.   Augusta inquired if he did not love river and forest scenery.

"I am neither a Triton nor a Robin Hood," replied the bachelor, "I am quite content with the Serpentine and the scenery of Piccadilly."

"But though you are not a Robin Hood," said Mr. Spread, "I don't think, Barker, you would object any more than myself to pass a jovial hour with Friar Tuck under the green-wood tree."

"Friar Tuck, were he living, would willingly exchange the green-wood tree for the Star and Garter.   That's the true charm of Richmond."

"But the associations of that beautiful neighborhood," said Mrs. Martin, didactically, "I mean the literary associations, Thompson, Pope—"

"Whom nobody reads," interrupted Barker; "people read Wordsworth and Tennyson, but they don't read Dryden and Pope. Inform the public that Alfred Tennyson smoked a dozen cigars in the park, or on the terrace, and the association will bring some few pilgrims.   But of the thousands who flock to Richmond by omnibuses, rail-ways, and steamers, week-day or Sunday, nobody thinks of Alexander Pope more than of Alexander Selkirk."

"Very true, generally speaking," said Mr. Spread; "however, we are a strong Popish party in this house."

"But I engage there is a Wordsworthian interest," said the bachelor, "a lambkin and donkey party."

"Indeed there is," said Mrs. Spread, laughing, "and a Tennyson faction, too.

Philip Spread avowed himself a Wordsworthian; Augusta declared herself a Tennysonian, and was supported by Adelaide Smyly, who honestly confessed she had never read a line of the bard of Twickenham, except the "Messiah," which she had learned by task-work at school.

"How I detested the nymphs of 'Solyma!'   I was regularly punished with Pope once a-week."

"As Elizabeth and I were with the church-catechism by Miss Stanley," said Philip.

"I was luckier than Adelaide," said Laura Smyly, "for I was corrected with 'Montgomery's Satan,' and 'Pollock's Course of Time.'   My unpleasant associations are all connected with poetry of that order."

"Quite right to make the birch disagreeable," said Mr. Spread;

" but it is too bad to make young people hate roses and myrtles by making rods of them, eh, Mrs. Martin?"

"Really," said Mrs. Martin, smiling at this appeal to her school-room experience, "I think I shall take a hint from the method pursued with Miss Laura Smyly, and cultivate a just taste in poetry by using the trash of the present day for a system of secondary punishments."

"Do," said St. Leger, laughing; "whip Theodore well with the ' Omnipresence.' "

"Give him the ' Excursion' smartly," said Barker.

"Or ' Bells and Pomegranates,' " said Laura Smyly.

"Lay both ' Mr. and Mrs. Browning' on him," said St. Leger.

"Would you call that a secondary punishment?" said Mrs. Spread from the sofa. "But, tell me, Mr. Barker, have you read this charming little red book?" alluding to the Christmas present which she held in her hand.

"I never read either red books, green books, or blue books," said the bachelor, "sentiment, sedition, or statistics."

"Do you approve the modern system of illustrating works?"

"A good pen doesn't want the help of the pencil," said Barker, "and a bad pen is not the better for it. Time was, Mrs. Spread, when books were illustrated by wit and common-sense."

"And now," said Laura Smyly, completing the antithesis, not, perhaps, without a wish to please Mr. Barker, "and now they are only illustrated by Crookshank."

The bachelor *did* look pleased; and, animated by Miss Smyly's support, jumped up from the table, strutted up and down the open area before the fire, and lanched into a sweeping, indiscriminate attack upon the literature of the day, in which there was, of course, a vast deal of unfair but amusing stricture, with a dash here and there of equally just and poignant remark. The company listened with profound attention. At length, Mrs. Spread desired to know what the bachelor thought of the " Cricket on the Hearth."

"Now listen to the *Critic* on the Hearth," whispered Laura Smyly to her neighbor. But as Barker turned to Mrs. Spread to answer her question, it unfortunately happened that he again trod upon Pico's tail. Pico snapped at his toe, and would probably have bitten it, if Mrs. Spread had not promptly interfered, by snatching her favorite up, and correcting him on her lap with a tortoise-shell paper-knife. This done she desired Philip to pull the bell for a servant to remove both the greyhound and the kitten. A footman obeyed the summons, and at the same time presented his mistress with a note, which turned the conversation of the evening into another channel.

It was a note in a showy blue envelope, smelling of musk, with a seal of pink wax, bearing the sentimental and original device of a Cupid shooting at a heart. It was evidently a note of invitation; but a very uninviting one, indeed. The girls watched their mother's countenance as she opened it, and looked inquisitive.

"The Narrowsmiths!" said Mrs. Spread, with the gesture of a person suffering with intense cold, and dropping the note on the sofa, as she might have dropped a lump of ice, or a cold pebble.

"Dinner?" said her husband, also seized with a shuddering.

"Worse," said the lady.

"Worse!" repeated Spread, as if he could imagine nothing worse than a dinner at the Narrowsmiths.

"A house-warming! New Year's Day!"

"House-warming!" cried the father of the family.

"House-warming!" repeated the daughters.

"A house-warming at the Narrowsmiths!" exclaimed Philip—"of all kinds of entertainment—imagine the Narrowsmiths giving a house-warming, the Narrowsmiths who know less about calefactory arrangements and thermal comforts than any family in England."

"Calefactory arrangements and thermal comforts," repeated Laura Smyly, laughing. "What hard words, Philip, you do use—do tell us what they mean?"

"The arrangements for heating a house to be sure; supplying it with warm air and water."

"Why, then, not say so, in plain English, Philip?"

Barker began to conceive a favorable opinion of Laura Smyly from this successful sally.

Mr. Spread now drew his chair close to his fair wife, and they talked awhile apart on the subject of the menaced hospitality.

"We won't go, of course," said the wife, suppliantly.

"I fear we must," said the husband; "remember, my love, we declined their invitation at Michaelmas."

"We shall get our death of cold," said Mrs. Spread.

"We'll muffle well, my dear, particularly as it's a house-warming," he added, his eye twinkling with humor.

"Muffle," repeated his wife, as if she thought that all the muffling in the house would not be enough for a dinner with her husband's partner in the month of January.

"Well, my dear, we have till morning to consider the question.

I grant you it is a serious one—a very serious question—but now for our whist. Come, Mrs. Briscoe, you love your rubber—sixpenny points. Come, St. Leger, you play."

But Mr. St. Leger either did not play, or preferred chatting with the girls, who were now re-established on the ottoman.

They were amusing themselves with a specimen or two of bad spelling in Mrs. Narrowsmith's invitation.

"There is no excuse for bad spelling," said Mrs. Martin, who was a disciplinarian in orthography.

"But some words are *so* difficult," said Adelaide Smyly.

"There is always a way of evading them," said St. Leger "as my countryman, Giles Eyre, did."

"How did he manage?" inquired Barker.

"A friend invited him to dine, and he wrote an answer excusing himself on the ground of a fit of the gout. Some time after, his friend met him, and expressed his surprise at his having had that complaint, as it was not in his family. 'That's the truth,' said Giles Eyre; 'none of us ever had it in the memory of man.' 'Then,' asked his friend, 'what did you mean by saying in your note that the gout prevented your dining with me?'. 'Och,' said Giles, 'that's aisily explained—would you have had me lose my time spelling *rheumatism?'* "

There was a good laugh at St. Leger's story, and then Mr. Spread renewed his endeavors to make up a whist.

Laura Smyly plays," said Augusta Spread.

"Very little, sir," said Laura, gayly; "but I'm at your service if I'm wanting.

The Smyly girls were up to any thing—girls of the world—no nonsense about them, extremely amusing and easily amused, the very girls for country-houses, buxom, handsome, frolicsome, mettlesome girls; they rode, walked, danced, sung, and were both capital talkers and capital listeners, the latter a valuable accomplishment in both sexes, and a rare one.

"But we want a fourth," said Mr. Spread, counting his numbers.

"Come, Barker, you must join us; Miss Smyly will not undertake dummy."

"Decidedly not, sir," said Laura, laughing.

Barker had no objection to cards, but he played whist vilely. Moreover, he was a little weary after the day's journey, and was disposed to be refractory; but Miss Smyly had impressed him favorably by her rebuke of Philip, and he liked her all the better for the good-humored alacrity with which she had consented to play. Determined by these considerations, he condescendingly sat down to play one rubber, every body marveling to see him so gracious.

Such a whist as it was! Miss Smyly and Mr. Barker *versus* Mrs. Briscoe and Mr. Spread. Every body was delighted when Laura cut with Mr. Barker. But not one of the four players had the slightest real knowledge of the game. Hoyle would have either laughed or wept, had he been a looker-on. There was a reciprocal disclosure of hands before three cards were played—at least, a whist-player of any acuteness might have concluded almost to a certainty how the several suits were distributed.

"I suppose *somebody* has trumps," said Mrs. Briscoe, commencing the conversation.

"I depend on my partner," said Mr. Barker.

"Don't depend upon me, sir," said Laura. "I always hold such abominable cards—don't I, Adelaide? She doesn't hear me, Mr. St. Leger is so very amusing."

"I say nothing," said Mr. Spread, puffing his cheeks, and looking mysterious.

"Have you no diamond, Miss Smyly?"

Mrs. Briscoe had just played a diamond, and Laura had played a heart.

"Diamond—to be sure I have—lots of diamonds."

"We'll forgive her this time," said Mr. Spread.

"I'll never do it again, sir, said Laura.

"Until the next time," added Barker, with a playful grunt.

"I'm sure I thought nobody had diamonds but poor me," said the old lady. "Where *can* all the spades be?"

"I know somebody could answer that question," said Miss Laura Smyly.

"Spades are trumps, are they not?" asked Spread. Certainly, it is of great moment at whist to know which suit is the trump, but there is not a little disadvantage in postponing the inquiry until the middle of the game.

"It makes very little difference to me," said Mrs. Briscoe.

"Nor to me, ma'am," said Laura.

"Whist is a scientific game," said Mr. Spread, revoking, as he spoke, in the most transparent manner, but nobody took the least notice of it.

"The rest are mine," cried Barker; "we make the trick."

"Pardon me, Barker, the trick is ours."

"Yours!—one, two, three, four, five, six, seven, eight—we make two tricks."

"And you had three honors," said Mrs. Briscoe, good-naturedly registering her adversary's advantages.

"Game!" cried Barker.

"I held the queen," remonstrated Mr. Spread; "it fell to Miss Smyly's ace, and Mrs. Briscoe played the knave."

"Then we are only four," said Barker, counting two by honors, on the strength of the ace and king. It passed *sub silentio*, and so ended the first hand. The remainder of the rubber, it may be supposed, was equally scientific.

The Spread girls, Adelaide Smyly, Mr. St. Leger, and Philip, had, in the mean time, been very pleasant on the ottoman, or round about it. Philip was rallying Adelaide on her having rejected the addresses of a certain Tom Unthank, the dwarfish and monkey-faced proprietor of an estate of three thousand a-year, in Hereford-shire. Among other things, Philip warned her of what was proverbially said to be the fate of old maids—namely, to lead apes in a certain place not to be named to ears polite.

"I don't know," said Adelaide, "whether I shall lead apes or not in the other world, but no ape shall lead me in this, I promise you."

"Bravo, Laura!" cried Philip.

"My name is Adelaide, not Laura," said the young lady, looking as if she was hurt by Philip's blunder. He was very much annoyed at having made it; it was the third time that evening he had con-founded the sisters.

CHAPTER IX.

I am the merry wanderer of the night.
Midsummer Night's Dream.

The Dispersion—Mrs. Briscoe's Anxieties about lazy Letty—The Smyly girls at Beauty-set—Mr. Barker in Bed—The Watches of the Night—Mrs. Briscoe's nocturnal Attentions to the Bachelor—Breakfast—Appearance of Owlet—The Pie of Pies—How Owlet ate it—Results of Mrs. Briscoe's Activity—Petrarch and Laura—What detained Mr. Owlet—Rehearsal of the Miracle Play of Balaam—Revival of an Eremitical Institution.

Now took place the dispersion to bed-rooms and dressing-rooms; the time was come for exchanging silks for dimities, and the arts of the milliner for the simplicity of nature.

"I dare say my poor Letty is asleep long ago," said good Mrs. Briscoe to Elizabeth Spread, as that young lady attended her up stairs.

"I'll send mamma's maid to you," said Elizabeth.

"No, no, Bessie, my dear, I can go to bed very well without assistance; I'm used to it, my dear."

Elizabeth marveled, if such were the case, why Mrs. Briscoe incurred the trouble and expense of keeping a lady's-maid. As they moved along a corridor, the repose of some very industrious sleeper was painfully audible, and Mrs. Briscoe instantly recognized her poor Letty.

"Poor thing, she is not well," said the tender-hearted mistress; "the journey was too much for her; how heavily she sleeps! Wouldn't you say, my dear, she was feverish?"—pausing, and hearkening with attention to the nasal performance of the slumbering maid.

"I should say, ma'am, she is very sleepy. Good-night, dear Mrs. Briscoe."

And Elizabeth went her way to the room she shared with her sister Augusta, paying the Smylys a short visit *en passant*, and a merrier pair of lasses, at beauty-set, than Adelaide and Laura, were not to be found north or south of Trent. Adelaide was maid to Laura, and Laura was maid to Adelaide. How they rated one another about broken laces and tangled bobbins, tapped and slapped each other with fans and bouquets, bandied charges of inattentions and depredations; wished each other married, called each other geese, and having said and done every thing gay and girlish, foolish and funny, how they made a race for bed, as the last up was always to put out the candle.   They almost died laughing when they heard of Mrs. Briscoe's anxieties for the health of Letty.

"I only wish she was asleep herself," said Elizabeth; "I fear she won't sleep to-night at all, she took such very strong tea."

"Why did Augusta give it to her?" asked Laura.   "She'll decidedly walk to-night," speaking of Mrs. Briscoe as if she was a spirit.

"I hope and trust she will visit Mr. Barker."

"What fun it would be," cried the other.

"Do you remember her at uncle Bedford's, Laura?" said Adelaide.   "She was always watching the watch-dog, nursing my aunt's nurse-tender, and doctoring the apothecary's boy at Richmond. And, such an ear as she had for a mouse in a closet—"

"Or a bow-wow in the yard," added Laura, jumping into bed. "Good-night, Elizabeth.   Adelaide, bolt the door before you put out the candle."

Mr. Barker, meanwhile, was slumbering not quietly but deeply. He reviewed, before he slept, the occurrences of the day, and found several departures from the fixed principles of his life to upbraid himself with; he had suffered himself to be betrayed into several instances of *bonhommie*, had behaved more as became Mr. Spread than Mr. Barker; in short, though he had not sinned altogether intentionally, he felt lowered in his own esteem, and made a thousand resolutions to be more inflexibly unamiable for the future.   It may well be supposed he did not forget, among other subjects of disagreeable reflection, the boorish simpleton in search of an uncle, with whom he had traveled part of the day.   But the more he thought about him, he felt less and less uneasy, and even began to laugh at himself for being so very weak, as even for a moment to fancy it possible, or even probable, that there could be any consanguinity between them.   Fear makes men as credulous as hope; and if he was to live in dread of being claimed as an uncle by the son of every man who chose to die in the colonies, a very harassing life he would have of it.   All this was mighty well, as long as he remained awake, but Queen Mab is, of all ladies, the least trammeled by logical rules, and, accordingly, no sooner did Mr. Barker fall asleep than there was an end to all sound reasoning, and he went through a series of imagin-

D

ary persecutions (exaggerations of the real annoyances of the day)
from a monster, in shape between a man and a bear (but sometimes
taking the form of Pico), who insisted on being related to him in
some shocking and inexplicable manner.

But Mab was not Barker's only female visitor that night.   Mrs.
Briscoe having dosed her maid (who had no other fever than that
which she might well have caught from the pile of blankets over
her) with a bottle which was to be taken every third hour, had
promised to return in due time to administer the second draught, and
had arranged that, should Mistress Letty be asleep, she would leave
a light in her room, and also her own watch, so as to enable the poor
thing (whose only complaint was laziness) to help herself to the contents of the bottle during the rest of the night.   Proceeding, about
two o'clock in the morning, to carry this design into execution, she
found her watch out of order, and it immediately occurred to her to
borrow a watch from one of the Smyly girls.   Mrs. Briscoe slept so
little herself, that she had no idea of the value set upon sleep by
other people, or what a grievance it is to have it chased from the
eyelids wantonly.

Tap, tap, tap, went the old lady's knuckles.

No reply; the sisters were sound asleep.

Tap, tap—louder than before.

Laura awoke, and turned upon her side.

Tap, tap, again went the knuckles.

Laura sat up in the bed, and inquired who was there.

"Only me—Mrs. Briscoe, my dear; the door is bolted, my dear."

"We are in bed, Mrs. Briscoe; we are indeed—what *is* the matter?"

"Nothing; don't be frightened, dear.   I only want the loan of
your watch.   Letty has to take her bottle every third hour; I hope
and trust she will be better in the morning."

Laura was highly exasperated, but got up, opened the door, and
handed Mrs. Briscoe what she wanted, wishing both her and her
patient devoutly with a certain spiritual personage more eminent
for his talents than his virtues.

The old lady trotted off with the watch, and, mistaking doors, entered Mr. Barker's room instead of Letty's.   The rooms were similar in size and furniture, and, by the dim light which the taper gave
(only, in fact, making darkness visible), there was no very striking
difference between the bachelor and the maid, buried as both were
under huge mountains of bed-clothes.   The old lady, accordingly,
having listened to Barker's breathing, and carefully tucked him in,

deposited the light (with a bottle and a spoon) on a small table which stood at the side of the bed, shrouded by the curtains; and, having placed the watch in a convenient position (not observing Barker's watch which was lying there too), retired noiselessly, highly satisfied with herself for all her benevolent arrangements. But several hours afterward, growing fidgety again, and thinking that the watch would be of more use to herself than to Letty, she returned, tucked Barker in again with the utmost tenderness, and carried off his watch instead of Miss Smyly's, which it resembled extremely. The man-servant, who came to the bachelor's room at eight o'clock the next morning (and a thoroughly English winter's morning it was, not very distinguishable from night), removed the candlestick, with the bottle and spoon; and when Mr. Barker rose, and had completed his toilet, he took up the watch which he found on the table, placed it in his waistcoat pocket, and went down to breakfast. Mrs. Briscoe, on her part, before she went down, was very particular in returning Miss Laura Smyly her property, or what she believed to be such.

On entering the parlor, Barker had the pleasure of being introduced to Mr. Owlet, who had arrived during the night. He was a tall, slender, grave, absent man, under thirty years of age, with long face and sallow complexion; his eyes small and abstract, diffuse hair, capacious mouth, and a voice as hollow and spectral as if it came out of the depth of those remote ages in the study of which he passed his life. A long, black frock, descending almost to his ankles, was the only remarkable part of his dress.

Mr. Spread's was the house for a breakfast; and, as Christmas is the time for good cheer at all hours, you may conceive what a breakfast Mr. Spread's was. None of your flimsy town breakfasts, only fit for invalids and women, exhausted rakes and jaded beauties; but the jolly, substantial breakfast of men of business, in the fullness of health and the plenitude of spirits. It was a breakfast of many breads and many meats, substantial as the prosperity, and various as the resources of England. A side-board, oppressed with viands, neither sighed nor groaned, because it is only in fiction that side-boards utter such sentimental sounds. Mahogany commands its feelings to admiration; but if oppression could have wrung a sigh from a side-board, the effect would have been produced that merry morning. In the center stood, or, rather, towered, a vast pie, which was surrounded with minor attractions, such as tongues, fowls, collars, and marmalades, just as a great planet is attended by a body-guard of satellites. But as Jupiter excels his moons, so did that pie surpass collars, fowls, and tongues in magnitude and glory. That was a pie indeed!—a subject for hymn and history; a pie to be held in such reverence as Mohammedans pay the Caaba, or Christians the chapel of Loretto—evidently the production of a great artist, a Palladio of pastry, or a Wren of cooks. It was more an Acropolis or a temple than a pie; worthy of being served to a Lord Abbot, amid anthems; not made to be opened with knife of Sheffield, but carved with blade of Toledo or Damascus. It might have been considered as a poem, a composition of talent and turkeys, of genius and grouse. Into such a pie was it that Bion, the philosopher, wished himself metamorphosed, that wisdom, in his form, might captivate the sons of men. Stubbles had been thrashed, covers ransacked, woods depopulated, and preserves destroyed, to furnish forth its mighty concave. It was a pie under whose dome you would have wished to live, or been content to die. Appetite grew by feeding on it; its very sight was better than to eat aught else eatable. It dilated the soul and exalted the character to be in the same room with so noble a creation of gastronomic mind.

When that pie was in ruins it reminded those who beheld it of the Coliseum.

Spread ate it festively.

Barker ate it critically.

Philip Spread ate it transcendentally.

Mr. Owlet ate it medievally and monastically, and a right hearty way it is of eating a Christmas pie, let me tell you. How he did eat it—with an appetite like zeal, with a zeal like fanaticism! As to the ladies, they only breathed its incense, and it was a meal, which, with coffee and toast, was solid enough for them.

Breakfast had not long commenced, when Mr. Spread and Mr. Barker fell to comparing London time with Liverpool time, and Philip commenced a lecture on the lunar method of finding the longitude. Barker produced Miss Smyly's watch, and Mrs. Spread, thinking it a pretty one, begged to see and examine it.

"It would be unfair to inquire who L. S. is?" said Mrs. Spread, observing those letters neatly engraved upon the case.

"L. S.!" exclaimed Barker.

"A gift from a fair lady, of course," said Mr. Spread. "Come, Barker, never blush; Mrs. Spread gave *me* a watch the week before I married her."

Barker looked cross, and denied that there were any such letters on his watch; but the letters were there to speak for themselves—L. S., in unmistakeable characters; and the watch went round the table, so that every body might see them.

"I protest," cried Laura Smyly, when it came round to her, "it is extremely like *mine*."

"It *is* yours," exclaimed her sister, examining it; "I should know it any where."

"Oh, ho!" cried Mr. Spread.

"And where is mine, then?" demanded Barker, in extreme perplexity.

"And whose watch can I have got?" asked Laura, equally confounded.

"It is easy to guess," said Mr. Spread.

"Mine!—impossible!" protested the astonished and much-embarrassed bachelor; but there was no denying it—P. B. standing for Peter Barker as palpably as L. S. stood for Laura Smyly.

"I think Laura has found a Petrarch," said Mrs. Spread, aside to Adelaide; but Barker overheard it, and was very angry.

As soon as Mrs. Briscoe's participation in the transaction was known, the mysterious exchange was soon explained. It was food for mirth during the holydays; and Mrs. Briscoe's narrative, aside to the girls, heightened the jest vastly. "Only think," she said, "my dears, of my tucking the gentleman in twice; but indeed he was very good-natured yesterday evening to poor Letty and me."

How Mr. Spread did enjoy it; how he shook and laughed in his Rabelaisian chair; and how mad it made the baccalaurean cynic!

It was very scandalous of the Rev. Bartholomew Owlet—his intimates called him Bat—not sooner to have joined the Christmas circle that assembled round the hearth of the generous Liverpool merchant. Mr. and Mrs. Spread were both hurt by his conduct, though they said nothing. As to Elizabeth herself, who ought most to have resented the delinquency, she took the most merciful view of it imaginable; far from uttering a harsh word, she never harbored a harsh thought of her intended, but argued herself into a firm belief that he who was so pious a priest could never prove an unfaithful shepherd. Mr. Owlet, however, might very well have suspended his somber pursuits during the holydays; it would only have been a reasonable sacrifice upon the altar of love—a shrine old enough, one would suppose, to command the veneration of the most enthusiastic antiquarian; but if he was for bowers at all, it was for ivy bowers; and he continued to mope in the cloisters of Salisbury until the old year was at its very last gasp, poring over manuscripts and missals, planning the revival of the Miracle Plays and Mysteries, and every now and then (accompanied by his friend and fellow-laborer, Lord John Yore) "complaining to the moon" of divers

bishops and deans, whose wretched, low-church bigotry led them
to regard with an unfavorable eye the pious mummeries that diver-
sified the religion of the chivalrous and feudal times.

Lord John Yore was the son of the Duke of Gonebye, a member
of the House of Commons, furious to repeal the laws of mortmain,
and as mad about Maypoles as Lord Dudley Stuart is about Poles.
Lord John believed in nothing more strenuously than that the glory
of England fell with the monasteries, and that a statesman could propose to himself no nobler object than to propagate a monkish spirit,
and remove the obstacles thrown by the barbarous policy of Protes-
tantism in the way of the re-establishment of the religious houses.
He had failed once or twice in experiments of his own to get up little priories in different places, as models for larger institutions, and
to direct the stream of public opinion into the same devout channel;
but, undeterred by his ill-success, he was now engaged, with only
redoubled ardor, in a similar undertaking, upon a part of his father's
estates—namely, to organize a peculiar species of eremitical institution of the most venerable antiquity ; it consisted of a collection of
cells, at some small distance from each other, each hermit having
his own, and providing for himself apart, the reverse of his usual
conventual system.   Several " egregious clerks" of Oxford, and two
or three layman of the Coningsby school, had already applied for
admission into this new fraternity.   But Lord John's warmest supporter was Elizabeth Spread's fantastic lover, and he, in his turn,
received from Lord John the most cordial aid and encouragement in
his battles with deans and chapters, to overcome their narrow prej-
udices against the conversion of cathedrals into play-houses.   His
lordship, indeed, went farther than merely advocating Owlet's views,
for he actually engaged himself to be one of the reverend gentleman's *corps dramatique*, and promised to take the part of the quadruped in the miracle play of "Balaam," in case no spiritual person
was to be found disposed to appear in it.   There had actually been
a rehearsal in Owlet's chambers, and the actors had complimented
one another highly upon the merits of their several performances.
Owlet had a magnificent beard, and his noble friend a superb pair
of ears.   Several good hits were made in the course of the piece,
but the audience (consisting of some dozen of tractarian divines,
friends of Owlet, and Young-England men, cronies of Lord John)
were particularly delighted when it became Owlet's duty to smite
his beast, and the latter requested the prophet not to hit so hard.
In fact, it was this rehearsal that detained the minor-canon from
paying his *devoirs* at the feet of his fair lady, who, perhaps, would

not have been quite so tolerant, had she known what sort of animal it was whose society he preferred to hers.

This important business, however, having been transacted, Mr. Owlet prepared to flit, and Lord John, being also bound to the north, they agreed to meet on a certain evening in London, and travel together by the night-train to Liverpool. Had the home secretary issued a search-warrant on that occasion to examine the luggage of this eccentric pair, the officers employed would have made some extremely curious and amusing discoveries. In Owlet's portmanteau would have been found the wild costume and enormous beard in which he sustained the character of Balaam, a change of hair-shirts, a discipline, a surplice, and a packet of letters containing his correspondence with the Mayor of Salisbury, relative to a procession of Flagellants, which the active canon had been desirous some months before of exhibiting in the streets of that ancient city.

CHAPTER X.

A wretched rascal, that will bind about
The nose of his bellows, lest the wind get out
When he's abroad. Sweeps down no cobwebs,
But sells them for cut fingers, and the spiders,
That cost him nothing, to fat old ladies' monkeys.
A slave and an idolater to Pecunia.

The Staple of News.

Christmas in the House of a Miser—Gripus and his Wife in Council—A Winter-piece—How Mrs. Narrowsmith affected the Thermometer—Who were to be asked to the House-warming—Proposition to invite the Bachelor to Tea—Isaac Narrowsmith resolves to give Champagne—His wife determines not to have Napkins—Character of Mr. Narrowsmith—Their Tea-table—How Providence sent the Miser a Silver Fourpence.

VERY different were the Christmas doings in the house of Mr. Spread's partner, the new house of the Narrowsmiths in Rodney-street. No comfort, no cheer, no charity. Neither hearts nor hearths were warm. No pleasantry brightened the countenance— no friends thronged the table—no pie towered upon the board— challenging attack, and throwing down the gauntlet to voracity. The house was a fair one enough—the rooms sufficiently large—all the permanent accommodations reasonably complete—but it was bleak and dreary; penurious fires drew forth the damp without dispelling the cold; stinted draperies gave easy access to the wintry winds through the crevices of the windows; threadbare carpets left the floors as chill as those of vaults or warehouses: deficient furniture of mean quality, grim without antiquity, and rigidly excluding all the warm colors, consummated the dreary effect, and made it one of the last houses of the land (of houses roofed and glazed) in which any body in good-humor with himself and the world would wish to entertain his friends, or be entertained by them. Every thing in Rodney-street was managed upon the greatest possible retrench-ment and the least possible comfort principle. Nothing was on a large scale but shabbiness; there was abundance of nothing but bad wine in the cellar and cold water on the table. This shivering and starving went, of course, as usual, by the specious name of economy, whereas it was extravagance and waste of the most absurd kind, for there are two ways of squandering the gifts of fortune; they may be wasted in avarice as well as in prodigality, by a Nœvius as well as by a Nomentanus.

In a parlor, figuratively called a dining-room, by the side of what, metaphorically speaking, might be said to be the fire, sat in domestic council Mr. Narrowsmith and his wife. It was quite a winter-piece. The painter, to take the picture, should have been one whose line was boors in a frost. The room looked funereal, as if it had been furnished by an undertaker, and a particularly gloomy one. The curtains, newly hung, were of some paltry drab-colored stuff, and as much too narrow and too short as it was possible to make them, without their ceasing to suggest the idea that they were designed for curtains. A wretched Kidderminster, the more wretched for being new like the curtains, and much too small for the space to be covered, had been violently stretched and tortured with tacks to make the most of it; and when the most was made, it left a broad track of board extending all round the apartment, as bare as the pavement in the street. This track was studded with dingy mahogany chairs, few and far between, a dozen being required to do the duty of twice that number, like a garrison after a bloody siege. The shriveled rug on the hearth-stone made as poor an attempt to cover it as the tortured Kidderminster did to cover the floor. The cold black stone was only about three quarters concealed by it, and a villianously meager cat—a cat as lean as Cassius—sitting right in the center of the rug, with her green eyes pensively fixed upon the grate, as if she was pondering upon the vice of avarice, plainly proved that not so much as a fat mouse did credit to Mrs. Narrowsmith's housekeeping.

Mr. Isaac Narrowsmith, a small, mean man, dressed in seedy black, with vulgar arithmetic in every line of his pinched and sallow features, little, sharp, suspicious eyes, and a nose not worth talking about, having made up his little mind to give a miserable dinner, was now debating with his worthy consort upon the guests to be invited, and the cheap dishes and false wines to be imposed upon such as should honor their bad cheer. It was to be at once their annual dinner to the Spreads, and a feast to celebrate their removal to Rodney-street from the baser quarter of the town where they had previously resided. If harmony of tastes is a pledge of happiness in the married state, Mr. and Mrs. Narrowsmith ought to have been happy as turtle-doves, for the lady was in her way, and in her departments, as pitiful and griping as the gentleman. They had but one soul between them, and that might have been lodged in a nut-shell. Mr. Spread (who, as we have seen, was one of the few who now condescend to read Pope) used to call them Mr. and Mrs. Gripus; and Philip, being fresh from the study of mechanics, gave them the sobriquet of the male and female screw.

Mrs. Narrowsmith was a tall, muscular, harsh woman, with flat, square, pale, rigid, frigid features; she would have made an admirable matron of a work-house or a jail. When Mr. Narrowsmith married her, she was the widow of a rich planter in the West Indies, and she looked like a woman who could brandish the whip and wallop her negresses. She was about as genial as an icicle, and as mild a creature as a white bear after a bad day's fishing in the frozen seas. She was even harder, colder, and keener than her husband. The thermometer fell in her neighborhood; she actually radiated cold, and people who sat beside her got sore throats. She had one good point, her hair—that was beautiful—a golden brown, and remarkably luxuriant; but, as it were, to compensate for its beauty, it was clumsily arranged; part held in awkward captivity by a comb of spurious tortoise-shell, part falling in graceless negligence upon a shoulder unworthy to receive it. Of the maternal air and aspect she had nothing. Who could fancy that dry, harsh, frigid woman suckling a babe? though you could easily figure her to yourself chronicling small, very small, beer.

What this incomparable lady wore upon the present occasion she almost always wore, except when she appeared at *fêtes*. It was an old black silk dress, which not a maid-servant in Mrs. Spread's house would have put on her back. It was very tight, very short, and not worth five shillings. Its shortness had the agreeable effect of exhibiting stockings of a very subdued white, and shoes that looked as if they had been made by her husband's shoemaker.

"How many shall we have?" asked the miser, chafing his skinny fingers, preparing to count the list of his company upon them. "Ourselves, two; Maria, three—"

Maria, or, more accurately, Maria Theresa, was the daughter and only child of the Narrowsmiths. She was twenty-three, and too like her mother to be much of a beauty, either in person or in mind; but she was too young to affect the thermometer in the same degree; besides, she had her mother's hair; and, having been three years at a boarding-school (where she learned to thump pianos, and call it music, to bedaub paper, and call it painting in water-colors), was considered in her circle a highly-accomplished young woman. Of course she was a great, that is to say, a rich match. She had not herself thought much about matrimony, but her considerate parents had been speculating for some time upon Philip Spread as an eligible husband for her. The Spreads had no notion that such a project was even in embryo.

" Ourselves three, the Spreads five," continued the penurious merchant.

" Only four Spreads—three and four are seven," said the lady.

" Seven—the Neverouts won't."

" Of course they won't ; they never dine out in winter."

Then why did Mrs. Narrowsmith invite them ? Simply because they never dined out in winter.

" What of the Marables ?"

" The Marables keep New Year's Day with old Mrs. Marable at Birkenhead. Maria ascertained it ; don't they, Maria ?"

" Yes, mamma," replied Miss Narrowsmith.

" But you asked them ?" continued Isaac.

" I did, of course. We were so long in their debt that I positively felt ashamed. Now the compliment is paid, there's a weight off my mind."

" Seven—George Voluble makes eight—the Crackenthorpes ten —Dr. and Mrs. Prout twelve. Will General Guydickens come ?"

" Yes, and Miss Guydickens—he never dines out without her, and we can't do without the general's man."

" Fourteen," said the miser, summing up. " I have been thinking it would be right to ask Mr. Spread's friend, Mr. Barker."

" Won't it do to ask him to tea ? The Reverend Mr. Thynne and Mr. Fitzroy, the commissioner, are only asked to tea. I'm told Mr. Barker is one of your London fine gentlemen, who cock up their noses at every thing, and can't dine without champagne and napkins. You can't be so infatuated, Mr. Narrowsmith, as to think of giving champagne ?"

The miser crossed his legs, twirled his thumbs, and looked very serious and miserable ; thinking of his partner's dinners, and of what was likely to be expected from a man worth a hundred thousand pounds. Then Mr. Crackenthorpe was a rail-way prince, and General Guydickens was a great rail-way man, too, and a sort of a nabob into the bargain. Isaac Narrowsmith was actually so infatuated as to be thinking of giving champagne, with some little fluctuation in his mind as to the question whether his champagne

should be French or British. Conscience and vanity pronounced
for the foreign article—avarice and meanness declared for our home
produce.

"Well," said the female screw, divining the cogitations of her
spouse as perfectly as if her soul was a portion of his, "I always leave the wine to you—only tell me if you make up your
mind to have champagne, that I may borrow Doctor Prout's
glasses." A bit of forecaste, on the part of the fair speaker,
from which the reader will probably infer that Doctor Prout's
table was not the most celebrated in Liverpool for the jovial size
of his goblets.

"Borrow them," said Mr. Narrowsmith, with admirable economy
of words, conveying both his determination to produce the sparkling
wine, and his concurrence in his wife's plan for restricting the
consumption of it within the closest possible limits.

"I positively won't have napkins, then," said Mrs. Narrowsmith,
her frugal mind jumping as nimbly as her husband's from one sordid
speculation to another.

On the evening of the same day, the Narrowsmiths were at tea
in the parlor described in the foregoing chapter, the drawing-rooms
being too fine to be lived in, and accordingly reserved for state occasions—weddings, balls, and house-warmings! The tea made by
Miss Maria Theresa was very different from that made by Augusta
Spread. It was a different leaf—perhaps that of another tree altogether; its price was three and sixpence the pound, and it was advertised and recorded in Messrs. Sloe and Twankay's list of teas as
" a good strong breakfast tea, earnestly recommended to the use of
families and *schools*." It was the very tea to be administered to
Mrs. Briscoe; there was nothing in it to agitate the nerves, or to
murder sleep, whatever other damage it might do the drinker's
constitution. The genial Mrs. Narrowsmith had just finished her
second cup of this innocent mixture, when two notes were handed
her by a not-overclean or well-appointed lad, intended to enact a
page, as appeared from the multitude of tarnished buttons on his
jacket—a jacket that was manifestly a resurrection in the jacket
form of one of the oldest of his master's old coats. The notes were
presented on a salver made of one of those wonderful metals which
(the public is assured by the patentees) is not only a "perfect substi-
tute" for silver, but more genuine than silver itself.

Every thing in the Narrowsmiths' house was either second-hand
or spurious; imitations, substitutes, things " as good as new," wonderful bargains, delft not to be distinguished from china, tallow can-

dles superior to wax, cottons equal to silks, "old lamps for new," German silver and albata plate.

One of the notes was from the Spreads—an acceptance. With what reluctance was that note written! The second was no sooner opened than it produced a sensation almost electric. It came from the family who had so cunningly been asked to dinner, because it was believed that they had accepted a previous invitation. The biters were bitten! The Marables were coming—all the Marables —Mr. and Mrs. Marable, Miss Marable, Miss Lucy Marable, and Master Frederic Marable—innumerable Marables; it was all a mistake about their engagement to Birkenhead. The miser looked tragically comic, his lady looked comically tragic, and, as to Maria Theresa, notwithstanding her imperial name, she narrowly escaped having her ears boxed by her mild mamma, who, excited by the spirit of parsimony, was much more like Xantippe than her husband was like Socrates.

Mrs. Narrowsmith said it was "A nice to-do!"

Mr. Narrowsmith observed, in equally classic phraseology, that it was "A pretty kettle of fish!"

The mother said the daughter was "a careless slut," and she could hardly have chosen an adjective and substantive more happily describing that young lady had she been professor of rhetoric in the college of Billingsgate.

The miser, as became his sex, was the first to recover his composure.

"It can't be helped," he said, philosophically, "we must only make the best of it."

"And, after all," said Maria Theresa, regaining confidence, "a dinner for twelve is a dinner for twenty—indeed, mother, I have heard you say so twenty times."

And in truth this was a doctrine which Mrs. Narrowsmith had frequently not only broached, but acted on, in her hospitable dispensations.

"We shall have twenty, if all come," said the merchant, lugubriously.

"James, remove the tea-things," said Mrs. Narrowsmith, with asperity. "Put that cold muffin carefully by; take care of the tea-leaves. Maria, go and look after the napkins—don't leave more out than will be absolutely necessary: eighteen will do. Wait till I give a dinner and ball again! What are you looking at, Mr. Narrowsmith? Do you see any thing on the floor?"

The merchant had just fixed his little keen eyes upon a small shining object at some distance from him, just where the tortured Kidderminster refused to go any farther. Mrs. Narrowsmith directed her tolerably acute visual organs to the same point; but Maria Theresa, who was leaving the room to execute the commission respecting the napkins, not only discovered what the object was, but picked it up, proclaiming the important fact, that it was a silver fourpence. Who could have dropped it there? Who could have been so profligately careless of their money? The Narrowsmiths disclaimed the ownership of the glittering fourpence, all of them; yet Mr. Narrowsmith made no scruple of seizing it to his own uses, and depositing it in his pocket, observing to his wife, as he did so—

"How providential that I saw it."

This was, perhaps, the only sentiment bordering upon piety which escaped Mr. Narrowsmith's lips during the entire of the sacred season, when, as "sweetest Shakspeare" says—

> "No planets strike,
> No fairy takes, no witch has power to charm,
> So hallow'd and so gracious is the time."

Isaac Narrowsmith was a merchant plebeian, not a merchant prince; he had the faculties for acquiring wealth, without the talents or the virtues to enjoy it. He was as narrow-souled as he was narrow-chested; efficient in his counting-house, out of it a nobody; he had none of the genial qualities, none of the literary tastes, none of the social dispositions of his partner. Reach of mind he was so deficient in, that he was always trying to overreach. With books he was totally unacquainted, save the waste-book, the day-book, and the ledger; as to the arts, he was only versed in the mean ones, and the only science he had ever studied was that false arithmetic which teaches men to be penny wise and pound foolish. Narrowsmith was a man of illiberal opinions, whom circumstances attached to the Liberal party. He voted with the Whigs, but the Whigs could well have dispensed with his ungracious and discreditable support. He was a Reformer, who sneered at Lord John Russell; a free-trader, who made light of Mr. Cobden and Mr. Villiers. But with all his meannesses as a private individual, and all his worthlessness as a public man, he was the darling of the lady on the wheel; she smiled on him, pampered, cockered him; the work

of his shriveled hands succeeded; all his speculations prospered.
He speculated widely, and often daringly, in all manner of securities
and insecurities; always wide awake upon 'Change, with an eye to
the main chance, and never for an instant diverted from his schemes
of self-aggrandizement by any consideration of humanity or sense
of moral obligation. In short, he was not much of a Christian,
although he went to church; but very much of a Jew, although he
did not frequent the synagogues.

CHAPTER XI.

Pennyboy Senior. Who can endure to see
The fury of men's gullets and their stomachs?
What fires, what cooks, what kitchens might be spared?
What ponds, what parks, coops, garners, magazines?
Hunger is not ambitious. What need hath nature
Of perfumed napkins or of silver dishes?

The Staple of News.

The Night before the House-warming—Mrs. Narrowsmith compared to Agamemnon—A Miser's Cook—Her Professional Career—Deeds without a Name—The Polar Expedition—The Miser's Company—A Cold Fire—Thirteen at Table—Who made the Fourteenth—A Monosyllabic Lady and a Dissyllabic Lady—Misconduct of Doctor Prout—Use of an Epergne—Pursuits of Literature at a Dinner-Table—An Irish Row—Mr. Barker on Absenteeism—Mr. Barker charms Mr. Crackenthorpe.

THE night before a dinner, in an establishment sorrily appointed, is only comparable in anxiety, bustle, and confusion to a night before a battle—such a night as Homer describes as passed upon one occasion by the Greek generalissimo, or that which preceded the fight of Agincourt, so marvelously related by the chorus in the play of Henry the Fifth. In humble imitation of the great dramatist, we must here give "a little touch" of Mrs. Narrowsmith "in the night," not omitting to invoke "a muse of *fire*," before we engage in so cold a subject.

She first reviewed her *batterie de cuisine*, which was not exactly in the state that M. Soyer would call efficient. She next inspected her cutlery, which, like bad writing, was sadly in want of brilliancy; but then, *en revanche*, it abounded in point, for the knives were beginning to look exceedingly like skewers, as if nothing, even a knife, could escape the emaciating influences of so niggardly a house. Then she marshaled the spoons, missed a couple, and made a fuss and uproar about them, as if they had been made of the gold of Peru, instead of the silver of Germany. The plates and dishes were reconnoitered next: three plates were cracked, two dishes were absent; perhaps they had absconded in company with the spoons, taking a hint from the runaway dish in the nursery rhyme, or prescient of the revolting uses to which their mistress meditated putting them.   These preliminaries having been dispatched, and Mrs. Narrowsmith having settled in her own mind from whom she should borrow the many necessary articles which were not forthcoming from her own stores—who was to be drawn upon for plate, who for china, who was to lend an epergne, who contribute a table-cloth of the size requisite, and who was to accommodate her with a second pair of nut-crackers—this paragon of wives and pink of housewives proceeded, in company with her cook and her daughter, to lay the foundations of the several made-dishes (as she called them), which were to form the lateral ornaments and attractions of the board.

Mrs. Narrowsmith's cook was as good a cook as was to be had for the wages which Mrs. Narrowsmith paid her.   In personal neatness, in culinary talent, and in moral principle, she was just the kind of cook that Swift had in his eye in those unlucky directions of his to servants, which are almost the only directions that nine servants out of ten ever attend to.   However, cook the lady was (for she was as much a lady as her mistress), cook by office, profession, and experience.   She had ruled the roast for a Welsh parson, which must have made her familiar with jovial diet; she had ministered in the kitchen of a half-pay captain of infantry, where she could not have failed to see lordly cheer; she had officiated for briefless barristers in lodgings, the best of all academies for the finer branches of gastronomy; and she had already lived in the unctuous service of the Narrowsmiths nearly four years, ample time to perfect her education, particularly as the climate of the kitchen was never of that high temperature which must so materially enervate a cook's frame, and embarrass her in the discharge of her focal duties.

Such had been the career, such the fortunes, of the enterprising and accomplished Dorothea Potts (for that was the name of the ingenious and exemplary woman), in concert with whom, alternately directing and directed, Mrs. Narrowsmith was now engaged in a variety of mysterious operations, over jars and saucepans, unthought of by Glass, unimagined by Kitchener.   It is sickening, nay, maddening, to think for a moment of the things that are occasionally eaten, or served up to be eaten, in this carnivorous, herbivorous, frugivorous, and omnivorous world, by the few who have the luck, or the ill-luck (as the case may be), to be born under an eating star.

There was fearful cooking that night in Rodney-street, mixtures of all things cheap and rancid, sweets that should have been sour,

and sours that should have been sweet; Mrs. Narrowsmith manufactured custards without precedent, Miss Narrowsmith fabricated
puddings without example, while th. *soi-disant* cook concocted inexplicable gravies and appalling soups. A dropper-in during the
orgies might well have cried,

> "How now, ye secret, black, and midnight hags,
>   What is't ye do?"

and the trio might, with equal propriety, have replied, like the
witches,

> "A deed without a name."

The setting-out of the Spreads for Rodney-street, when the inevitable hour came, was not unlike the departure of a crew of hardy
adventurers upon an overland journey to the pole. The muffling
was prodigious; the demand for furs, flannel, inside-waistcoats,
lambs'-wool hose, shawls, boas, all the warm clothing reconcilable
with the semblance of dinner-dress, was very brisk indeed. Mr.
Spread fortified himself with worsted stockings under the silk, and
put on an additional shirt; Mr. Barker, who had with difficulty
been prevailed upon to go at all, re-enforced his ordinary raiment
with a couple of supplementary vests; and Mrs. Spread looked
quite portly in the voluminous petticoats which she thought it discreet to wear, starting, as she was, upon an expedition to the frigid
zone. Mrs. Martin had not been invited even to tea, at which Mrs.
Spread was much displeased; but the governess herself was very
well content to stay at home, as she was never happier than when
she was ruling her little kingdom, or composing some work upon the
rights and prerogatives of woman.

The table was spread for twenty, but the party that assembled
was considerably under the mark. Of the formidable Marable family, only two, the old people, made their appearance; they were
the first arrivals; the little Spread faction were the next, Barker
keeping close to Mrs. Spread, determined to have her for his neighbor at dinner. Then were announced Major-general and Miss
Guydickens, the former, a parched old East-Indiaman, rigid as a
poker and dull as a door-post; his daughter, a young lady six feet
in altitude, with a neck like a crane's, and competent to talk of nothing in the world but Dost Mohammed and her cousin Lieutenant
Curry, who shot a tiger and wounded a hippopotamus. These
were followed by Doctor and Mrs. Prout, who never entered a
room together, Mrs. Prout always hanging in the rear to adjust a

preposterous cap, and stick the last pin in her stomacher.   Then came Tom Voluble, and had not been two minutes in the room before he touched upon the weather, the funds, Irish distress, French politics, gun-cotton, rotten potatoes, President Polk, and Miss Cushman.   The Crackenthorpes were the last—they always were ; Mr. Crackenthorpe blamed his wife, and Mrs. Crackenthorpe blamed her husband ; then both blamed their watches, and while they were thus occupied, dinner was announced by the gentleman in soiled gloves, who acted butler upon this solemn occasion.   The Narrowsmiths had made no arrangements for the pairing off of the company, so there was a scramble of gentlemen for ladies, and this was fortunate for Barker, who secured Mrs. Spread for himself.   Mr. Narrowsmith gave his arm to Mrs. Crackenthorpe, because she was glowing in crimson and rubies.   The Prouts and the Marables exchanged husbands and wives.   Tom Voluble went off chattering with the fair Maria Theresa, who was gorgeously attired in expectation of Philip Spread, and grievously chagrined at his non-appearance.   Philip had been formally and even pointedly invited to dinner but preferred accompanying his sisters and the Smylys to the evening-party.   The never-failing courtesy of Mr. Spread would have made him offer his arm to the miser's wife, even had she not been so refulgent as she was in yellow satin, with a turban on her head, which would have electrified the streets of Bagdad. But just as the portly merchant was advancing to execute his polite intention, Mr. Crackenthorpe stepped before him, and Spread had no resource but the graceful Miss Guydickens, the cousin of the officer who shot the tiger and wounded the hippopotamus.   The East-Indiaman went down to dinner alone, as it was often his lot to do.

The Spreads had predetermined not to try the soups.   However, the Marables and Crackenthorpes seemed to think them excellent. Major-general Guydickens bellowed for cayenne-pepper ; but there was none to be had for his bellowing, so he did without it, which was very philosophical for a major-general.

Mrs. Spread, drawing her shawl well about her, took the interest of a curious observer of social phenomena in reveiwing the array upon the table ; and she thought, upon the whole, that it looked surprisingly well : the cloth was whiter than she had anticipated, the glass brighter, and the argentine and albata did their best to look silvery—what could albata and argentine do more ?   Then there was a splendid epergne, borrowed from the Prouts : it was stocked with evergreens—the ivy, the arbutus, and the holly ; they looked

wintery, certainly, but then they were fresh and healthy, and for
Mr. Barker they produced the very desirable effect of interposing
between him and the polar Mrs. Narrowsmith's hideous head-gear.
Barker was very cold, and as he sat with his back to the fire-place,
he turned round to see how it was that no heat reached him.
There was a fire in the grate, but it had evidently been lighted not
an hour before. It yielded a great deal of smoke, but no warmth
whatever. While he was directing Mrs. Spread's attention to these
agreeable incidents of a house-warming, the page put a finishing
touch to the piece, by running up and asking the bachelor, " Would
he like to have a fire-screen?"

While they were enjoying this serious jest, up jumped Mrs.
Marable, in considerable excitement, and proclaimed the astound-
ing fact that the party consisted of the ill-omened number of thirteen.

There was a general movement. The superstition is a prevalent
one. Of course, neither the Spreads nor Mr. Barker were so
weak as to feel very uneasy at the circumstance, nor did Major-
general Guydickens betray any very strong emotion; but the rest
of the company were not so philosophical; and as to the hostess
herself, she was made utterly miserable by the discovery.

"Shall I make Grace come down, mother?" inquired Maria
Theresa, hitting on a mode of meeting the difficulty.

Barker growled and glanced at Mr. Spread.

" It's a very good suggestion, my dear," said Mrs. Narrowsmith,
quite relieved by her daughter's felicitous proposal. " I'll fetch
her myself," she added; and, rising from the table, she left the
room.

" Who can Grace be?" said Mrs. Spread to Mr. Barker.

" One of the daughters of the house—I think it's an ice-house,"
replied Barker, shivering, and glancing again at the cold fire.

" Cold enough for one," said Mrs. Spread—" but Mr. Narrowsmith has only one daughter."

The hostess re-entered at the moment, leading by the hand, not a
handsome, but a singularly interesting and quiet-looking girl, of fifteen or sixteen, whom Barker did not immediately recognize as the
young person who had occupied the corner of the carriage on his
journey from town, and whom he had, with astonishing civility,
conducted in safety to the place of her destination. Mrs. Spread,
with the quick perception of her sex, discovered, almost at a glance,
that the little girl, for whose presence she was indebted to so odd
an accident, was no second edition of Maria Theresa, or a work of

the same class at all. Though dressed with the utmost simplicity, in a frock that would have been a very plain one even in the morning, and with no ornament but a mean necklace of blue beads, which had obviously been huddled on her neck by way of compensation for the frugality of the rest of her attire, she was at once distinguished and fascinating. It was a puzzle to Mrs. Spread to account for so gentle and refined a little girl being related or connected with a family so coarse as the Narrowsmiths. Who could she possibly be? What might be her history? How did it happen that she had never been seen, her name so much as breathed, or her existence even hinted at before? She expressed her surprise at, and admiration of Grace, in smiles and becks at Mr. Spread, who replied, in the same language, that he concurred in his wife's approval and participation in her astonishment.

There is a magnetic power in genuine worth and delicacy which attracts the notice and sympathy of the same qualities, whenever they come within the range of its influence. Mrs. Spread could scarcely keep her eyes for a moment off the new-comer: she was the only thing feminine in the room which it was possible to regard with interest—indeed, even with complaisancy.

The bachelor pleased Mrs. Spread greatly, by recalling to her memory the exquisite lines of Ben Jonson—

> " Give me a look, give me a face,
>   That makes simplicity a grace ;
>   Robes loosely flowing, hair as free
>   Such sweet neglect more taketh me,
>   Than all the adulteries of art ;
>   They strike my eyes, but not my heart."

The miser asked Barker to take wine—sherry. Mrs. Spread could evidently see that Barker would have given the wine another appellation. In fact, it was a mixture of the grapes of Cadiz and the Cape. Mr. Narrowsmith was as roguish about wine, and as practiced a garbler of the grape as the most disingenuous vintner in Liverpool.

Now the fish came, a magnificent turbot, to do the miser justice, but it was a little overdone, and the sauce was execrable.

Mr. Spread had been separated, by some accident, from the fair East-Indian, and sat between Mrs. Crackenthorpe and Mrs. Marable. The one was a dissyllabic, the other a monosyllabic lady.

" You find this frosty weather agreeable, I hope," to Mrs. Marable.

" Very."

" I should think there must be skating in some places."

" Do you?"

" I was fond of skating in my young days."

" Were you?"

Then he tried Mrs. Crackenthorpe.

" Have you been lately in London?"

" No."

" Your sister lives in London, if I remember right?"

" Yes."

" You know my friend Upton, I think?"

" No."

" Don't you think this room a little cool?"

" Yes."

" You find your new house comfortable, I hope, Narrowsmith," said Mr. Spread, giving the ladies up, and making one of those remarks indispensable at house-warmings.

" Very," squealed the host, in his wiry, gibbering voice; ".warm and comfortable—very—don't you think the atmosphere of this room agreeable? Well, I assure you, it's the coldest room in the house."

" Except the kitchen," muttered Barker, to his fair neighbor.

" We found it not easy to warm the house we lived in before," said Mrs. Narrowsmith.

" Did she ever try coals?" growled Barker again.

But the guest that most annoyed the Narrowsmiths during the repast was Doctor Prout, who, when he was not talking of hydropathy (for he was a furious advocate of water *externally*), was always calling for something that was not to be had. After the soup he called for cold punch; when he was asked what wine he would take, he replied Burgundy; he asked three times for cucumber; and at the dessert, he begged Mr. Spread to help him to a peach, mistaking, or pretending to mistake a pile of apples for one of the rarer fruit.

The Prouts would not have been asked at all, but that their epergne was in requisition; a splendid article, which (being very obliging people) they were always ready to lend a dinner-giving friend, for the reasonable consideration of being invited along with it. The epergne *never* dined out without the Prouts, and the Prouts *seldom* dined out without the epergne.

Mrs. Spread was wretched about her husband, and was continual-

ly saying to Mr. Barker—"I fear he will get his death of cold—do
you think the window behind him can be open?—how happy I am
Augusta is not here."

Barker made no reply; he was paying critical attention to something on his plate, which Mrs. Narrowsmith had just recommended
to him as "*one of Madame Maintenon's cutlets*." Having removed
the envelope with his fork, he turned to Mrs. Spread, and with the
oddest conceivable mixture of disgust and enjoyment in his countenance, directed her attention to the unfolded paper.

"What! I protest there is writing on it—in the name of all that
is comical, try to make out what it is."

Thus adjured, Mr. Barker looked narrowly at the scrap of paper
in which the cutlet had been dressed, and had no great difficulty in
reading nearly the entire of the Crackenthorpes' answer to the Narrowsmiths' invitation. The cutlets just at that moment taking their
round again, Mrs. Spread resolved to have one, to try her chance of
a literary document, where nobody could have dreamed of meeting a
thing of the kind. It was a very diverting occupation this, for a dinner-table."

"Well, what have *you* got? is it *mine*?"

"*Ours*," said Mrs. Spread, recognizing the hand of her daughter
Elizabeth upon the wrapper of the exquisite *morceau* before her.

"Mrs. Spread, will you take a glass of champagne with me?"
squeaked the miser, from the foot of the table. He had deferred
the production of the champagne until the latest possible moment,
from which Mr. Spread, who well knew his habits, inferred, and
correctly, that he had screwed up his courage to give a tolerably
fair wine. And it was really so; Barker had a glass of it after Mrs.
Spread had been helped, and he liked it so well that he invited
Spread to join him in another, after which he had some venison,
which was not bad, considering that it had been roasted in a grotto;
and then (undeterred by the looks of his host, who, he made no
doubt, was scowling malignantly at him) he looked round the table
for a supporter in a third glass, when, his eye resting on the little
Grace, who sat nearly opposite to him, he began to recall the features
of his fellow-traveler, and good-naturedly asked her to take wine, at
the same time ordering the flask to be carried round to her, which
was done, before Mrs. Narrowsmith could interfere to prevent it, or
recommend Cape Madeira to her *protégée* in place of the champagne. Mrs. Spread remarked how the attention of Mr. Barker
flushed the cheek of the little girl, and with what a singularly sweet
smile she returned the bachelor's courtesy.

General Guydickens, meanwhile, asked Mr. Marable to take wine.

"Try that Maderia," cried the host—"the Madeira to Major-general Guydickens."

Mr. Marable, however, was a tea-totaller, and would drink nothing more generous than cold water.

"I'm *sworn*," said Mr. Marable, "not to touch *wine*."

"There is not a headache in a hogshead of *that*," said Narrowsmith.

"Nor a *perjury*, either," said Barker, in Mrs. Spread's ear.

The second course was worthy of the first, and the dessert of the second course. As handsome a dessert might have been provided in the wastes of Arabia Petræa. The mistakes and vulgarities of the day, amusing at first, became at length intolerably fatiguing. Who can endure a five-act farce? Poor Mrs. Spread, suffering very much from cold, and thinking of her fireside and her happy children at home, stole little agonizing looks from time to time at her husband. Barker was tired of grumbling, and became moody and silent. There was some stable-talk between the major-general and Mr. Crackenthorpe; Miss Guydickens told her tale of the tiger and Lieutenant Curry; and as to Mr. Voluble, he continued to chatter like a flock of sparrows under the eaves of a barn.

But it was a tedious, heavy, chilly affair altogether, and Mrs. Spread thought that Mrs. Narrowsmith would never give the signal for the rising of the ladies. The truth was, that Mrs. Narrowsmith was uncertain whether she ought to look at Mrs. Marable, or Mrs. Spread, or even at Miss Guydickens. At length, it was over; the ladies went, the gentleman remained; a bottle of claret was produced; Mr. Spread said it was corked—another—Mr. Spread made the same remark—a third—it was a wonder it had escaped the same criticism, for there was very little wine *uncorked*, in any sense of the word, in Mr. Narrowsmith's establishment. The third, however, was not a very bad bottle, and it promoted a little conversation.

Mr. Barker had what Spread called an Irish "row" with the doctor, who was a quack, out of his calling as well as in it. Eventually, more of the party became involved in it, as often happens in rows of another kind.

The conversation commenced good-humoredly enough. Somebody observed, that what the Irish were most deficient in were habits of prudence and foresight.

"Bad calculators," said Mr. Narrowsmith.

"I don't think we can say that of them," said Mr. Marable; "at least, I'am sure they multiply fast enough."

"And the tithe system," said Barker, "must have made them tolerably quick at decimals."

"Their divisions, too," added Spread, "are quite as remarkable as their multiplications."

"A complete system of political arithmetic," said the bachelor. "I wish they were equally celebrated for their political economy."

"The less of that they have the better," said Mr. Marable, who plumed himself on being a practical man; "at all events, I trust the principles of political economy will not be regarded now, when there is every prospect of the country being visited with famine."

"Very like saying that the principles of navigation ought to be disregarded by the mariner in a storm," said Mr. Spread.

"What Ireland wants, sir, is a vigorous government, a good sound despotism," said the doctor; "put down assassins, that's what I say."

"Put down exterminators first," said Barker.

"What you call extermination, I call improvement," said the doctor.

"Then, I say, put down improvement," said Barker.

"Doctor, you are for bleeding—it is quite natural," said Spread, good-humoredly.

"A little of the doctor's immersion, too," said Mr. Crackenthorpe, "would, I think, do Ireland no harm; I am quite of the late Sir Joseph Yorke's opinion, that an hour's ducking in the Atlantic would do her a great deal of good."

"I don't know," said Barker, "what the effect of *cold* water would be, but I must say the country has been kept in *hot* water long enough."

"By the priests and the agitators, sir," said the doctor.

"By the absentees," said Crackenthorpe.

"By the clergy," said Marable.

"By the Whigs," said Narrowsmith.

"By quacks," said Barker.

The word quack is a most unmusical one to the ear of a doctor, particularly when he is a professor of hydropathy, and therefore Mr. Spread, who always exerted himself to keep the peace at the dinner-table, as well as in other places, diverted the physician's attention by asking him whether he did not agree with Mr. Crackenthorpe, that absenteeism was in a great measure what kept up the supply of "hot water" in Ireland.

E

The doctor entirely concurred with Mr. Spread, who then added, " My friend Barker is, I know, of the same opinion."

Here the spirit of contradiction manifested itself in the Bachelor of the Albany in a manner that was truly scandalous. A thousand times had he agreed with Spread in inveighing against the Irish absentees; yet now, to his friend's infinite astonishment, he wheeled right about, and took up the opposite position fiercely.

" Quite the contrary," he said; " absenteeism is one of the few blessings that Ireland enjoys. The more absentees the better. The question lies in a nutshell. An absentee is either rich or he is poor. If he is rich, he must be a rascal to desert his native country; and there is sufficient resident rascality, I think, at present, without taking measures to increase it; if he is poor, on the other hand, of what use can he be at home—what can a pauper landlord do for a pauper tenantry? The question lies in a nutshell."

Spread stared, and blushed for the bachelor, but said nothing.

The doctor observed, with great justice, that all Barker had said was arrant sophistry; that there was no more deceptive form of argument than that which the bachelor had employed, and that he would come down upon the absentees with a thundering tax.

" Every owner of a landed estate," said the doctor, " ought to reside upon it."

" And by parity of reasoning," said Barker, " every man who has property in the funds ought to live in Threadneedle-street."

So saying, he rose from the table, and followed the ladies. The general feeling was strongly against him; but Marable and Crackenthorpe, being crotchety men themselves, were quite charmed with the bachelor, and Crackenthorpe said he was just the man for Boroughcross, a town in Yorkshire, which was just then in want of a representative.

" Eh, Marable, what do you think?"

" I agree with you," said Marable.

" We'll both talk about it to-morrow," said Crackenthorpe; " no time ought to be lost."

CHAPTER XII.

A violet, by a mossy stone,
  Half hidden from the eye;
Fair as a star, when only one
  Is shining in the sky.
                          WORDSWORTH.

The Miser's Salons—Mrs. Narrowsmith's Taste in Colors—Fascinations of Maria Theresa—Historiette of a Shipwrecked Girl—Laura and Petrarch have a Tête-à-tête—A Monster-Meeting—Mrs. Narrowsmith is caught doing Something very shabby—Mr. Barker retreats—His Retreat is intercepted—He refuses to sing, but is forced to dance—He is confounded by a Name in a Stranger's Hat, and wishes himself back in the Albany.

THE drawing-room!—a withdrawing-room would have been a better name—for there was nothing to draw any body to it, and every thing to induce people to withdraw from it. To Mrs. Spread it was bleaker than the dining-room many times. A few pompous pieces of furniture only drew attention to the shabbiness of their associates. There was not a picture, or even a print upon the walls, or any thing to cover their nakedness, save a single very large looking-glass in an ostentatious frame, a looking-glass quite out of keeping with the other details of the apartment, and which only served, in fact, to double the dreary effect of the surrounding objects. The space between the windows was occupied by tables of a whitish-gray marble. On one of these cold slabs lay one or two annuals of years gone by, probably bought at a stall for a shilling apiece. A tawdry prayer-book and an album in half-binding, gaudily lettered with the name of Miss Maria Theresa, glittered and shivered upon the other. The room was newly and (if you will take Mrs. Marable's word for it) "tastily" furnished. The governing tint was drab —all drab, drab walls, drab carpets, drab every thing. It made one think of the men of Pennsylvania, or the Society of Friends. Drab was Mrs. Narrowsmith's color; her very soul must have been drab; it was a cheap color, and what she called a fast color; a color, too, that bore dyeing and turning, and all the metamorphoses to which

fancy, inspired by meanness, could subject stuffs. Pendent from
the ceiling by a green cord, was a system, or constellation of glass
prisms and sockets, capable of holding some eight or ten candles.
It was dignified with the name of a chandelier, and held in such
veneration by the Narrowsmiths, that it was only illuminated upon
gala occasions like the present; at all other times kept as religiously
veiled as the relics of Aix-la-Chapelle, or the Holy Coat of Treves.
When Mrs. Spread entered the drawing-room, this superb affair
had only two candles lighted; Mrs. Narrowsmith, however, ordered
the page to illumine the rest forthwith, explaining to the matrons
round her that the candles were "patent amandines," the advantages
of which over wax were incredible; and looking, when the operation of lighting was complete, as vain as the wife of a Mandarin
presiding at a feast of lanterns.

This splendid room communicated by a folding-door with another
still more spacious, embellished with the same severe taste, and in
an alarming state of preparation for music and dancing. Here stood
Miss Maria Theresa's second-hand Broadwood (a very *grand* piano,
indeed), bought at an auction for twenty guineas, with a pile of
music books near it, containing all the odious overtures, rascally
rondos, and snobbish sonatas, composed for coarse ears and red
fingers, to enchant the low-countries of the musical world. These
horrors of harmony were all in readiness, upon this occasion, to
tickle the ear and melt the heart of Mr. Philip Spread, into whose
breast it was only natural to think a passion for the fair daughter of
the house would creep all the easier for having the various entrances
previously unlocked by that accomplished young lady herself, with
her own ivory keys. However, she did not rely, or her mother for
her, solely upon her melodious powers, for a table, in a corner of
the same room, was covered with unequivocal proofs that she could
astonish the eye with colors, as well as the ear with sounds. In
fact, Miss Narrowsmith was decidedly a magnet with two poles, the
only misfortune being that they were both repelling ones. At least
they had no other effect that evening upon the young man whom
she had laid so extensive a scheme of conquest. The conduct of
Philip annoyed all the Narrowsmiths extremely. He never vouch-
safed a glance at Maria's paintings; never once peeped into her
album; and while she was performing the overture of Der Frei-
schutz, his back was turned upon the executioner, and he was
engaged in conversation with his mother, and at one time (of all
people in the world) with little Grace Medlicott. So piqued was
the miser's daughter at this negligent behavior, that she positively

refused to sing, although, in the opinion of her own circle, she was little short of a Prima Donna.

Grace Medlicott was the name of the girl whom nobody cared for in the coach, and for whom nobody seemed to care in the house to which Mr. Barker had been so strangely instrumental in conducting her. Directly Mrs. Spread entered the drawing-room, and could disengage herself from the vulgar attentions of her hostess, she approached Grace, and got into conversation with her; having previously ascertained her name from Maria Theresa, who spoke of her, not with any positive slight, but as if she was a person who was not in a position to excite any feeling at all, not so much as scorn. Mrs. Spread, it may well be supposed, asked no probing, or even leading questions; and the reserve with which the young girl confined her explanations respecting herself to such points only as it would have been rudeness not to have elucidated, gave Mrs. Spread a very favorable opinion of her taste and judgment. The particulars of her story which Mrs. Spread was enabled to collect that night amounted merely to this:—that she was an orphan, nearly related to Mr. Narrowsmith, and under his protection, if not legally his ward. She had lately returned from one of the colonies, in the care of a person who had been a steward or domestic of her father. The ship had been wrecked upon the Cornish coast (it had been a remarkable shipwreck, and Mrs. Spread was familiar with its details from the newspapers); the loss of lives had been very great, and among those who perished was the person who had charge of Grace. Her own personal share in the dangers and horrors of the wreck had been considerable. How she had escaped she scarcely knew; and, after her life had been preserved, she found herself a young and timid girl, cast upon the shores of a country where she was not acquainted with the face of a human being; the tempest that destroyed the vessel still howling, and not so much as the body of her unfortunate attendant rescued from the waves. In this state of destitution she had not been without several offers of assistance; but with instinctive prudence she had selected, as the most eligible, that of the clergyman of the parish in which the calamity had occurred. He was a young, but a married man, almost as poor as his divine Master, whose doctrines he preached, not ineloquently, in the pulpit, but with ten times more power in the silent rhetoric of his life. To the charity of this gentleman she was indebted, not merely for a temporary asylum, but for the recovery of some few articles of property, including a box, containing several papers, of more consequence than Grace, at the time, was aware of. Among the rest

was a letter directed to Isaac Narrowsmith, esq., of the firm of
Spread and Narrowsmith, Liverpool.   She understood it to contain
her recommendation to the care of her father's only, or nearest
relative in England; and to avail herself of that gentleman's friendship, became, of course, her primary concern.   The good Mr. Ramsay (that was the clergyman's name) would gladly have acted still
as her protector, but Grace could not consent to burden, for more
than a few days, the benevolence of a person upon whom she had no
claims, and who could but very ill afford to indulge in the romance
of hospitality; she therefore determined to repair at once to Liverpool, where there could be no doubt that her relation, from his eminent mercantile position, would be discovered with ease.   She had
barely money enough remaining to defray the expense of the journey; and she was so deficient in clothes (having none but those
which she happened to wear upon the fatal night of the shipwreck),
that she was constrained to accept a few indispensable additions to
her stock from the scanty wardrobe of the vicar's wife.

While Mrs. Spread was gleaning these few particulars, which
interested her extremely, Mr. Barker was ranging the rooms in a
savage humor, which was, however, somewhat mollified, upon his
descrying the agreeable Laura Smyly, who had established herself
in a corner, where she was at once aloof from the vulgar and
enabled to observe all that went on.   The bachelor observed that
" she did not dance."

" *Dance!*" exclaimed Laura, "*here!*"

These two monosyllables, with the emphasis upon them, explained
Laura's reason for not dancing in the most satisfactory manner.
Perhaps it was the allusion to dancing; but certainly Mr. Barker
at this precise moment (unused as he was to trouble himself about
the feet of ladies) *did* cast a glance at the foot of the sprightly girl,
as, refulgent in a satin shoe, it came peeping, like a plump white
mouse, from under her satin petticoat.   Another thing is equally
incontestable: the thought passed through his mind that the foot
which thus peeped out was too pretty to trip on Mrs. Narrowsmith's
drab carpets, although it was not so fairy a foot as to dance on the
sands without leaving a print behind it.   No! it was the pretty foot
of a pretty woman, a much better thing than that of a nymph, a fay,
or a goddess, whatever Mr. Barker may have thought upon the subject.   But perhaps he thought so too.

" Are you well acquainted with Liverpool, Miss Smyly?"

" Pretty well; we are a good deal with the Spreads."

" Do you know many of these strange people?"

" A few only : you may suppose Mrs. Spread keeps such monsters at a respectful distance. She is well abused for it ; they call her proud and upsetting because she refuses to know such enormities as those women you see sitting on that sofa opposite."

" She is perfectly right," said the bachelor. " Those Narrow-smiths and Marables are very good company—for one another."

" I think this might be called a monster meeting," said Laura. " Look at that trio on the sofa, a sphynx, an ogress, and—I don't know what to call the third—can you help me ?"

" She reminds one of the fabulous account of Scylla, her face is so fishy ; and those frightful curls, of which she is so prodigal, are the hell-dogs barking about her."

" That will do admirably," said Laura, smiling most graciously, as she commended the classical similitude.

Mr. St. Leger now came, and prayed Laura to dance with him ; but his suit was rejected.

" Who is that giantess who dined here—*there*, bobbing her head up and down ?"

" Oh, Miss Guydickens, the giraffe : is she not the image of a giraffe? She is going to be married to the priggish pigmy she is dancing with. Lord John Yore ought to have secured her, he is so mad for maypoles."

" Ha! ha! Who is the priggish pigmy ? I hear him talking of Palmerston and John Russell as if he was in the cabinet himself."

" He *is* some small official ; he has some little mission, or pretends to have one, from the Home Office, relating to the scarcity, they say."

" He has come to a very good place for collecting details upon *that* subject," said Barker.

" My sister knows him," continued Laura ; " he came once on a visit to a house where she happened to be, in Suffolk, and he had immense packets, in official envelopes, coming down to him continually, marked ' private, immediate, and confidential,' with sometimes a ministerial frank in the corner. Adelaide suspected that he was not the very great man he set up to be ; and one morning, with some other girls to support her, she insisted on seeing the contents of a packet (I believe it was a box), more than usually consequential ; and what do you suppose the box contained ? Some gloves, a parcel of cigars, and a white waistcoat !"

" I have known a treasury messenger dismissed for not forwarding a red box containing a bouquet. Fans and bracelets are frequently expressed from the Home Office, and a clerk of the Ordnance

will sometimes put on all the steam of the department to transmit
an aunt in the country a case of gunpowder-tea."

Laura laughed heartily.

" Who is the lady in black, yonder, talking so fluently—handsome
—what a brilliant complexion !"

" A Mrs. Miller—one of our rich widows—do you think her
pretty ? She *is* clever—very accomplished : she plays—sings—
paints."

" Mr. Voluble seems to be paying her attention ?"

" He is engaged to her ; they will talk each other to death before
the honeymoon's over—it's like a match between a macaw and a
parrot ; but do, Mr. Barker, do look at Mr. Narrowsmith putting out
the candles."

The miser had just extinguished the two lights of the constellation
called a luster, believing that nobody was observing his proceedings.

Barker was extremely amused by his fair companion ; and, indeed,
Laura Smyly was uncommonly lively and entertaining, with as good
a knack at a nickname as any lady in England. It was no wonder
she had not been married, for she was too poor for some men and
too clever for others ; besides, she was not the sort of girl to fancy a
briefless barrister, or elope with an *aide-de-camp*. Mrs. Spread
used to say she had a great deal of the character of Beatrice—a
shrewd tongue, with a good understanding and a warm heart.

Though St. Leger had failed with Laura, Mr. Philip Spread
thought he might succeed in winning the other sister for a set, so
he advanced to *Laura*, and respectfully inquired, " Would Miss
Adelaide Smyly dance a quadrille with him ?"

" I can't answer for my sister," said Laura, as demurely as she
could ; " but I see her yonder talking to your mother, and she looks
disengaged."

Philip retired, discomfited and piqued ; and, accusing Laura of
preferring her conversation with Mr. Barker to a dance with *him*,
he revenged himself, on joining his mother, by throwing out a hint
that the clever young lady in question was " throwing her cap at the
Diogenes of the Albany," as if Laura Smyly was the girl to throw
her cap at any one, and as if Barker was a man to have caps thrown
at him.

The preliminaries of a concert of vocal and instrumental music were
now painfully audible ; this was, of course, a signal to Barker to
make his retreat ; which, on every account (except, perhaps, that it
terminated his agreeable *tête-à-tête*), he was happy to do.

The Spreads were people who, when they did a civil thing, did

it as handsomely as they could, and therefore when they decided on
dining with the Narrowsmiths they made up their minds also to remain the due length of time under their roof—a term of punishment
which was extended on the present occasion, on account of the evening party which followed the dinner.   Barker, however, was under
no recognizances to submit to the same amount of personal suffering; so the first notes of the approaching squall no sooner reached
his ears than he bowed ceremoniously to the young lady with whom
he had been conversing, and made his way out of the room, with a
nod and a bitter smile at Mrs. Spread as he passed near her chair.
As he went down stairs, he encountered a group of noisy young
men, who had just arrived to grace Mrs. Narrowsmith's festive
circle.   These were Tom Trombone and Dicky Horne, who were
in requisition for the concert, besides several other exquisités of
Liverpool (many of them suitors to Maria Theresa), in all the fla-
grancy of provincial dandyism.   Trombone's shirt-studs were actual
rocks of Irish diamond, and the hair of the whole phalanx had evidently been diligently dressed for the occasion by some elaborate
coiffeur of Deane-street, publicly pledged to cut gentlemen's hair
after the newest Parisian fashion, for the moderate charge of sixpence.   Up they came to Mrs. Narrowsmith's brilliant salons, bois-
terously gay, laughing, jesting, playing practical jokes upon each
other, particularly Horne, Trombone, and another, who kept vocif-
erously singing snatches of the glee of "Glorious Apollo," which
was probably in the musical bill of fare for the evening.   They
halted in a body on the first landing-place (which was not very wide),
as it were to perfect themselves in their horrid melody before they
proceeded farther.   First, Trombone would come out with his part,
in a deep bass voice, as loud as thunder; then Horne, who was a
tenor, and a terrible one, would strike in; and, finally, all three
would unite their powers, until the bleak house actually shook and
rung with the performance.   Poor Mr. Barker, having to pass this
agreeable knot of revelers, edged close to the wall, and moved as
rapidly as he could, to get out of their reach and hearing as soon as
possible.   He was on the point of succeeding, and just turning to
descend the second stair-case when the third vocalist, a particularly
noisy young man, evidently flushed with bad wine, or with something still more exciting (as indeed were his comrades also), rushed
forward, slapped him on the back, grasped him by both the hands,
and claimed acquaintance with him as his friend and fellow-traveler.
Imagine the dismay with which the justly-incensed bachelor recognized, in the perpetrator of this audacious rudeness, the owner of

E*

the three-barreled pistol—the nephew in search of an uncle! The youth, who was as strong as a Hercules, held Barker like a vice, laughing and shouting so immoderately, that neither the remonstrances nor the struggles of his captive produced the least effect.

"You musn't leave us—stay for supper—you're a jolly, gay fellow."

"Jolly companions every one."

burst from the whole orchestra.

"Does your friend sing?" cried Horne.

"You sing, jolly old fellow, don't you? You know you do," cried the chief persecutor, unhanding Barker, but planting himself so as to cut off his escape down stairs.

"We'll not go home till morning,"

chanted Trombone, the leader of the band,

"Till morning—till morning.
We'll not go home till morning,"

was then executed in full chorus, Barker in vain trying to escape from the ring.

"Well, you can dance, old fellow, if you can't sing," and no sooner said than done: the bachelor's rail-way acquaintance seized him by both hands again, and compelled him by main force to dance a hornpipe, or something of the kind, upon the lobby. Barker's torments were only terminated by the interposition of Miss Maria Theresa Narrowsmith, who, being anxious that the music should commence in the drawing-room, appeared at the head of the stairs, and called to Signors Trombone and Horne to "have done with their nonsense," as "mamma wanted them instantly." Trombone and Horne obeyed the summons with a hop, step, and a jump; but Mr. Barker's more particular friend insisted upon embracing him affectionately, squeezing his hands, and clapping him on the back a dozen times before he gave him his freedom.

The state the bachelor was in, after such rude treatment and violent exercise, may easily be conceived. He was in a fever, and scarcely able to articulate with vexation. There was considerable difficulty, too, about finding his hat. His name, however, was written in it, and he told the servant what it was. A hat was soon handed to him—a hat in which he would not have walked a hundred yards for a thousand pounds. It was not a sportsman's hat, or a waterman's hat, or a bishop's hat, or a coachman's hat, or a prize-fighter's hat, but one that combined the oddities of those and all other hats that ever were invented.   Barker, of course, repudiated it ferociously, and charged the servant with not being able to read.

"Alexander Barker," said the servant, to repel the attack upon his learning.

Barker winced.

"It is not Barker—it's Parker," said Mrs. Narrowsmith's page, peeping into the hat which the other servant held in his hand.

Barker had the curiosity to examine the inscription himself, and found it impossible to decide whether it was Parker or Barker; but the Alexander was not to be mistaken, and unfortunately Alexander was his brother's name.   Meantime, his own hat was produced, and he rushed from the house, heartily wishing that he had never left his chambers at the Albany.

CHAPTER XIII.

Here let us sit, and talk away an hour,
On this and that, of something or of nothing;
Be't sense, or nonsense, any thing for talk;
Mine shall be free, and yours shall be malicious;
I tell you, Blanche, I'm talkative to-day.
The Spinsters.

Chat about Grace—Mr. Spread and Mr. Barker differ about the Amount of
Villainy in the World—The Bachelor sets the Breakfast-table in a Roar—
He is humiliated by Mrs. Martin—Mrs. Martin delivers a Lecture on the
Art of Conversation—Theodore meditates an Outrage to the Bachelor, and
is brought before Mrs. Martin's Correctional Tribunal—Mrs. Spread visits
Mrs. Narrowsmith—Mrs. Spread takes a bold Resolution—Grace discovered
to be a Heroine.

MRS. SPREAD, though the most devoted of mothers, had room
enough in her affections to interest herself, occasionally, in the children of other people, whenever she found intellectual superiority
combined with simplicity and truth of character; but particularly
when, either through misfortune or neglect, innocence was left
without protection, or merit without a friend.   Her heart was so
free from every thing selfish, and her mind from every thing narrow
and vulgar, that there was ample space in both for every kindly feeling to expand itself; throwing out attachments and sympathies in all
directions, as some fair plant in a roomy conservatory, where all is
warm and lightsome round about, branches freely in every direction,
with infinite tendrils, to seize and fasten upon whatever is sweet and
beautiful within its reach.   Of all the young persons she had ever
met, she had been most struck with Grace Medlicott, and the feeling
was shared by her husband and her daughters.   Mr. Spread suspected that Grace was niece to Mr. Narrowsmith; he had some recollection of having heard, many years before, that his partner had a
brother, with whom he had quarreled, and who, after some years of
struggle at home, as a literary man, under a feigned name, had ultimately obtained a colonial appointment, and disappeared from England.   The recollection was a very faint one.   Narrowsmith had

never alluded even to the existence of a brother, and Mr. Spread had totally forgotten the assumed name, if, indeed, he had ever heard it. All agreed that Grace was a remarkable girl, intelligent beyond her age, which it was not very easy to determine. One said sixteen, another thought she was not so much, Mr. Spread was of opinion she might be "in about her eighteenth *winter*."

"Winter, indeed—you may well say winter, my dear," said Mrs. Spread; "if the poor thing continues with her friends in Rodney-street, she is not likely to know much of any other season."

"I certainly think," said Mr. Spread, "that to be under the protection of the Narrowsmiths is as like being unprotected as it well can be; at least, against cold," he added. "I hope, in other respects, the poor girl will not be so badly off."

"Imagine Mr. Narrowsmith being guardian to any one!" exclaimed Augusta.

"Imagine Mrs. Narrowsmith supplying the place of a mother!" said Elizabeth.

"Come, girls," said their father, who never encouraged gloomy or uncharitable views in his children, either of persons or things, "come, we perhaps do the Narrowsmiths injustice; after all, there is not so much villainy in the world as we are too apt to think."

"Ten times more," said Barker, who had hitherto been breakfasting in moody silence—"ten times more villainy than you, or I, or any body, has any notion of. The secret history of the world remains to be written."

"I admit he's a miser—Narrowsmith *is* a miser," said Spread, not much disposed to be disputatious, and not very clear but that the bachelor was in the right.

"A miser!" repeated Barker. "He is *miserrimus*."

And then he drew a picture of the previous day's entertainment —so true, so vivid, so piquant, so full of minute detail, so highly, though unintentionally, comic, that, while full of gall and bitterness himself, he set the whole breakfast-table in a roar. It was like an actual *rechauffé* of "Madame Maintenon's cutlets," and Mr. Spread declared it made him feel over again as if he was seated on an iceberg, eating his soup with a hatchet.

"I trust that poor girl," said Mrs. Spread, returning to the subject of Grace, "whoever she may be, is not entirely dependent upon the bounty of her relations; she looks like a person who would soon sink under hard or unkind usage."

"Then she will sink soon enough," said Barker. "What other treatment will she meet from that she-driver?"

"We must only hope the best," said Mr. Spread. "And now, Miss Laura, what have *you* to say for yourself? Why, you are as silent as my Bessie there, this morning. How did you like Mrs. Narrowsmith's ball? Who did you dance with?"

Laura laughed, and said she had not danced at all.

"She was more agreeably employed," said Philip, maliciously.

Barker had no notion that he had been alluded to, as having contributed to Miss Smyly's entertainment; it would have made him extremely angry, which Mrs. Spread knew so well, that she intimated to Philip, by a look, that he was not to venture upon such tender ground again. But Laura thought a maternal rebuke was too slight a correction for Philip's impertinence; she was not a young lady to be assailed with impunity, so she begged to have a list of young Mr. Spread's partners on the previous evening, first desiring to know who was the beauty in pink with whom he had danced—*twice?*

"And the beauty in blue, whom you waltzed with?" inquired Adelaide.

"I can tell you, Philip, you *ought* to have danced with Miss Narrowsmith; it would have been only polite," said Mrs. Spread.

"But only think, mamma, of his having never once danced either with Miss Marable or Bessie Bomford, the whole night," said Augusta.

"Phil, my boy," said his father, rising, "I fear you are a Sir Proteus. You remind me of a humorous rhyme in one of Sheridan's letters to Swift:

"'You are as faithless as a Carthaginian,
  To love at once Kate, Nell, Doll, Martha, Jenny, Anne.'"

"That's in a letter of Swift to Sheridan," snarled Mr. Barker.

Mrs. Martin now rose, with her usual dignity, and, in rising, signified, *sotto voce*, to Elizabeth Spread, that she wished to have a little private conversation with her, upon a subject which she said had been suggested by the remarks that had just been made upon the inconstancy of men. Elizabeth, being satisfied of Mr. Owlet's constancy, did not exactly see the appropriateness of the theme selected for the private lecture, but was too respectful to decline attending it. As Mrs. Martin was leaving the room, she missed her black silk reticule; it happened to be hanging on the back of Mr. Barker's chair, and, in rather a lofty way (forgetting, perhaps, that it was not a gentleman in petticoats she had to deal with), she motioned to the bachelor to hand it to her. There is no avoiding sometimes obeying little orders of this nature; but while Barker was making the circuit of the table to do what civility required, Mrs. Martin, instead of waiting, kept moving briskly forward, talking to Elizabeth, so that he had to submit to the indignity of following with the reticule, and still following, until the commanding governess reached the top of the first flight of stairs, when, at length, remembering the reticule, she turned round, and extended her hand to receive it, acknowledging Mr. Barker's courtesy only with a dignified inclination of her head. It made the proud bachelor very sore, and the Smyly girls were in ecstasies.

Mrs. Martin, having made Elizabeth sit down beside her, on the *causeuse* in her dressing-room, proceeded, with great solemnity, to introduce the topic of the approaching nuptials with the Canon of Salisbury, and to impart her own profound views of the line of conduct to be pursued by a married woman, desirous of maintaining the influence and dignity of her sex.

"Depend upon it, Elizabeth dear," she said, "domestic government is a science; when I say government, you must not suppose me to mean that a woman ought to seek to rule her husband; in fact, my dear, when I use the word government, I mean *system*; it is not too much to say, that the happiness of the married state depends entirely upon the *system* pursued by the lady, and what that system should be it has been the great object of my life and writings to establish. You have read my work on the ' Matrons of England ?' "

" Yes, madam, with great interest."

" And my work on the ' State and Dignity of the British Wife ?' yes, I know you have read both; now, my dear, if those works have any value, it is, that in them I have unfolded the principles of what I call my system with husbands; and I firmly believe that its general adoption by our sex would do more than any thing else (unless any measure could be introduced in parliament—your father doubts it) to cure married men of that indifference and proverbial inconstancy which we are all so ready to complain of, without taking the pains we ought to correct and remedy. Now, attend, my dear—my first principle is *design*; let there be a *design* in every thing you say and do."

Perhaps Elizabeth looked as if she thought this rather a singular precept for so great a moralist as Mrs. Martin, for that lady paused a moment, and added, parenthetically, " Of course, I distinguish between having *a design* and being *designing*; the design I speak of is merely the improvement and moral elevation of your husband, which you must always, my dear Elizabeth, keep steadily before your eyes."

Elizabeth had always been of opinion that she was rather to look for improvement and elevation to her husband; so this part of the system not a little surprised her. However, she did not interrupt Mrs. Martin, who thus proceeded:

"Conversation is as much a science as mathematics or geology. It is upon your conversation (you are deficient, Elizabeth, in this—you are too reserved—too silent) that you must rely for carrying out the *design* I have explained. Now, listen, my dear; mark what I say upon this vital subject: I have reduced the art of conversation to three simple rules, nothing can be simpler; the first is adaptation: study your husband's tastes and character, and adapt your conversation to them; the second is, to be always lively and animated—here, my dear girl, you are not all that I could wish you—and the third is this, in all that a woman addresses to her husband, she should aim at either *the establishment of a fact or the deduction of a moral.* Now, go, my love, and reflect upon what I have said; write down as much of it as you can. I shall apply the rule of adaptation to your particular case in my next lecture."

Elizabeth went her way, very much entertained, if not equally edified, by Mrs. Martin's discourse, and just at the same time Mrs. Briscoe's lazy maid came to lodge a very serious complaint against Mr. Theodore Spread, whom she had caught in the act of putting a mouse into one of Mr. Barker's boots. Letty was grateful to the bachelor for his services on the night of her arrival, and took this opportunity of showing it. Only fancy Mr. Barker finding a mouse in his boot—and in the model-house of Mrs. Spread. To be sure, such things will happen in the best regulated familes, and would take place much oftener were it not for the Mrs. Martins. Theodore was on the point of undergoing the extreme penalties of the law, when Laura Smyly opportunely interposed, and at her suggestion a whipping was commuted into ten lines of Montgomery's "Satan," the rigid infliction of which had the excellent effect of making the offender abominate both Montgomery and Satan all the days of his life.

Mrs. Spread knew too well what a dinner is to a family like the Narrowsmiths, to think of visiting there the day after the banquet. The next morning, however, she resolved to perform that duty, with an interest she had never before felt in going to the house in Rodney-street. Mrs. Narrowsmith was "not at home," such was the allegation of the page; the fact being, that Mrs. Narrowsmith *was* at home, but "not fit to be seen" (so she elegantly phrased it herself), as if she had ever been in that lady-like state since the day of her nativity.   A day or two after, Mrs. Spread called a second time, and was admitted, but she failed in her principal object, which was to see Miss Medlicott.   Grace, of course, was talked of, and all that fell from Mrs. Narrowsmith's pinched lips respecting her, not merely corroborated what Mrs. Spread had already learned, but alarmingly confirmed her apprehensions that the fascinating little girl had found relatives not friends, and a house, not a home, in England.

"A poor relation of Mr. Narrowsmith's—not a sixpence in the world.   How people could die and throw their children upon other people, she could not imagine.   Yes, the shipwreck was a very dreadful thing indeed; a visitation of Providence, she had no doubt; every body that goes to sea is liable to be shipwrecked; for her part, she could not tell why Grace Medlicott was sent to England at all; they had orphans enough at home to provide for, Heaven knew."

"Heaven knew" much more about orphans than Mrs. Narrowsmith, who was a very, very religious woman in her own way, and went twice to divine service every Sunday, with the tawdry page carrying the tawdry prayer-book behind her; but Mrs. Narrowsmith's religion was limited to church-going; she was not on visiting terms with the fatherless and the widow.

An allusion of Miss Spread to Grace's personal attractions, which were just those to strike people of refined taste, and to make no impressions on Marables and Narrowsmiths, excited Miss Maria Theresa's spleen considerably.

"Pretty!—do you think so?" with the genuine boarding-school toss of the head, supposed to be the finishing-touch of a young lady's physical education.

"I do, indeed," said the calm Augusta, in her soft, equable voice, without motion enough of her head to agitate a thread of her hair; "more than pretty," she added, "at least *I* think so."

"Only think, mamma, of Miss Spread calling little Grace Medlicott a beauty;" and the fair Miss Narrowsmith giggled in a fascinating way she had, as she made this unfair representation of Augusta's opinion.

"Your brother seemed to think so, at all events," said the mother, tartly, addressing Augusta.

"My poor Philip," said Mrs. Spread, smiling; "he changes his notions of beauty so very often, he can't well be said to have an opinion on the subject at all."

There was some comfort in this. Since Philip was so changeable, the time might come when Maria Theresa might be the "Cynthia of the minute."

This thought occurred simultaneously to both mother and daughter, and they inwardly resolved that Philip had carefully noted the important facts—that Philip had only spoken to Grace while his mother was conversing with her, and that none of the girls he had danced with had fortunes, or, at least, any thing to be compared with hers.

The visit was soon over; Mrs. Spread found it too cold and too disagreeable to tempt her to renew it speedily ; so, being anxious to know more of her new acquaintance, she resolved on rather a bold step, which was to invite the Narrowsmiths to an evening party, which, upon other accounts, she wished to give.

Meanwhile, a little incident occurred at the counting-house, which tended to increase the interest already taken by the Spreads in the unfortunate *protégée* of Mr. Narrowsmith. The counting-house of a great firm is a place of vast resort, frequented by merchants, bankers, brokers, notaries, captains of ships, and hundreds of people connected, in one way or another, with mercantile or monetary transactions. Among others who called that day, on various matters of business, was a man who had been one of the few passengers saved in the wreck of the *Indestructible*. He was relating to Mr. St. Leger the appalling scenes he had witnessed, describing, to the best of his power, the tremendous force of the gale, the frightful commotion of the sea, the uproar, the confusion, the terror, the agony, the hope, the fear, the awful pauses of the storm, the terrific renewals of its violence, the dastardly bearing of some, the cool intrepidity of others, specially mentioning such instances of steadiness and bravery as he himself had the opportunity of noticing. Among other cases, he spoke with enthusiastic admiration of a very young girl, who had from first to last exhibited a degree of courage and self-possession to be admired even in a man, and which had enabled her to be of signal service to the other female passengers, the lives of one or two of whom she actually saved, by her presence of mind, at a particularly critical moment. It immediately occurred to Mr. St. Leger that this might have been the girl of whom he had heard the Spreads speak with interest ; and upon introducing his informant to Mr. Spread, the description tallied so perfectly with that of Miss Medlicott, that no doubt of their identity remained. Grace, accordingly, was now invested with a double interest—she was not only an outcast, but a heroine.

"Poor, fragile thing," said Mrs. Spread, when she heard this account of Grace's noble behavior; "one would think a breath would shatter her to pieces; she looks so meek, too, and so timid."

"The timidity of modesty," said Mr. Spread, "not that of fear. I hope we shall soon see her again."

The delicate spirits of the world are the gallant likewise; the gentle, the modest, the unselfish, compose its chivalry. Let the coarse do its coarse offices: a Caliban will serve to "fetch in our wood;" but give us an Ariel for the higher ministries.

CHAPTER XIV.

Lysimachus. Oh, here is
The lady that I sent for. Welcome, fair one!
Is't not a goodly presence?
Hel. A gallant lady.

    Pericles, Prince of Tyre.

Omens of a happy Summer—Mr. Spread's Attentions to Mrs. Martin—A
Laughing Dinner-table—Spread on Epergnes—Definition of good Table-
talk—what spoiled the House-warming in the Opinion of the Bachelor
and Laura—Laura's Superiority to Elizabeth Spread in the Art of Adaptation—Mr. Barker plays the Critic again—Grace Medlicott's cold Boudoir
—Laura's Sobriquet for Mrs. Narrowsmith—Observations on the Thermometer—Music.

THE day fixed for Mrs. Spread's "at home" was to be the last
of Mr. Barker's sojourn in Liverpool. There was a great deal of
conversation about the Rosary; and whether it was the genial climate,
both moral and physical, of Mr. Spread's house, the agreeable vivacity of Laura Smyly, or that the wind was *in the northeast*, the
bachelor was wonderfully placid and propitious. Ten days had
elapsed since the fatal house-warming, and he had once more
thrown off his mind the incubus of an imaginary nephew. The
Smyly girls, who knew every thing and every body, were not only
intimate with the family of Dean Bedford, the late tenant of the
Rosary, but relations of Mrs. Bedford, with whom they were going
to pass part of the summer, so that there was every chance of the
Spreads commencing their rural lives under the auspices of Euphro-
syne. The dean, who had removed to a neighboring villa, called
Far Niente, was, by all accounts, the heartiest and goodliest of
churchmen; Spread foresaw that Barker would derive immense
satisfaction from having always at hand, in a flourishing and luxurious ecclesiastic, food for his caustic humor and exercise for his sa-
tirical talents.

When dinner was announced, Mr. Spread presented his arm to
Mrs. Martin, with as much respect as if she had been the Duchess

of Sutherland.   Mr. Barker conducted Mrs. Spread, who had first
to remind Owlet that it was his duty to escort Elizabeth.   Philip
had the two Smylys, and the tall Augusta fell to the lot of Mr. St.
Leger.   The dinner was served on a round table, which, with the
snowy whiteness of the cloth, the sparkling of the glass, and the
brilliancy of the plate, seemed actually to smile, and welcome the
company as they gathered about it.   Owlet said a tractarian grace
in his deep sepulchral voice, which nobody but Elizabeth thought
particularly harmonious.   The dinner was plain and elegant, like the
service.   You could neither cry "*aufer opes*," or "*pone dapes*,"
which has been happily rendered "more carving and less gilding."

Barker was pleased to observe that there was no *epergne*, now that
it was not Mrs. Narrowsmith, with her turban, who sat on the opposite point of the compass, but one of the Smylys—which of them he
hardly knew, for they had dressed critically alike, to plague and per-
plex Philip.

Spread disliked *epergnes*, too.

"I object to them," he said, "on free-trade principles: they interrupt the commerce of the table; I can't allow prohibitions on
eyes, Mrs. Martin; how are looks and smiles to be exchanged
through a forest of camelias and chrysanthemums?"

"How few understand the art of conversation, particularly table-
talk," said Mr. St. Leger.

This drew forth Mrs. Martin, who treated the company to an abstract of the system she had unfolded in her morning lecture.

"The best description I know of good table-talk," said the merchant, "is given by Don Armado, in 'Love's Labor Lost:' 'a
sweet touch, a quick venue of wit, snip, snap, quick and home; it
rejoiceth my intellect, true wit;' the don, however, talks himself
in another style."

"A round table has great advantages for conversation," said Mrs.
Spread; "do you like a round table, Mr. Barker?"

"I attach more importance, Mrs. Spread, to the social circle about
it."

"I am for a round table and a round of dinners," said Mr. St.
Leger.

"When people know how to give them," said Barker.

"And whom to ask to them," said Laura Smyly.

"Which very few do," said the bachelor.

"The circle," said the mathematical Philip, "is the perfect figure."

"The social figure, at all events," said Spread; "and now,

Mrs. Martin, take a glass of Madeira with me, that has gone the rounds.

"And send it round to Mrs. Spread and me," suggested Barker.

"After all, Barker, old Narrowsmith gave us one or two fair bottles of wine."

"They must have *spoiled* the dinner," said Laura Smyly.

The remark tickled Mr. Barker; Laura was gaining ground rapidly in his good opinion.

"What a cynical remark," said Mrs. Spread.

"I agree with Miss Smyly," said Barker; "it reminds me of what Launce says—'I would have one that *takes upon him to be a dog*, to be a dog *at all things.*'"

"Elizabeth, my love," whispered Mrs. Martin to that too taciturn young lady, "why don't you talk to Mr. Owlet? say something improving or entertaining."

Elizabeth reasonably thought that Mr. Owlet should rather be saying something instructive or entertaining to her; but the reverend gentleman was just getting into a medieval discussion with Laura Smyly, who had a scrap of intelligence on most subjects, and perfectly understood Mrs. Martin's principle of *adaptation*.

Mrs. Martin paid close attention to what passed between Owlet and Miss Smyly, simply with the view of finding an opening through which she might again urge Elizabeth to take part in the conversation; and, whenever she saw what seemed a fair opportunity, she kept nudging and pinching the poor girl, dinning in her ear, "Establish a fact, my love," or "Now do, my dear, deduce a moral."

The party that assembled in the drawing-room was not a large one, having been invited chiefly for the sake of Miss Medlicott, who occupied a larger space in Philip's consideration, now that he found she had claims to be considered a heroine. Mrs. Narrowsmith thought it strange that Grace should have been invited at all, and had, with the ready concurrence of her amiable daughter, fully determined to leave her behind; but this was overruled by Mr. Narrowsmith, who perceived that it would be displeasing to his partner, and he happened to have several petty reasons (pending the proceedings to dissolve the partnership) for doing every thing to conciliate and propitiate Mr. Spread. Accordingly, at the proper hour Grace proceeded to her room, to make preparations for the party at the Spreads.

It was no fit bower for a girl of delicate constitution, and the tastes and habits of a lady; a garret, adjacent to that occupied by

Mrs. Dorothea Potts, and not very superior in its furniture and accommodations.   There was a small bedstead, scantily curtained with dingy blue-white dimity ; a few sorry chairs ; a mean dressing-table, with a paltry looking-glass ; a rickety chest of drawers, a few odds and ends of well-worn carpeting, no fire in the grate, and on the chimney-piece some miserable fragments of knick-knackery, which had formerly decked the drawing-room, a fire-screen of rice-paper, a stone peach, and a tea-cup of Nankin china, without a handle.   The chronic chill of this wretched chamber was aggravated by a broken pane of glass, which an effort had been made to repair with an old newspaper and a few wafers ; but one of the wafers had yielded, and the paper was flapping to and fro, while the wind amused itself by blowing about the flame of the solitary end of candle, by whose capricious glimmer the niece of one of the wealthiest merchants in England was struggling to make her evening toilet.

But when, bringing up the rear of the miser's party, she entered Mrs. Spread's drawing-room, what a charming contrast she was to her forward cousin, arrayed in bright blue muslin, with a bunch of gaudy roses in her hair, an unwieldy amethyst brooch stuck at her waist, and flourishing a bouquet of the ghastliest flowers.   Mrs. Narrowsmith again glistered in her yellow satin, now in its third season, with the turban on her head that would have astonished the Turks.   She, too, had her broom to brandish, wintrier still than Maria Theresa's.

Mrs. Spread's invitation had named nine o'clock, but the Narrowsmith's did not arrive until ten, which they thought a stroke of " gentility," as people like the Narrowsmith's and Marables uniformly do.

Laura Smyly was sitting near Mr. Barker, as Mrs. Narrowsmith swaggered in.   Laura called the bachelor's attention to a small thermometer, which hung on the wall behind her, and pretended that it was sensibly affected on the entrance of the miser's wife.

The fair Miss Narrowsmith was grievously disconcerted at finding that there was to be no dancing : Narrowsmiths and Marables have no notion of an evening party without dancing ; and how they do dance when they set about it !   However, there would have been a quadrille that evening (so good-natured and complaisant was Mrs. Spread), only that Philip could not be prevailed on to dance with Maria Theresa, which would have been an indispensable civility.

Fortunately for Mrs. Spread, there was no great necessity to dedicate herself very long to Mrs. Narrowsmith, for that incomparable woman was not very fond of conversation with people who either did not, or could not, talk of dyeing and turning, the misdeeds of servants, and suits for spoliated kitchen-stuff. Besides, there was a certain Lady Wrixon in the room, the wife of a beknighted London alderman, and Mrs. Narrowsmith soon began to rub her yellow satin skirts against this personage's crimson velvet ones, partly because the "city madam" was dignified with a title, and partly with a view to get a correct picture of fashionable life in London, which her ladyship could not but be familiar with, as she had a grand house in a grand square, being no other than Finsbury. Thus Mrs. Spread was enabled to have a long chat with Grace Medlicott, and did not leave her side until she saw that Philip coveted her place, having found five minutes' colloquial commerce with the pitiful merchant's daughter business enough in that line for a single evening.

Philip now monopolized Grace in his turn, and made her go over her shipwreck again, expressing in the most ardent terms his admiration of her fortitude and gallantry; and puzzling her a little, too, now and then, with questions respecting "the law of storms," and the "rotatory motion of hurricanes," which (although practically acquainted with the subject much better than he was) she did not find herself competent to answer. Among other incidents which she related in her account of that fearful night, she mentioned the fact of a lady, one of the passengers, who, in the mental aberration or delirium produced by excessive terror, sang several snatches of songs with a voice of great power and feeling. This suggested to Philip the inquiry whether Grace sang herself. She replied, bashfully, that she did sing a little, but had not sung for a long time. He pressed her a point beyond the bounds of politeness, and it ended by her consenting to try a simple air, if she had not forgotten the words.

Meanwhile, Mrs. Spread had been anxious to have a little music, in order to afford Miss Narrowsmith an opportunity of displaying her powers, more particularly as the syren of Rodney-street had been disappointed in her expectations of a ball. Mr. Spread made some objection on the part of Barker, who detested the piano as much as cowards do the trumpet that calls them to the battle-field; but Mrs. Spread would not hear of it; she had no notion of humoring one of her guests, no matter how old a friend, at the expense of the company in general; and her husband could not demur to so just a decision. Spread himself liked music in a pleasant, social, unmusical sort of way : that is to say, he liked without understanding it, preferred an old ballad to a modern melody, and thought the words of a song a very important part of it.   Miss Narrowsmith was a songstress of too much consequence to sit down to the piano without repeated solicitations ; but Mrs. Spread, knowing her to belong to that school of young ladies who are never more resolute to sing than when they urge twenty reasons for not singing, took care good-naturedly to press her request the proper length, and Miss Maria Theresa was ultimately prevailed on to favor the circle with

"I dreamed that I dwelt in marble halls,"

which, after several graceful oscillations of her head, a few preliminary false statements to the effect that she had several varieties of colds, and the playful toss of her ghastly bouquet down on the instrument, she proceeded to execute, in her most brilliant manner, the tip-top *bravura* style of the boarding-schools.

There were several people in the company, particularly Lady Wrixon, the Crackenthorpes, and the Hooks, who thought the performance very good.   Maria Theresa's voice, in fact, was not a bad one.   Had her vocal powers been under the direction of a correcter taste, they were capable of considerably better things ; indeed, even such as they were, she would have displayed them that evening to much better advantage had she not been annoyed and distracted by observing that Philip Spread was paying no attention whatever to her strains, but entirely absorbed in conversation with Grace Medlicott.

Mr. and Mrs. Spread, however, had been "all ear" from first to last, and it was in the social merchant's most Grandisonian manner, and with his blandest smiles and politest compliments, that he took the red right arm of Miss Narrowsmith, and led her from the piano to a seat by the side of her mother, in a distant corner of the room.

Poor little Grace took the vacant place at the piano, unnoticed by any of the Narrowsmiths, or, indeed, by any one but Philip and his mother.   A group in the middle of the room intercepted her from the view of Mr. Narrowsmith and Maria Theresa.   Barker was one of the group, and had just engaged in a peppery discussion with a Mr. Hooke and a Mr. Crooke, upon some of the political questions of the day.

Perhaps the reader may remember, or may not object to have recalled to his memory, the following passage from the fable of "The Flower and the Leaf," where the "rude performance"

F

of the goldfinch is contrasted with the finished melody of the nightingale :

> " Thus as I mused, I cast aside my eye,
> And saw a medlar tree was planted nigh ;
> The spreading branches made a goodly show,
> And full of opening blooms was ev'ry bough.
> *A goldfinch there I saw, with gaudy pride*
> *Of painted plumes, that hopp'd from side to side,*
> Still pecking as she pass'd ; and still she drew
> The sweets from every flower, and suck'd the dew ;
> Sufficed, at length, she warbled in her throat,
> And tuned her voice to many a lively note,
> But indistinct, and neither sweet nor clear,
> Yet such as soothed my soul, and pleased my ear.
> Her rude performance was no sooner tried,
> When she I sought—*the nightingale*—replied
> So sweet, so shrill, so variously she sung,
> That the grove echoed, and the valley rung.
> And I, so ravish'd with her heavenly note,
> I stood entranced, and had no room for thought."

This was just the case with Philip Spread, when Grace warbled the first words of that exquisite Shakspearian wood-note,

> " Hark, hark ! the lark at heaven-gate sings,
> And Phœbus 'gins arise,
> His steeds to water at those springs,
> On chaliced flowers that lies."

It was magical, electrical. Even Barker felt it, and stopped wrangling. The question ran through the room, " Who is it ?" The applause was no longer confined to Crackenthorpes—there were exclamations of rapture from all quarters, and Mrs. Narrowsmith and her daughter (echoing the voices about them) had just pronounced the words, " enchanting and divine," when the group in the middle of the apartment suddenly opened, and disclosed to their astonished view that it was their despised relative who had presumed to sing.

Not until that moment had any of the Narrowsmiths been aware that Grace possessed the talent which she now exhibited in such perfection. Her triumph was not the less complete that it was timid and unintentional. Unfortunately, she gained two victories by one achievement.   Her cousin was eclipsed, and Philip Spread was at her feet.

No female accomplishment excites so much attention as that which this modest and retiring girl had unexpectedly shown herself mistress of.   She became at once an object of intense curiosity and interest to all who either heard her performance, or whom the fame of it reached.   Every tongue was busy; people were no longer content with the vague account which seemed to be all that the Narrowsmiths were disposed to give of her.   In short, there was a resolution to know as much about so attractive a young woman as could be ascertained; and as all were not as delicate as the Spreads in prosecuting inquiries into family matters, a good deal of additional light was thrown on the subject in the course of a few days.   Although she went by the name of Medlicott, she was (as Mr. Spread had suspected) the daughter of a brother of Mr. Narrowsmith.   But she was related to his wife also.   Her father, after a series of struggles in the paths of literature, to him more flowery than fruitful, had left England and settled at Bermudas, where he married a Miss Montserrat, a lady in possession of a large fortune, which was, however, disputed by another branch of the family, the representative of which was the father of Mrs. Isaac Narrowsmith, her first cousin.   As Mrs. Isaac was an only child, her personal interest in this dispute was a deep one, and a considerable part of the expense of the law proceedings, which were instituted in the colonial courts, was secretly borne by her wealthy and rapacious husband.   The cause came to final adjudication on the very day that Grace Medlicott was born.   The decision was against her father; it was a heavy blow, but it was accompanied by one heavier beyond measure.   The same hour that deprived him of his wife's fortune bereaved him of herself.   Against the latter sentence there was no appeal; against the former he was advised to seek relief from the tribunals of England, and for his daughter's sake he ought to have done so; but he had always been deficient in energy, and, now completely paralyzed by affliction, he suffered the law to take its course without a struggle.   Nothing remained but a small appointment which he held under the crown.   It enabled him, however, with strict economy, to give his daughter the education of a gentlewoman.   He lived until she reached her eighteenth year, when he was carried off by a severe and sudden illness, which scarcely afforded him time to execute a will which he placed in the hands of a trusty servant with instructions to conduct his daughter to England, and commit her to the care of his brother at Liverpool.

Long before the date at which this story commences, Mrs. Nar-rowsmith had inherited, upon her father's death, the estate in Ber-mudas which the father of Grace Medlicott had surrendered with-out opposition. It was worth a thousand pounds a-year, and had been settled upon the miser's daughter. All this was soon known, and (as such matters usually are all over the world) was much talked of in Liverpool circles, suspicious and ill-natured people not being slow to hazard a variety of unfounded observations, reflecting upon the share the Narrowsmiths had in the transactions in question. As to Mrs. Spread, she merely expressed her anxious hope that the rights of Miss Medlicott had not been sacrificed.

" We must presume the contrary," replied her husband; " at all events there is no ground whatever for imputing any thing improp-er to her relations; it is no fault of theirs that the colonial lawyers decided in their favor."

" No; but, my dear, suppose the decision of the colonial lawyers to be wrong?"

" How is it to be reversed, you mean—who is there to act for Miss Medlicott?"

" I see a difficulty there, I confess; but come, my love, we must not let our feelings transport us too far, and, above all things, we must avoid intermeddling in the affairs of our neighbors."

CHAPTER XV.

Some men are born great, some achieve greatness, and some have greatness thrust
upon them.   *Twelfth Night.*

The Furies of the Real World—Further Acquaintance of the Spreads with
  Miss Medlicott—The Trials of that Young Lady—Her Conquest of Philip
  —Mr. Barker returns to Town—How he performed the Duties of a Printer's Devil—How he acted as a Common Carrier—Mrs. Harry Farquhar
  again—Portrait of that Lady—The Bachelor pays for interfering in the
  Question of the Spreads' Change of Residence—He gets a smart Scolding,
  and narrowly escapes something smarter still—Fortune thrusts Honor and
  Responsibility upon him—Mr. Spread perplexed—Mysterious Disappearance of Grace Medlicott and Philip Spread.

MALICE, envy, and uncharitableness, you are the furies of the real
world.   There needs no Alecto, with her discordant trump, no ad-
der-crowned Megæra, no Tissiphone with scorpion whip, to vex, to
poison, and torment us.   You, with the aid of the money-fiend, are
sufficient for all mischief; and the four of you have now taken possession of the Narrowsmiths, and formed a league against an unprotected girl.

Into the gloomy interior of a mansion infested by these evil spirits
it is not our pleasure, and fortunately not our business to penetrate.
This is a tale of the Bachelor of the Albany, not of Grace Medlicott;
and our preference of summer to winter, and of the sunny points of
life to its cold hollows, disposes us to keep as much as possible in
the company of the Spreads and Smylys, and associate as little as
can be helped with the Narrowsmiths and their friends.

But a few particulars more of the history of Miss Medlicott it will
be proper to relate, before we lose sight of her, as the Spreads
themselves soon did, ignorant of her fate, and almost uncertain of
her existence.

She never sang again in Liverpool, save once or twice at Mrs.
Spread's, when there was no company; but it was only once or
twice that this occurred; indeed they would have seen very little

more of Grace, after the evening of her fatal triumph, had it not
been that fortunately Mrs. Narrowsmith and her daughter went for a
few weeks to London, on a visit to Lady Wrixon, and then there
was both increased facility of access to Rodney-street and less difficulty of getting Miss Medlicott to come to Abercromby Square.

What strongly excited the attention of Mrs. Spread, in the com-
mencement of her acquaintance with this young person, was her
seeming unconsciousness of the iron natures of the people with
whom she lived, while no other eye could help perceiving that
she was indebted to her sordid relatives for little more liberality
and attention then she would have found in a common asylum for
female orphans. It takes time to open the pure eyes of generous
and unsuspicious youth to the meannesses and inhumanities of the
world. Grace had slowly to be convinced that she was irksome to
the relations whose duty it was to cherish and protect her. She
was a burden in the house of which she was the only embellishment
and honor. The narrow economy of the entire establishment
blinded her to the fact that, toward her, parsimony was more than
parsimonious. She felt herself pinched without knowing who it
was that pinched. She was grateful for ill-usage, and returned
coldness with warmth. " How few people," she argued, " were
like the Spreads! Discomfort was the custom of the house, and
why should she (a dependent though a relation) be more comfortable than the rest of the family ; as to the tempers of her aunt and
cousin, those were little failings of character upon which she, of all
people living, ought not to be severe."

But there was no mistaking the real state of the case, when malice
and envy came into play. She then ceased to be the object of a contemptuous protection, and was elevated into an object of jealousy and
rancor. On the morning of the next day but one that succeeded
Mrs. Spread's party, Mr. Narrowsmith, fumbling in his pockets in
search of some small piece of money, for some indispensable dis-
bursement, produced the self-same silver fourpenny, the finding of
which on the carpet, about a fortnight before, he had piously ascribed to a direct intervention of Providence. He recognized it by
a small hole drilled through the center. So did Grace Medlicott; it
was hers; the only property she possessed in money when she arrived in Rodney-street: yet she did not, she could not, bring herself to
claim it—it went as her anonymous contribution to the weekly ex-
penses of the opulent miser.

From that hour her bread was bitter, and would have been so, had
it been that of the royal table. From that hour it became a steep

and wearisome journey up to her dreary attic; and wearisome it
would have been had it been the bower of Rosamond, or the chamber of an Infanta. But she did not reveal the bitterness of her lot
to the Spreads, not at least with her lips, or intentionally even by
her looks. Those looks, however, told her tale in a language which
Mrs. Spread, with her quick-sighted tenderness, understood as well
as if it had been written for her reading. Of all the Spreads, Philip
was the last to take an interest in Miss Medlicott. She had no pretensions to beauty, and, though shipwrecked in a tempest, she was
unacquainted with the theory of storms. The Smylys were both
handsomer and wittier; and then he was confessedly "in love with
Miss Marable, or at all events with Bessie Bomford." But Grace
had her advantages, too. Nature did not write the word gentleman
more legibly on the brow of Uncle Toby than she had written that
of lady on the forehead, indeed in every feature, of Miss Medlicott.
She was artless, pure, fresh, and thoroughly unworldly and unselfish; the very incarnation of truth and modesty. In the one accomplishment which she possessed, she was unrivaled; and then she
was an orphan, a wanderer, like a casket of pearls without an owner,
cast by the waves upon a savage shore. These were powerful attractions; and they did not fail, after some time, to make an impression upon the susceptible *mind* of Philip, who was musical, romantic, and had all the benevolence of his father in his blood. The impression once made, grew deeper and deeper rapidly; every meeting with Grace strengthened, every song she sang improved it, until
at length the feeling extended itself toward that warm region of the
mind which borders upon the heart's territory, and Philip was
wounded for the first time with the "rich golden shaft." It "killed
the flock of all other affections in him;" he flirted with the Smylys
no more—thought no more of Miss Marable, or Bessie Bomford.

It was a most indiscreet attachment, but it was not the less strong
upon that account.

> "Will Love be controlled by advice?
> Will Cupid our mothers obey?"

All the members of Philip's family had, by their admiration of
Grace, and their enthusiasm about her, unwittingly contributed to a
result which they deplored extremely, as soon as their eyes were
open to it. The previous character of Philip's love affairs—the impetuosity with which they commenced, and the levity with which
they were abandoned—made his friends inattentive to symptoms

which would otherwise have excited their suspicions. Then parents, in such cases, are commonly as blind as love itself; and they are blindest precisely where they ought to be most quick-sighted, where the attachments formed by their children are most irreconcilable with prudence. The Spreads were far from being worldly people, but they were as far from despising wealth as they were from worshiping it. With all the interest they took in Mr. Narrowsmith's niece, and, notwithstanding the high opinion they entertained both of her heart and her understanding, they considered the young lady a very ineligible match for Philip; and it deeply distressed them to perceive, as at length they did, that it was no longer possible to cultivate her society with a due regard to the welfare of their son.

But we return to the Bachelor of the Albany. Fortune had still several tricks to play upon him, though she suffered him to return in peace to his London lodging, with the single exception of influencing Mrs. Martin to make him the bearer of some corrected proofs of her "British Stepmothers." The reader is left to guess whether it was under the control of Fortune or Discretion that Laura Smyly at the same time repressed a strong inclination she had to beg of Mr. Barker to be the carrier of a small parcel, which she was anxious to forward to a friend of hers at Brompton. That Mr. Barker *offered* to execute, and actually *did* execute, that commission, surprised nobody that knew him: they put it down to the very perverseness of his humor.

But our Diogenes had not been three days in his tub before his temper had to undergo a very rough trial indeed. In crossing the designs of Mrs. Harry Farquhar, by influencing the Spreads to settle at Richmond instead of Norwood, he involved himself in more difficulties than one.

. Mrs. Harry Farquhar, the pretty little Amazon of Norwood, after storming about the room for several minutes, rung the bell waspishly, and ordered her pony-phaeton. The phaeton was at the door in a quarter of an hour. Mrs. Harry jumped in, whip in hand, and looking as if she was very much inclined to use it on the person of a quiet, respectable gentleman who stood by, doing his best to be civil, as became a dutiful husband, for that was the humble situation he held in his lady's household.

She was a pretty, a wickedly-pretty woman, with an insolent eye, and a glowing, passionate complexion. Like Hermia, in the "Midsummer Night's Dream,"

"Though she was but little, she was fierce."

She had a pert, expert, and malapert tongue that could libel or scold one in a leash of languages. When she was coquetish, she prattled French; when she was transcendental, she chattered German; she rated her servants, including Mr. Farquhar, in plain English. You saw by her toilet she was a termagant; she was too hasty for buttons, and too violent for hooks and eyes. She wore the prettiest of bonnets, but wore them awry. There was generally a trail of black ribbon at her heels; and her dress behind was always open—to observation. In one point, however, she excelled: she knew how to put on a shawl—a rare knowledge with our countrywomen. She was commonly, too, *bien coiffée* and *bien ganté*, except when she tossed her hair, or tore off her gloves in a conjugal *fracas*.

Leaving her ponies in charge of her servant, standing at the entrance to the Albany in Piccadilly, she strutted, whip in hand, in her brazen, fearless way, toward the bachelor's chambers, the number of which she had first learned from the porter.

Reynolds answered her bold knock and her sharp application to the bell.

"Is Mr. Barker at home?"

Reynolds hesitated, and was lost. In a moment the bachelor was startled from a chapter of Rabelais, which he was devouring, by the apparition of a lady in his *sanctum-sanctorum*, and the last lady he would have coveted a visit from. She bustled in, affectedly smiling and simpering, but with half an eye you could see the snake among the flowers.

"You are surprised at a visit from me, Mr. Barker—no, thank you, I shan't sit down. You never come to see me, Mr. Barker."

Barker had never been so completely thrown off his center before; he muttered something about being glad to see Mrs. Farquhar, and an humble inquiry as to the fortunate circumstances to which he was to ascribe the honor she had done him.

"Perhaps I'm come to give you a little bit of a scolding, Mr. Barker," still smiling, but the snake more visible every moment.

Barker bit his lip, grew a little white, and said that, "Ignorant as he was of having given any offense, he hoped she would see the propriety of reserving her favors *of that description* for Mr. Farquhar."

This stung her little ladyship, but she passed it over in her eagerness to come to the main point, which was her desire to know what he meant by interfering in the affairs of her sister's family.

"Madam!" said Barker, not perceiving her drift.

"The Spreads must live at Richmond to please you, Mr. Barker;

they can't take a house at Norwood, near *me*, because you presume to intrude."

" The intrusion, madam, is not upon *my* part," said Barker, bowing, and almost glancing at the door.

" To meddle in what's no affair of yours," continued the pretty vixen, slapping her dress with her whip.

" Really, Mrs. Farquhar," said Barker, with the severest gravity, and anxious to disembarrass himself of his visitor, " I can discover no adequate motive for this strange proceeding on your part, unless, indeed, you are come to horsewhip me."

" Now, don't you deserve it, sir?" said the pretty little Amazon, again slapping her dress; but now she did it rather playfully, and with a simpering laugh, beginning to be sensible that she had placed herself in a false position, and that her best course was to laugh herself out of it. Barker ought to have built a bridge of gold for the flying enemy, but he could not resist the temptation of replying, and he made the reply in his acrimonious manner.

" I have not the honor to be your husband, Mrs. Harry; if I had—" glancing at the horsewhip, with the plainest intimation that in that case it would infallibly change hands.

" If you had, you would know better than to interfere in what is none of your business, Mr. Peter—Peter the Hermit—we all know what kind of hermits you bachelors of the Albany are—your characters—"

" Take care of your own character, madam; you will have no sinecure office," rejoined Barker, vehemently.

" My character is in no great danger *here*, at all events," retorted Mrs. Harry, with a look so point-blank at Mr. Barker's grizzled hair, that never did arrow go directer to the mark. She was so content, indeed, with the blow, that she accompanied it with a contumelious courtesy, and thought it a good opportunity for retreating, which Reynolds, who had witnessed the scene (not without apprehensions for his master's safety), gave her every facility for doing. However, she did not return to her ponies without several brandishes of her whip, and a muttered volley of " mischief-making bachelors" and " Peter the Hermit," three times over.

As to Mr. Barker, being of the more laconic sex, he vented his wrath in the single exclamation,

" Why the fiend does not that booby, Lord John Yore, revive the good old English institution of the ducking-stool." He then turned savagely upon his man, and Reynolds was very near being cashiered for keeping the door so carelessly.

Your short woman is more effective in the world than your tall one.   The Vastabellas and Altadoras have something masculine about them, which puts us on our mettle, and makes it a point of honor to have our own way with them.   But the Parvulus and the Minimas are women all over; they rely on their sex alone, and manhood less firm than Mr. Barker's has no chance against them. The ascendency of woman is inversely as her strength and stature. The lofty beauties are most stared and marveled at; but it is the small, tight woman that sways the world—we mean, of course, when she is pretty and piquant, *bien chaussée, coiffée, ganté,* and Mrs. Harry Farquhar sometimes was all that.

But this visitation was mere child's play compared to the inhuman sport which our bachelor's evil genius was preparing to make with him at the self-same moment in another and a distant place.   His journey to Liverpool had already involved him in several embarrassments; he had been threatened with a most objectionable nephew, entrapped into a most perilous flirtation, turned to the uses of a printer's devil by a blue-stocking governess, and now his malignant star stands right over the House of Commons, menacing a still more direct and flagrant violation of his deep-laid scheme of life, but continuing all the while to entangle his fortunes with those of the fair sex, the most embarrassing course that the fortunes of a Benedick could take.

It will be remembered, that at the moment Miss Medlicott sat down to sing at the late eventful party at Mrs. Spread's, Mr. Barker was engaged in a warm political squabble with two or three gentlemen, who occupied, in a group, the center of the room.   A few days subsequently, Mr. Spread was waited upon at his counting-house by two of these gentlemen.   They were intimate friends, and their business was to consult him about the selection of a fit and proper person to represent a borough in Yorkshire, in which they were interested, and with which Mr. Spread was well acquainted. In fact, they came as a kind of deputation from the constituency of the borough.

"Have you any body in your eye?" asked the merchant.

"Why, we have," replied Mr. Crooke, one of the deputation; "we have a friend of yours in our eye, but we wish to do nothing without your advice and approbation!"

"Who is your man?" inquired Spread.

"A gentleman whom we met the other evening at your house," said Mr. Hooke, the other deputy.

"Sir George Wrixon?"

" No."

" Mr. Motherwit!"

" No, no."

" Who, then? I can't guess."

" Why—Mr. Barker, to be sure," said Crooke.

Spread had as hearty a laugh as he ever enjoyed in his life. When he had laughed enough, he frankly informed the deputation that they possibly could not have thought of a gentleman worse qualified for a seat in parliament, to say nothing of the fact of his having an insuperable objection to office or business of any kind.

Both Hooke and Crooke were of opinion that it would be easy to overcome an objection of so vague a nature.

" But," said Mr. Spread, " the character of my friend Barker is no secret. It would be the most mistaken delicacy on my part (since you have done me the honor of asking my opinion) not to state to you frankly, that he is far too impracticable and crochety a man to make a useful member of parliament."

" We are a crotchety constituency ourselves," said Mr. Hooke, laughing.

" We won't quarrel with him at Boroughcross for being crotchety and impracticable," said Hooke's colleague.

" Upon my word, then, gentlemen," said Mr. Spread, with his laughing eye, " my friend Barker is just the man to suit you; only the misfortune is, that you would easier persuade him to go up in a balloon than to go into the House of Commons."

" We'll engage to return him without a shilling expense," said Mr. Crooke.

" He wouldn't go into parliament for ten thousand a-year," said Spread, speaking seriously, and rising at the same time, in order to put an end to the conference, as he had important business on his hands.

Messrs. Hooke and Crooke retired, and Mr. Spread thought no more of their ridiculous project. But just as he was on the point of leaving the counting-house to return home to dinner, the same pair of commissioners called again, with Mr. Crackenthorpe and Mr. Marable along with them, and Mr. Spread could hardly believe his ears when he was assured, by all four, that nobody else in all England but Barker would be likely to carry the election for Boroughcross; and that they had, accordingly, resolved to propose him, *nolens volens*, or, rather, without giving him any intimation of the honor designed him.

" Well, gentlemen," said Spread, " take your own way; but remember, I warn you, that you will only throw away your time and money.   You might just as well return General Tom Thumb."

"Now, Spread," said Mr. Crooke, "all we request of you is, that you will keep the thing quiet—not a word to Barker for your life."

But Spread, very properly, declined to make any such promise. It was, indeed, a grave question, whether, knowing Barker's almost fanatical repugnance to duty of all kinds, he ought to suffer him to be brought into the position of embarrassment, where (as a tribute to the crookedness of his politics) the eccentric electors of Borough-cross seemed determined to place him.   No doubt the honor would be very considerable, of being returned to Parliament in the manner proposed, and it was just possible that it might act upon Barker's vanity, so as to induce him to retain the seat, once "thrust upon him," like "greatness" upon poor Malvolio.   In fact, Barker was a very difficult man to understand or deal with.   It was hard to know "where to have him."

Upon the whole, Mr. Spread was in a state of no little perplexity that evening.   His love of the comedy of life half disposed him to assist fortune in playing a practical joke upon his friend, and he was powerfully supported in this merry view of the matter by Adelaide and Laura Smyly, who had fun enough in them to chase the tragic muse out of the world.   Mrs. Spread, on the contrary, whose good-humor never made her forget her benevolence for a moment, was of opinion that her husband should immediately apprise Mr. Barker of what was going on.   Always disposed himself to the straight-forward course in every transaction of life, and doubly pleased when he took the right way, with the sanction or at the suggestion of his wife, Spread made up his mind to write the next day to Barker; and if he did not keep his resolution, it will be admitted that there was excuse enough for his breaking it, and, indeed, for losing sight of the subject altogether, for before breakfast the following morning the startling news was received that Grace Medlicott had suddenly and mysteriously disappeared from her uncle's house, and this was quickly followed by the equally alarming and unaccountable discovery that Philip had started for London, by the express-train, at day-break—the first independent step, amounting to a seeming breach of filial duty, which Philip had ever taken.

The first impression naturally was that this double flight was the result of concert between the fugitives; but a letter which Philip left for his mother dissipated that suspicion, and satisfied all his family that, having received intelligence of the step taken by the unprotected girl, he had merely followed her with the chivalrous design

of guarding her amid the perils of the metropolis.   A perilous place
London certainly is for defenseless maidenhood; but when innocence and beauty are championed by love and romance, the protector
is generally in greater danger than the *protégée*.   The recollection
of this made the Spreads very unhappy about their son.

As to the cause of Grace's disappearance, it was only too easily di-
vined.   Mrs. Narrrowsmith had returned to Liverpool, and no doubt
the unfortunate girl had no longer been able to endure the tyranny
of her protectors.   Mr. Spread, upon reflection, thought it likely that
she had resolved upon turning her talents to account, and supporting
herself in the situation of a governess.   But still drearier explanations naturally occurred to the minds of other members of the family.   A bush in the dark, as the poet says, is easily mistaken for a
bear.

CHAPTER XVI.

*Sous quel astre, mon Dieu, faut il que je sois né,
Pour être de fâcheux toujours assassiné ?
Il semble que partout le sort me les adresse,
Et je vois chaque jour quelque nouvelle espéce.*

                                        MOLIÈRE.

The Topic of the Clubs—Mrs. Harry Farquhar electioneering—Masculine Women and Ladylike Men—Perverse Purity of the Electors of Borough-cross—Tom Turner writes a spicy Article—How Mrs. Harry went down to the Borough, and in what State she returned to Town—The *Times* of the 10th of February—How Barker was advertised for—How he was affected by his Return to Parliament—His Correspondence with Mr. Spread—Troubles of Parliamentary Life—The Bachelor becomes the Topic of the Day—Receives a letter from his old Writing-Master—Takes the Oaths and his Seat—Is invited to the Rosary—Is advertised for again.

THE *bruit* soon ran through the clubs, that Barker of the Albany was coming into Parliament. Great was the mirth, many the speculations to which the rumor gave rise.

"Returned by Wormwood Scrubbs, I presume," said Saunter, a lounging lord of the Treasury, and member for Lazenby.

"I should guess Bath," said Will Whitebait, a porpoise and a dandy. "I can't imagine a fitter colleague for Roebuck."

"I'm told," said Tom Turner, another Treasury lord, a lady's man, "that he knows nothing of what is going on; and that if he is returned, he will throw up his seat—take the Chiltern Hundreds."

"No," said the first Treasury lordling, "he won't do that, for fear of being called on for an account of his *stewardship*."

It happened that one of these gentlemen, Tom Turner, was a great friend and ally of Mrs. Henry Farquhar, who, for some time back, had been extremely desirous to push her noodle of a husband into Parliament. On the same day that the above short conversation took place, Turner was visiting at Norwood, and suggested to Mrs. Harry that she would have a very fair chance at Boroughcross, it would be so easy to convince the electors that their votes would be only thrown away upon the individual they proposed to return, as he had an insurmountable objection to public life, and would positively never take his seat. "The expense may be about five or six hundred pounds," said Mr. Turner.

Mr. Farquhar ventured to observe that he thought this a reasonable sum; but his wife looked as if she did not care a fico what he thought upon the subject. A hubbub among the little Farquhars happening to be audible at that moment, she directed her husband to go and restore order.

"Indeed," she said, "the day is so fine, I think you had better take the coach, and give the children an airing. I shall ride out with Mr. Turner."

Mr. Farquhar was submissively proceeding to execute this mission, so becoming of a man and a would-be senator, when his wife called him back, and added—

"Now, I beg you won't let Helen take cold; and remember, either going or returning, to call at Surgeon Dent's, and get him to look at Louisa's teeth."

"Who is our opponent?" said the manly Mrs. Harry to Tom Turner, after her ladylike husband had left the room.

"A man you know—Barker."

"Barker! what Barker?"

"Of the Albany."

"Barker of the Albany! Is he the man?" cried the termagant Mrs. Harry, vixenishly and exultingly, plucking off her right-hand glove at the same time, and tearing it in two places. She broke herself in gloves, at exciting junctures.

The electioneering arrangements were all completed in the course of a pleasant ride, and a gay dinner after it, at which Will Whitebait and Saunter assisted, as well as Tom Turner. Not one of the three exchanged a syllable the whole evening with Mr. Farquhar, but, by way of atonement, they drank his champagne and claret generously. A stranger to the institutions of the country could have come to no other conclusion than that the British House of Commons was a lady's chamber, and the Government of England a petticoat one. Well—the election was to take place in three days; and on the following day, Mrs. Harry and Tom Turner posted down to Boroughcross—Turner with a thousand pounds in his pocket, in crisp Bank-of-England notes, the property of a quiet, biddable gentleman in the dickey, who was no other than Mr. Barker's competitor for a seat in the legislature.

But it was too late: Messieurs Hooke and Crooke had been too active. The reputation of the crotchety bachelor, backed by the

name of Spread, were too strong for Mrs. Harry, even with the lord
of the Treasury and a thousand pounds to boot.   Some of the most
corrupt electors, out of sheer perverseness, refused to be bribed.
Cautionary notices to the constituency were posted through the
town, all to no purpose.   Mrs. Harry herself would have made a
speech from the hustings, had she received the least encouragement,
but not receiving it, she supplied Tom Turner with a number of
malignant anecdotes of the bachelor, most of them sheer fictions,
which that light-fingered gentleman rapidly manufactured into what
he called a " spicy article" for a journal, styled the *Boroughcross
Independent*, which published it for the consideration of fifty pounds.
Calumny, however, proved as ineffectual as corruption.   Barker
was returned ; and Mrs. Harry, with scarce a button left on her
traveling dress, drove back moodily to town, having spent five hundred pounds in futile bribery, and five pounds additional in French
gloves.

The *Times* of the morning of the 10th of February was fraught
with matter of grave import to Barker.   He happened first to glance
at the advertisement columns, and there, among hues and cries after
revolted poodles, and lamentations for prodigal sons and wives errant,
he read the following, with feelings which (as penny-a-liners say)
" were too deep for words :"

" Should this meet the eye of a gentleman named Barker, whose
brother died some time since at Bermudas, he is requested to communicate with Mr. John Ramsay, No. 96, Chancery Lane, by whom
he will be made acquainted with something in which he will probably feel himself *deeply concerned*."

The countenance of the bachelor fell.   The nephew in search of
an uncle was now evidently taking active steps.   Barker rapidly
recalled all the vexatious circumstances which had signalized his
two meetings with the young man, by whom, or upon whose behalf
(there could be no doubt) the above advertisement had been inserted ;
he trembled to recollect that his Christian name was Alexander, and
how one of the passengers, on the journey to Liverpool, had actually
advised him to avail himself of the columns of the *Times*, to discover
his relative and natural guardian and protector !   Scarce had he
regained, in some degree, his composure, after this shock to his
nerves, when his eye was again saluted in another part of the same
great journal with his own name, repeated several times, in an article headed " Election Intelligence."   There was nothing in this to
surprise him ; but presently he encountered the name of Spread,
which struck him as an odd coincidence, but no more.   However,

when, a few lines farther down, he saw an allusion to the Albany, his curiosity was at length excited—he read the paragraph with breathless haste, and, to his boundless astonishment, found his own unquestionable self—Peter Barker, esq., of the Albany—Peter Barker, trumpeted as the friend of Arthur Spread, the great Whig merchant of Liverpool, declared duly elected a burgess to serve in Parliament for the town of Boroughcross ! ! !

Amazement engrossed him for a considerable time, to the utter exclusion of every other feeling. Indignation succeeded; and such a storm of it, that Reynolds hid himself in all manner of corners; and the man-mastiffs at the gates of the Albany skulked and trembled, as something fiercer passed them. Barker had obviously been made the victim of a most unjustifiable practical joke, and he instantly accused his oldest and best friend of being at the bottom of it, without a tittle of evidence beyond the statement in the speech of his proposer, Mr. Crooke, that the gentleman whom he had the honor to recommend to his brother electors was the friend of Mr. Spread, of Liverpool, whose name was a guaranty for the honor and respectability of every body connected with him. In the fever of the moment, he addressed the following short, but virulent letter to Spread, which was the first intimation Spread received of the return of Barker.

"The Albany, Feb. 10.

"Dear Spread—This is an infamous conspiracy and a vile trick. I can not acquit you of participation in it. Who the d—l are Crackenthorpe, Hooke, and Crooke ? I presume the fellows are friends of yours, so please to inform them that I shall certainly never sit for their confounded borough.

"Yours, &c.,
"Peter Barker.

"To Arthur Spread, esq.,
"Abercromby Square, Liverpool."

To which rude and unwarrantable letter Spread returned the following answer :

"35, Abercromby Square, Liverpool.

"My Dear Barker—I am sincerely grieved at what has taken place at Boroughcross, involving you so unexpectedly and disagreeably. That I had some intimation of what was intended is true, but far from having any share in it, I was on the point of giving you timely notice, when my attention was distracted by very distressing private circumstances, with which I shall not now trouble you. I was not aware of the fact that my wife's brother-in-law was a candidate, so engrossed have I been by the events I allude to. The use of my name on the occasion was utterly unauthorized, as you ought (I think) to have taken for granted. If there is any thing I can do to extricate you from this embarrassment, you will find me

" Your's, most truly,

"ARTHUR SPREAD.

" To Peter Barker, esq., M. P.,
    The Albany, London."

Now, let Mr. Peter Barker's future course be what it may, he is legally, and to all intents and purposes, a member of the imperial legislature, charged with serious responsibilities, saddled with momentous duties, liable to serious penalties, and, moreover, a kind of target set up by the Constitution for the political bores of all England to shoot at, besides being in a special manner the property of the bores of Boroughcross.

In the course of a very few days his breakfast-table began to be covered with letters, applications, petitions, suggestions, communications of all kinds, pertinent and impertinent to his new station. There were a dozen applications for civil offices from independent electors, and three modest requests that the bachelor would step down to the Horse-Guards and get cornetcies and other commissions for sons of the writers; there were two petitions, in tin cases, against a standing army; three for the instant removal of the bishops from the House of Lords; two for the erection of maypoles in rural districts; and a very voluminous one from the ladies of Boroughcross, praying the House to prohibit the importation of cigars, and remove, at the same time, all restraint upon the trade in Flemish lace and Dutch tulips. At the sight of this multitudinous correspondence Barker felt bewildered, as if he had been dreaming, and he actually laughed hysterically as he turned over the papers.

As a matter of course, he would accept the Chiltern Hundreds, and shake himself free from all this embarrassment, as he would throw off the oppression of a nightmare. This was the simple, natural, obvious course; but is it the uniform way of the world to take the simple, natural, obvious course? At all events, Mr. Barker did not take it, and the reason why he did not (at least the only reason assignable with any degree of probability) is now to be stated. Mr. Spread, upon receiving the hasty letter which the reader has just perused, lost no time to communicate to the electors of Boroughcross the flat refusal of his friend to avail himself of the honor they had done him. Mrs. Harry Farquhar and her Treasury lordling

were instantly in the field again, and Mr. Barker, though so celebrated a cynic, was too little of a moral philosopher to resist the
temptation of revenging himself upon the pretty shrew of Norwood,
which he did most amply, by determining to retain his seat for
one session at least.   The *Boroughcross Independent* had been duly
forwarded to him, containing Tom Turner's "spicy article," and
Barker would have had no difficulty in discovering Mrs. Harry's
smart hand in it, even if it had not been entitled "*Peter the Hermit.*"

Perhaps, had the secrets of his heart been known, some degree
of personal vanity would have been found conspiring with vindictive-
ness, to suggest the strange resolution to which Barker came upon
this occasion, so utterly inconsistent with the principles and course
of his past life.

Among the numerous annoyances, great and small, to which he
had now become exposed, in consequence of his entrance into public life, were the repeated allusions in the newspapers to his movements and intentions, what motions he was to make, what party he
was to act with, what bills he was to introduce.   Many of these
teasing paragraphs were inserted designedly to plague him; his ec-
centricities and morbid hatred of publicity being well known in the
clubs and political circles.   One day he read in the *Morning
Post :*

" Mr. Barker, the new member for Boroughcross, has arrived at
his chambers in the Albany."

Another day he saw in the *Globe :*

" We have reason to believe that the question of vote by ballot
will be brought before the House after Easter, by the member for
Bath, and it is said the motion will be seconded by Peter Barker,
esq., M.P. for Boroughcross."

A few days later he found the following in the *Daily News :*

" Mr. Barker, M.P., is about to accept the high and *responsible*
office of Steward of the Chiltern Hundreds; there will positively
be a new election for Boroughcross."

It was probably to this announcement that he was indebted for the
following letter, which he received shortly after :

March 15, 23½ Silver-street.

" HONORABLE SIR—I trust your goodness will excuse the liberty
I take of intruding on your valuable time, now the property of your
country ; but your kindness to me on a former occasion emboldens
me to apply to you again, now that Providence has placed you in

the high position to which you talents justly entitle you; and to which, knowing your honorable ambition, I always predicted that, sooner or later, you would arrive. Finding, from the organs of public intelligence, that you are about to accept the lucrative and influential situation of the Children Hundreds (which I presume is an office connected with the all-important subject of national education), I am induced humbly to beg you will cast a favorable eye upon my poor nephew, Alexander, who now writes an excellent official hand (having been instructed by myself), and is otherwise competent to fill the office of Private Secretary, or confidential clerk, beside being particularly fond of children, which would, of course, be expected in your department. I beg to inclose specimens of my boy's chirography, with twenty-three testimonials of his moral character, and trusting again that you will pardon this intrusion—'*Cum tot sustineas*'—as Horace says,

> "I have the honor to remain,
> "Your grateful and obedient servant,
> "MATTHEW QUILL,
> "Your old writing-master.

"To the Right Honorable Peter Barker, M.P., &c., &c., &c.,
"The Albany."

Owing to a concurrence of circumstances not unusual in the political world—two changes of administration in three weeks, and the usual Easter recess—it so happened that the spring was pretty far advanced before Barker took the oaths and his seat for Boroughcross. It was on a Friday; and the same evening he received, to his considerable surprise, the following short note, in a well-known manly, honest hand.

"The Rosary, April 21.

"MY DEAR BARKER—Here we are—pretty well settled—come down to us to-morrow and stay until Monday. I would offer you the haunted chamber, but we have not discovered it yet. There will always be a tub for you here, where you can lie all day in the sun, snarling at the Irish church, and wrangling with Mrs. Spread —like Dean Swift and Lady Acheson.

> "Ever yours,
> "ARTHUR SPREAD.

"Peter Barker, esq., M.P., The Albany, London."

The bachelor felt half disposed to decline this friendly invitation; not that he was offended at the free allusions to his cynical character, but that he felt somewhat ashamed of himself in his altered, almost revolutionized, position, and had a little fear of encountering his old friend, whose perception of humor he knew to be keen, and who might well be excused indulging in a little banter upon the rapid decline, if not the complete fall, of Barker's vaunted system. But then, on the other hand, he knew by ample experience, that Spread was never the man to push the fairest jest beyond the limits of good-nature and good-manners; and, further (what probably ultimately decided the point), he always felt himself comfortable under his friend's roof, and had found it particularly agreeable during the last visit. Whether that was owing to Mrs. Briscoe's attentions, or to Laura Smyly's charms, is not a question into which we are called upon to enter.

On the Saturday morning before he started for the Rosary, the member for Boroughcross again saw in the *Times* the alarming advertisement which has already been extracted from the columns of that newspaper. It was beginning to make him seriously uneasy, and the more so, because, on several occasions, as he walked the streets, he saw (fortunately without encountering) the identical young man to whom, it was so clear, that the advertisement referred. The bachelor, with this fair nephew dogging his steps, felt like Frankenstein, pursued by the misshapen creature of his hands; and, far from thinking himself " *deeply concerned*" in accepting Mr. Ramsay's invitation, he never, in all his life, experienced so little desire to visit Chancery-lane.

CHAPTER XVII.

Now turning from the wintry signs, the Sun
His course exulting through the Ram had run,
And whirling up the skies, his chariot drove
Through Taurus and the lightsome realms of love,
Where Venus from her orb descends in showers
To glad the ground and paint the fields with flowers.

The Flower and the Leaf.

The Rosary—The Spreads at Breakfast—Their Visitors, feathered and un-feathered—Finches and Smylys—Laura Smyly stays at the Rosary—Mr. Spread escorts Adelaide back to Far Niente, the seat of Dean Bedford—The Dean and Mrs. Bedford in their noontide Slumbers—Mrs. Harry Far-quhar imitates Mohammed—Arrival of the Bachelor—Owlet appears in the Twilight—Explains the Religious Uses of Church Theatricals—Barker's Hit at the Deans—More detailed Account of the Rosary, and what made it a particularly pleasant House.

THE Rosary, to which Barker was now about to be introduced, and where important events were destined to take place, was exact-ly the place for a family like the Spreads, with ample means, hos-pitable habits, elegant tastes, and cheerful dispositions. The do-main was extensive, undulating, and not overplanted; it extend-ed to the river-side, and abounded with walks and terraces, shady without gloom, and courting the sun, without being exposed to the unkindly blasts. Embraced from northwest to northeast by rising grounds, and imbosomed in woods, from every malignant point of the compass it was screened completely. There were two spa-cious gardens, laid out with an equal eye to productive power and picturesque effect. There were hot-houses and green-houses, graperies and pineries, a dial for Philip to regulate with his sextant, and an apiary, under a sunny wall, to aid his researches into insect-mathematics. In fact, it would be hard to say what the Rosary had not—a wash-house, a tool-house, a cow-house, a pigeon-house, a boat-house, a brew-house, an ice-house, and a bake-house, a dairy, and an aviary, a fowlery, and a piggery. Then there was nothing naked, unsightly, or neglected in any corner of the place; not a bit of bare wall visible, no ragged hedges, not a fence unrepaired, no vegetation out of place upon gravel walks. There was no such soft, fresh, bright turf any where.

A lawn sloped at the gentlest angle, from the house to the river's side, shaven with such precision, that it seemed the work of the razor, not the scythe, as if a coiffeur, or barber of Paris had performed the mower's duty. Immediately beneath the windows the smooth grass rose, and swelled like long sofas of green velvet, only interrupted by a few low steps of white marble, by which you gained the principal entrance, which was itself nothing but a more spacious window, under a porch of trellis-work, interwoven with climbing-plants, now beginning to flower, and evidently tended with such nicety that none but gay and beautiful insects, the exquisites of the entomological kingdom—a beetle covered with diamonds, a butterfly in ball-dress, or a Brummell moth—would presume to visit there. The place was populous with birds, now beginning to carol their hymn to Spring in every bush. The thrushes and blackbirds considered the Rosary their own, and in fact they held it in joint-tenancy with the Spreads, who were as kind protectors of birds as Mr. Waterton himself. It was certainly a delightful transition from Liverpool, and it was marvellous how soon the town mice got into the ways and habits of mice who had lived all their lives in the country. There was something to hit every body's fancy. Augusta had the loveliest of all arbors, promising to be as rosy as Gulistan and odorous as Sabæa, to carry on her operations in embroidery. Mrs. Spread had the sweetest boudoir, and most charming conservatory, forming a wing of the principal drawing-room. There was an ivied ruin, supposed to be that of a church, in one part of the grounds, for the antique-minded Owlet; and Mr. Spread used to promise to cut down a clump of trees at a particular point, so as to admit a breath or two of the fragrant and salubrious northeaster, to regale his honorable friend, the member for Boroughcross.

Within, every thing was as near perfection as the interior of any country-house could be brought by skill and taste of the first order. It was the best lighted, the best warmed, and (without the slightest assistance from Dr. Reid) the best ventilated villa in the kingdom. But it was commodious, without being regular; a house for incident as well as comfort, for adventure as well as convivial enjoyment. Some houses are evidently built for the Prims and Humdrums, houses where you must be always grave and demure, where the comedy of life is altogether out of the question, the rooms are so square and decorous, the stairs so methodical, the passages and galleries so correct and formal.   There is no satisfaction in a house where one can not occasionally make a geographical blunder.   One likes, now and then, to make an innocent error of a door or two in the navigation of a strange corridor; it is so comical, novelish, Don-Quixotish, and all that sort of thing, which is so very pleasant.   There can be nothing duller, when you are bedward bound, than to be assured by some Malvolio, that you "can not possibly go wrong."   Now, you could easily go wrong in parts of the Rosary.   It was not, like the mind of its proprietor, a place without nooks and corners in it. There were turns and returns, up and downs, ins and outs, crypts and turrets, front stairs for strangers, and back stairs for the household.   In fact, it was no easy matter to make your room without being out in your reckoning once or twice, often with heart-breakers ahead, the Dimity Isles on the lee-bow, or sometimes even speaking a strange craft like Owlet, or a piratical kitchen-maid on the larder tack.   Mr. Barker, the correctest of men, was always stumbling on the Abigails and Mopsas.

There was one particularly cheerful thing about this and every other house occupied by the Spreads: the number of smart, tidy, good-looking maids they had, never in one's way, or seemingly out of their proper places, yet for ever tripping up and down, popping out of doors, or into them, in spruce caps, with smart ribbons, aprons white as snow, and faces bright as morning ought to be.   They formed a most agreeable background, as it were, to the family picture, and made you feel merry and pleasant in spite of yourself. There was Mrs. Spread's maid, her daughter's maid, the nursery-maid, laundry-maids, and house-maids, and chamber-maids; two Lucys, three Marys, an Ellen, and a Kitty; Mrs. Spread's maid's name was Harriet.   Some were arrant coquettes, not a doubt of it; one was all eyes, one all ears, one all tongue; not one of them but had some fault of her own, as a set-off to her pretty face or her plump figure.   Not a maid of them all was perfect!

On the morning when Barker was expected down, the Rosary looked particularly beautiful.   It was April (almost May); and occasionally, even in England, April is a month which does not altogether belie the character which poets are unanimous in giving it.   At all events, it was a sunny and a genial day.   The Spreads had breakfasted in the hall above described, with the glass-door thrown wide open, so as to allow a couple of inquisitive finches to hop in and out, as it were to see whether the new-comers were likely to be agreeable neighbors. However, just as the repast was over, a still more interesting, and wholly unexpected pair of visitors bounded in—two charming girls,

G

in green silk dresses, with pretty pink bonnets, and the family party
jumped up with one accord, to greet the radiant and ever-wel-
come Smylys.   They were on a visit at Far Niente, a villa at some
little distance, occupied, as has been mentioned before, by Dean
Bedford, the former proprietor of the Rosary.   What chatting and
gossiping there was that lovely morning upon the natural couches of
green velvet, swelling and sloping down to the lawn.   It may well
be supposed that the conversation was not all mirthful.   The Smylys were eager for intelligence about Grace Medlicott, and Mrs.
Spread had none to give them.   They spoke of that hapless and interesting girl for a long time, recalling the minutest particulars of
their too brief acquaintance with her, speculating upon her fate, and
inveighing against the abominable conduct of the heartless Narrowsmiths.   At length, by mutual consent, the subject was dropped, as
a painful one which had been sufficiently dwelt on, the discussion
of it being calculated to lead to no useful result.   Adelaide was the
first to notice the absence of Philip ; but she perceived, directly she
mentioned his name, that there was something mysterious and embarrassing connected with it, which made her instantly change the
subject, by remarking some of the beauties of the spot.

" Now, girls," said Mrs. Spread, one of you must do me a *great*
favor.   I am not so unreasonable as to want to deprive the good
dean of you both at once ; but (as there is no company at Far
Niente) will one of you stay with us until Monday, and help us
to get through a very dull party this evening, and to amuse poor
Mr. Barker to-morrow ?"

At the mention of the bachelor, whose singular adventures they
were no strangers to, the Smyly girls laughed, until the Spreads
thought they would never stop laughing.   Then Adelaide wanted
Laura to remain, and Laura wanted Adelaide, and they had a good-
humored battle about it, in the course of which Adelaide made one
or two little hits, which threw Laura into slight confusion, and deep-
ened the roses of her cheek a shade or two—at least Mrs. Spread
thought so, and she had a shrewd eye for phenomena of this kind.
The end, however, was, that Laura remained at the Rosary, and
Mr. Spread, after luncheon, escorted Adelaide back to Far Niente,
where, indeed, he was almost a dayly visitor, so much had Dean
Bedford, the comeliest and courtliest dignitary of the most " gentle-
manlike" church in Christendom, gained upon his affections since he
became a settler upon the banks of the Thames.   However, upon this
occasion, Mr. Spread had not the pleasure of conversing with his very
reverend friend and neighbor, for it was, unfortunately, just the hour

when it was his innocent and canonical custom to doze in his great easy-chair, his venerable brows covered with Mrs. Bedford's cambric handkerchief to protect them from the sun and the flies. Adelaide, as she and Mr. Spread drew near the cottage (for so it was called, although a more comfortable house did not exist in the country), knew, by the disposition of the blinds and curtains, that her uncle was enjoying his quotidian nap, and taking the retired merchant to a particular window, through which a peep was to be had into the interior, she pointed to a spectacle which Spread always spoke of afterward as the most exquisite picture of still life he had ever seen. The portly divine, immersed in a sea of cushions, was taking his noon-day nap, his hands folded on his apron, the very type of prosperity in repose; while on a full-swelling sofa near him, good Mrs. Bedford, a comely woman of considerable tunnage, habited in rich purple silk, sympathetically slumbered. She seemed to have struggled against the drowsy influences; her spectacles lay on her ample lap, as if they had just tumbled from her nose; her massive right arm was dropping to her side, and her fair, fat, dimpled hand was evidently on the point of losing its hold of a volume of Madame de Sévigné's letters, which the excellent lady nodded through once a-year. The room was voluptuously and soporiferously furnished: it was the dean's library, where many a theologian of celebrity *continued* to sleep in morocco leather. The artificial twilight which Mrs. Bedford had made, before she sat down to doze over her "one book," was perfection—the sort of sunny shade, with a twinkle in it, which affects the eyelids so very drowsily in silent places. The mind of Mr. Spread traveled back to the galleries of Holland, and thought of fat kine, at the passage of a brook among the alders, the study of a Cuyp, or the theme of a Potter.

"I must take Barker to see this," whispered Spread to his fair cicerone, with a face that would have been worth a thousand pounds at the Haymarket.

"Do," said Adelaide, in the same subdued tone. "Laura has got such a capital name for Far Niente:—the *Cottage of Indolence.*"

"Capital—that will delight Barker; by-the-by, let me tell you, Miss Adelaide, that your sister is the only woman whose conversation I ever knew Barker really enjoy. Mrs. Spread says so, too. What does Laura think of *him?*"

"Oh, I don't know that she thinks of him at all; at least she says nothing to me, if she does; we joke about him now and then, that's all."

They now glided noiselessly from the library window; Spread

bade adieu in humorous dumb-show, and Miss Smyly crept into the house with similar comic action.

Mrs. Spread received, during her husband's absence, an alarming note from Mrs. Harry Farquhar, from which it appeared that Mrs. Harry was so bent upon being near her sister, that she had taken a small cottage on the very edge of the river, at about a quarter of a mile from the Rosary, and had already removed her children to it, in charge of a new governess, whom she had recently engaged for them.

" Since the mountain won't come to Mohammed," said Mrs. H., " Mohammed must only go to the mountain."

The necessity for such a movement was by no means obvious to the Spreads, and it annoyed Mr. Spread particularly, as he foresaw it would have the effect of discouraging Barker's visits to the Rosary. While he was deploring this result of his termagant sister-in-law's pertinacity, the bachelor arrived; he was soon followed by Sir Blundell and Lady Trumbull, neighbors of the Spreads at Oxford House; Mr. Periwinkle, the celebrated conchologist; Mr. Spunner, an eminent equity lawyer, and his wife; and, lastly, by Mr. Spread's old friend Upton, member for Tarlton, who brought his son with him, a daring, precocious boy of twelve or thirteen, that never left any house he visited without leaving a lasting reputation behind him by playing some laughable trick, or performing some mischievous exploit.

Upton, the father, deserves to be briefly sketched. He was a man of business, an able man of business, but a mere man of business. His understanding was a chamber with but one window, looking to business. There were no side-lights, no scholarship, no science, no wit, no taste.

The minds of scholars are libraries; those of antiquaries, lumber-rooms; those of sportsmen, kennels; those of epicures, larders and cellars; but the mind of Upton was an office. It had been an attorney's office formerly; it was a parliamentary office now. His knowledge was of Hansard, his reading of blue-books, his memory of votes and standing orders. It was a pigeon-holed, alphabeted mind, as full of bills and reports as the scrutoire of the Abbé de Sieyes was of constitutions. The common associations of Upton's ideas were of red tape, the finer ones of green ribbon.

Barker was soon tolerably at his ease. His altered position was treated as one of the ordinary vicissitudes of life, and no disposition was evinced by any one to banter him upon a change so broadly at variance with his boasted system of independence and irresponsibility. It was, of course, impossible to avoid politics, for both Upton and Trumbull were members of parliament, and Mrs. Martin was feverishly anxious about the rights of women, and in hopes of getting the bachelor to bring in a bill to declare and protect them. Indeed, the bachelor was not a little worried at dinner, between Mrs. Martin on her hobby, and Owlet on his ass. Owlet arrived in the twilight, just as dinner was announced.

Now, it was seldom that a dull dinner-party assembled round Mr. Spread's table, and, before they sat down, he took Barker aside and apologized for it. Trumbull, Periwinkle, Upton, and Owlet (to say nothing of the equity lawyer), would have required, at least, a score of Spreads and Smylys to counteract them. The quadruple alliance of a man of crops, a man of cockles, a man of blue-books, and a man of the dark ages—Laura compared it to two pair of wet blankets, Mr. Spread to four acres of poppy, and Barker to four tuns of lead. Trumbull *would* talk of nothing but the potato-rot; Periwinkle *could* talk of nothing but testacea and crustacea; the member for Tarlton was forever dragging in, head and shoulders, his report upon metropolitan sewerage; and Owlet was still discoursing, in deep, monotonous voice, of nothing but his hermitages and his miracle-plays. In fact, the only scrap of interesting conversation that Barker heard during dinner was upon the latter subject, between the Canon of Salisbury and Laura Smyly.

"Can you really be serious, Mr. Owlet, in desiring to see our venerable cathedrals profaned by dramatic performances?"

"Not profaned. The acting of a miracle-play, as they were acted in the great days of the Catholic church, would not profane our cathedrals, while it would purify and exalt the drama."

"But of what use could it be, Mr. Owlet?"

"Of the same use as in the olden time—afford a pious amusement, and diffuse a knowledge of the Scriptures."

"But surely the Bible Societies accomplish the latter object, do they not?"

"Not half so well as the ecclesiastical drama would. I am now in correspondence with the Bible Societies on the subject. I want them to devote a portion of their funds to the encouragement of church theatricals."

"In what part of the cathedrals," inquired Lady Trumbull, "was it the practice to have the miracle-plays acted?"

"In the nave," replied the Canon of Salisbury.

Mr. Periwinkle, who knew nothing beyond his crustacea, in-

quired what part of a cathedral that was, and Owlet was only too
happy to enlighten his ignorance.

" I had always been of opinion until now," said Barker, " that the
(k)nave of a cathedral meant the—dean !"

The canon made no defense for the deans, having been mortified
by the conduct of those dignitaries, whom he had failed to imbue
with a taste for theatricals. But Spread laughed, and said he would
introduce Barker to-morrow to a dean, of whom nobody ever said,
or could possibly say, a hard word."

" The dean who is so spiritual as to believe in ghosts," said
Barker. " Well, Spread, you are indebted to his superstition for a
tolerably comfortable dining-room, at all events."

The rest of the evening passed no less heavily. Barker fell into
one of his silent fits ; the room had been darkened to accommodate
Owlet, whose eyes were dim with his monastic researches ; Sir
Blundell Trumbull was fast asleep ; and, as to Mark Upton, he was
boring the ladies to the very death, with abstracts of his bills and
quotations from his parliamentary reports, particularly that upon the
engaging subject of Metropolitan Sewerage.

There was no withstanding so many slumberous influences. What
with those who talked, those who did not talk, and the dim religious
light of the drawing-room, the evening became as drowsy, toward
ten o'clock, as it could have been at Far Niente itself. Laura
Smyly was relating to Lady Trumbull the singular incident to
which the Spreads were indebted for the discovery of the Rosary,
and Mr. Spread was trying to rouse himself to converse with Periwinkle on shells, and with Spunner upon chancery costs, when a
shrill and piercing scream was heard from a remote part of the
villa, and the whole party, in an instant, became wide awake. Another and another cry succeeded ; the voices were evidently those
of the Kittys and Marias. Mrs. Spread distinctly recognized the
voice of her own woman, Harriet, having often heard her shriek at
mice and spiders. The first thought that occurred to every one was
fire. Mr. Spread ran to the door that communicated with the din-
ing-parlor. All in that quarter was dark and quiet. Mr. Spunner
ran to a door in another corner, which communicated, by a corridor,
with the wing of the Rosary where the guests were usually lodged.
The corridor was lighted, and he ran to the farther end of it, followed, at a distance, by Upton, who snatched up an expiring lamp ;
and by Lady Trumbull, Mrs. Martin, and Augusta, carrying candles. The screaming was now very distinct, and mingled with
other sounds still stranger and more alarming. Spunner forced

open the door at the farther end of the passage, and, directly he did so, something monstrous rushed toward him, something evidently not human, of a dark-gray color, and with a noise quite hideous enough to justify the terror of the maids.   Mrs. Martin and Lady Trumbull no sooner saw what was careering toward them than they screamed also, dropped the lights from their hands, and retreated to the drawing-room; Mr. Upton tried to do the same, but he was thrown down, the lamp shattered to pieces, and the gray specter, goblin, or whatever it was, trotted over him.   Augusta Spread escaped the same fate by getting behind the door just in the nick of time.   The apparition pursued the party into the drawing-room, which was now nearly as dark as a vault.   Mr. Spread's first impression was, that his little daughter Catherine's Shetland pony had escaped from the stables.   The Reverend Mr. Owlet (who, though constitutionally a craven, felt a demonological satisfaction in thinking that the Rosary was, indeed, haunted) never stirred from his seat from the beginning of the commotion, and sat now with his small eyes riveted upon the mysterious object, his elbows planted on those of his chair, his hands crossed on his breast—a comical figure of curiosity and cowardice, had there been any one present to sketch it.   The mysterious object, however, made toward him instantly, jumped on his lap, struck one of its fore-feet upon each of his knees, thrust its nose within an inch of his, shook an enormous pair of ears, and brayed in his face.   As there were no asses on the farm, the Spreads were totally at a loss to conceive how such a brute could have found its way into the house.   Still the animal maintained its place, with its hoofs on the minor canon's lap, braying at him pointedly.   Owlet shrunk as far back in the chair as he could, but the donkey only thrust his nose the closer.   The other gentlemen now approached to pull the animal away by the tail, and extricate the poor canon from his unpleasant situation.   The donkey kicked Barker, and Barker was seizing the poker to retaliate, when Owlet gasped out, in his hollow sepulchral tones—

"It is—it must be—Lord John Yore!"

"Lord John Yore!" exclaimed every body present, more amazed at the name of the player than they had previously been at his performance.   Before, however, it was possible to make any verification of Owlet's conjecture, the donkey wheeled round and cantered out of the room by the way it came, putting the shrieking Abigails and Mopsas again to flight, until it disappeared by a door beyond the passage, which led to the bed-chambers.

It was soon ascertained, however, that the actor in this impromptu representation of a miracle-play was not the noble lord whom Owlet naturally concluded him to be.   The fact was, that the reverend gentleman had carelessly left his theatrical properties in an open trunk in his room, where they had been discovered by Lucy, the nursery-maid, who was a Paul Pry in petticoats.   Lucy could not resist the temptation of exhibiting such diverting articles to Theodore, who in his turn revealed them to Master Freddy Upton, by whom the idea of playing the ass's part " for one night only," was not only conceived, but executed.

Trivial as this incident may appear, the ridicule of it (for Barker and Upton related it wherever they went), had the effect of putting down the attempts of the tractarian divines and the Young-England-men to revive the ecclesiastical drama.   You no longer hear a syllable breathed upon the subject, and many will stoutly deny—with what truth the reader is qualified to judge—that such a scheme was ever on foot.

The only sufferer by the exposure was Upton, who hurt his shin by his fall, and had his clothes drenched in the oil of the lamp which he was carrying; but Barker consoled him by telling him that his son would have the glory of laughing down church theatricals; and Upton solaced himself, before he went to bed, with a few pages of his own report upon Metropolitan Sewerage.

The ladies sat for a while in a circular group upon an ottoman, chatting, laughing, and composing their nerves before they retired for the night.   Somebody inquired for the conchologist, who was missing.   It was presumed that he had gone to bed.   Presently a subdued sneeze, or a stifled groan, was heard; the ladies listened, and Mrs. Spunner and Lady Trumbull began seriously to think that something was not quite right with the Rosary.   The same noise recurred in a few moments.   Mrs. Martin jumped up, protested that there was somebody under the ottoman; and, being a prompt, intrepid woman, pulled up the chintz without a moment's hesitation, and discovered the head of Mr. Periwinkle, who had sought an asylum there during the reign of terror.   The ladies, by sitting down in a circle, had prevented his escape; and he would have remained in durance until the room was deserted, only that a hair had tickled his nose, and forced him to make the noise, which revealed at once his retreat and his poltroonery.

CHAPTER XVIII.

The doors, that knew no shrill, alarming bell,
No cursed knocker ply'd by villain's hand,
Self-open'd into halls, where who can tell
What elegance and grandeur wide expand,
The pride of Turkey and of Persia land ?
Soft quilts on quilts, on carpets carpets spread,
And couches stretch'd around in seemly band,
And endless pillows rise to prop the head,
So that each spacious room was one full, swelling bed.

The Castle of Indolence.

Mr. Barker's Parliamentary Portrait—Doctor Bedford's Preferments in the Church—The Villa of Far Niente—Barker and Spread visit the Dean—Curious Instance of bad Memory—What became of Barker's Motion for a Reform of the Irish Church, and what became of the Ballot Question.

Mr. BARKER's parliamentary career was in several respects sufficiently disreputable. He had always been a perverse politician, and, as such politicians invariably do, plumed himself on not being a party man. He was a Whig when the Tories were in power, but very much disposed to turn Tory when the Whigs returned to office. He had too sharp an eye for abuses of all sorts not to be a reformer; but then he would reform no abuses, except at his own time, which was just when the public mind was least prepared, or in his own way, which was always the most impracticable mode imaginable. When parliamentary reform was the question, Barker would hear of nothing but free trade ; when the country was thinking of nothing but free trade, he talked of nothing but vote by ballot ; and when the potato failed in Ireland, and all the intelligence and humanity of the empire was concentrated upon devising means of averting the horrors of famine, Barker took up the church question furiously, and would have wheeled the ministry out for not reviving the appropriation clause. When he came into the House he had ample opportunities of being as crotchety in practice as he had previously been in theory. He seldom seconded a motion, without strongly reprobating the grounds stated by the mover ; and never supported

a bill without either attacking the motives of those who introduced
it, or giving them fair warning that he meant to strike its main provisions out in committee.   He was always making cross remarks
from the cross benches, or crossing the House to say something cross,
to cross somebody.   He commonly commenced a speech by saying,
"I rise, sir, to make an unpleasant observation;" or, looking vinegar at
the Treasury benches, "I am about to ask the noble lord, or right
honorable gentleman, a question which I know will be excessively
disagreeable."   Then there was no such moral lecturer as he was:
he was always schooling the House, and laying down severer principles of ethics for their guidance than he found it convenient to act
on himself.   By his own account, he was the only logician and the
only moralist in the House; indeed, so satisfied was he with the ac-
curacy and justice of all his own views, that he felt himself warrant-
ed to place all who dissented from him in the flattering dilemma of
knave or fool; he was too polite not to give them their choice of the
horns.   Then, when any member adopted the language of Billingsgate, Barker was so sore offended that he would rise and correct
him in the vocabulary of Wapping.   When a member was assailed
by a public journal, and wanted to have the editor or the printer up
for a breach of privilege, it afforded the bachelor an occasion, which
he always seized, for proving his zeal for freedom of discussion;
but, on the other hand, he was also so jealous of the dignity of the
House, that, when he was attacked himself by the newspapers, he
manfully asserted the privileges of parliament, besides feeling strongly that the licentiousness of the press is prejudicial to its liberty in
the last degree.   No man discovered more mare's-nests; no man
threatened ministers so frequently with impeachment, moved oftener that the House be counted, divided it oftener upon frivolous points,
or called for half so many useless and troublesome returns.   Upon
one occasion, being annoyed by an unmeaning quotation from Virgil,
he moved for a return of the number of lines of Virgil quoted by
members of the House, from the year 1688 to the present day,
specifying the lines in each case, the name of the member who
used them, and the particular poem from which each quotation was
taken, whether "Æneid," "Georgic," or "Bucolic."   The result
was, of course, very nearly a complete edition of the Mantuan bard,
in the form of a blue-book.   Barker was hardly ever in majorities,
and very seldom even in minorities of more than four or five.   More
than once he went out alone into the lobby; but for a considerable
time he and Mr. Buckram, M.P. for Wells, pulled wonderfully together, being two of the crookedest and crabbedest men in the king-

dom. Among other questions which they agreed to introduce together, at the most unseasonable juncture imaginable, was that of vote
by ballot. As to talking to either of them of expediency, or the danger of permanently damaging the cause by an untimely agitation of
it, you might as well have discoursed with a Jew about pork, or a
Pennsylvanian on probity. Another question to which Barker devoted himself as inopportunely as he well could, was that of the
Irish Church. Spread cordially agreed with him, that no estab-
ishment in the empire was so repugnant to every sound principle, both of religion and of politics, but pressed him to consider that
its reform was neither demanded by the people of Ireland themselves nor agreeable to the present temper of the people of England.
But the member for Boroughcross was impracticable. The 2d of
May was fixed for the ballot question, when Barker was to second
the motion of Mr. Buckram, and on the tenth of the same month
the bachelor was to move for leave to bring in a bill (not even Buckram having yet volunteered to stand sponsor to it) to retrench the
temporalities of the church in Ireland, and apply its surplus wealth
to general secular uses.

They were chatting on the subject as they walked over the next
day to Far Niente, to pay Dean Bedford a visit, or, at least, get a
peep at him through the casement, enjoying his canonical repose.

The slumbers of this excellent dignitary were neither the symp-
tom of any bodily ailment nor a luxury enjoyed at the expense of
duty. He was Dean of the Cathedral Church of St. Ormond, in
the diocese of Kilfenora, of which his father had been bishop in his
time. The deanery was reputed one of the best in Ireland ; first,
because it produced its incumbent a clear thousand a-year ; and,
secondly, because the dean had a treasurer, a chancellor, three preb-
endaries, five canons, and three vicars-choral to aid and assist him
(which they did most efficiently) in doing what was called "cathedral duty," the closest approximation to doing nothing attainable at
the present day, unless the Puseyites and Lord John Manners shall
succeed in reviving monastic institutions. The dean, however, had
other preferments ; a prebend in one diocese, a chancellorship in
another, two rectories in other sees, with cure of souls in contem-
plation of law, and in addition to these numerous good things, he
was vicar-general of the Diocese of Kilfenora aforesaid, a spiritual
territory, where we may mention, in passing, that a Protestant of
the established church was as rare a phenomenon as a unicorn or
a phœnix. Even the *net* income derivable from all these sources
was so *gross*, that the dean soon discovered it to be more conducive

to his ease to enjoy it on the banks of the Thames, than on those of
the Shannon, or even the Liffey. A pastoral staff should certainly
be a tolerably long one to reach from Richmond to St. Ormond, but
the dean had no occasion for a pastoral staff at all; for where he had
a few straggling sheep to feed, the shepherd of a neighboring parish
tended them for a consideration so trifling as to show clearly enough
that there is nothing so cheap as the actual cure of souls, when the
charges are left to be settled and defrayed by the ecclesiastical
authorities themselves. Doctor Bedford was a clergyman of the old
school; he had entered the church at a period when public opinion
was not so influential and exacting as it is at the present day; ere
the lives of deans, and even bishops, were discussed in newspapers,
and the vulgar doctrine of the wages of labor began to be applied to
the relations existing between the priesthood and the people. But
he was by no means one of the worst specimens of Irish pluralists.
He was neither proud nor rapacious; he was no reviler of the Catholic clergy while he enjoyed the revenues which had once been
theirs; he took legal proceedings to enforce his pecuniary claims as
sparingly as possible, and never took violent steps at all; he was not
only too benevolent, but too indolent to play the wolf in his own
fold. In a word, Dean Bedford had too much, and he was—content.

When he first imparadised himself at Richmond, he measured not
more than a yard and a half in the girth, not by any means an unreasonable circumference for an ecclesiastic of his rank and fortune;
but a life of ease and luxury, passed between the couch and the
table, rapidly increased his bulk: at the end of the third year his
tailor raised his prices; at the close of the fourth the buxom dignitary saw his knees for the last time; and ere a fifth had expired, it
was a favorite frolic of his wife's merry nieces (the Smyly girls), to
span him with their united arms; and it was not without considerable effort—at least so they pretended—that the tips of their fingers
were brought into contact.

Far Niente may be described in one word. It was all a bed-room!
The genius that furnished it must have been the very genius of
repose. You could not move in any part of it at a quicker pace than
a lounge; you were tempted to rest yourself every ten steps you
took; there never was house or cottage so voluptuously fitted up for
indolent enjoyments of all kinds. It was so well cushioned and pil-
lowed, rugged and carpeted, sofaed and bedded, that there was not
a nook or corner, not to say in drawing-rooms and bed-rooms, but in
halls, vestibules, and corridors, where you did not feel that it would

be delicious to throw yourself for a siesta; downy chairs were every where at hand to catch you in their fat arms; couches of resistless *embonpoint*, Dudus of couches, provoked you in all directions; but indeed you would have been quite content to fling yourself down on the Axminster at your chamber door.

If a bell was ever heard, it sounded as if it were muffled, or tinkled like the small silver bells at a private mass in a cardinal's closet. There was not a clock in the house except the chronometer in the kitchen; and the voice or the foot of a servant was never heard from Christmas to Easter, and from Easter back to Christmas. Indeed, as to the sound of footsteps, the perfect carpeting of the villa, combined with the solidity of the floors, would have made the steps of giants inaudible.

There was but one point on which Doctor Bedford and his wife ever differed—a fortunate circumstance in the matrimonial state. This was about the irregularities of Mother Church. Mrs. Bedford would never admit that the old lady had any, while her candid husband invariably took the Whig side of the question, and, with a jovial frankness that was charming, acknowledged himself to be an epitome, and by no means a small one, of the great flaws and undeniable abuses of the Irish ecclesiastical system. To hear Mrs. Bedford indignantly reading some speech in parliament, or extract from a pamphlet, where the case of the Deanery of Ormond was detailed to illustrate what the orator, or pamphleteer, would probably call " the colossal vices" of the Church Establishment, and to listen to the dean's commentary upon each statement—to see how benignantly he listened to the invectives of which he was the object, and how he laughed, and shook his fat sides, in his cosy chair, at what he considered a fair hit at his pluralities, or a humorous caricature of his person, was better than most scenes in modern comedy.

Spread and Barker were fortunate enough to catch Doctor Bedford just a few moments before he sequestered himself in his library for his nap. They made, therefore, but a short visit; indeed, Mrs. Bedford received Mr. Barker very coldly, being aware of his hostile intentions toward the established church. But the dean's warmth and *bonhommie* made up for his wife's frigid behavior.

" Is there any Irish news, Mr. Barker? I hear seldom from Ireland now."

" None, doctor; at least, nothing very new. There has been a fatal collision between the people and the police at Kilpatrick, in one of the southern counties."

" Where is Kilpatrick, Lizzy ?" said the dean to his wife.

Adelaide Smyly smiled.

" Why, uncle dear, you ought to know, I think; it is one of your own parishes."

" Ho, ho, ho," laughed the dean heartily—" I don't think I ever was there; I don't recollect any thing about Kilpatrick.   One of my own livings, is it ?—ho, ho—very likely—I dare say Miss Smyly's right."

The dean was much too courteous to allude to Barker's intended motion in parliament, but Mrs. Bedford would probably not have exercised the same self-command, had not Spread judiciously abridged the visit, and taken leave ; not, however, before the kind dignitary made Barker promise to meet the Spreads at dinner, at Far Niente, upon an early day.

" That's perfect, Barker," said his friend, as they sauntered back through the meadows.

" Apoplectic, I fear," said the bachelor.

" The churchman, or the church ?" said Spread.

" Both," replied Barker; " bleeding would do neither any harm— in the *temporal* artery."

" There is certainly room for retrenchment," said Spread ; " but I still think that the present is not the time for agitating the question."

" What I have seen," said Barker, " does not in the least alter my views upon that point; but I own it has shaken my opinion on another head.   I doubt if my motion goes the proper length."

It ended in Barker letting his motion for retrenchment drop. Another member snapped it up, and Barker gave it his most strenuous opposition, on the ground that, when an institution is objectionable in principle, it ought either to be utterly abolished or maintained in all its vicious perfection ; there was, there could be, and there should be no middle course.

" Join me," said the reformer, " in doing away with deformities."

" They are the beauties of the system," cried Barker.

" Let me use the pruning-hook," urged the other.

" The ax, or nothing," rejoined the member for Boroughcross.

The ballot question met a different fate.   Mr. Barker and Mr. Buckram assembled at the Crown and Anchor on the morning of the day appointed for the motion, to settle matters of detail, and make their arrangements preliminary to the grand debate.   The meeting lasted for some time.   Upon the main points they were agreed, and all went harmoniously enough, until they came to discuss

what wood was the best for ballot-boxes.   Buckram said oak, because
it was British; Barker was for cedar, because it was antiseptic.
Buckram could see no sense in cedar, and Barker thought oak the
height of absurdity.   Neither would give up his crotchet, and at
length they split upon the wood.   The ballot party broke up into
two furious factions; each called a cab, and went home in it; and
the question of secret suffrage received a blow which it did not
recover for three sessions.

CHAPTER XIX.

Neque virgo est usquam, neque ego, qui e conspectu illam amisi meo.
Ubi quæram ubi investigem, quem percuncter, quam insistam viam ?
Terence.

> I've lost the lady, and in losing her
> Have lost myself.   Where shall I seek her now ?
> Of whom inquire ? · I know not where to turn.

Retrospective—Philip and Grace—a Dangerous Crisis—A bad Cook proves
a good Woman—Escape of the Miser's Niece—Grace is pursued by Philip
to London, and from thence to Germany—Overtakes unfortunate Miss
Medlicott at Baden-Baden—What she was doing when he found her.

THE day of the dinner at Far Niente was big with important incident. · In the morning of that day Philip Spread rejoined his
family, looking worn, fatigued, and dejected.   His pursuit had been
as fruitless as his love had been imprudent.   His conduct had occasioned a great deal of uneasiness to his family, and would have distressed them a great deal more had their confidence in Miss Medlicott's firmness of character, high principles, and superiority to every
selfish consideration been less than it was.   They only did the fugitive girl justice.   The circumstances attending her flight from her
uncle's house, and the fruitless chase of her lover are now to be
briefly related.   Philip had not only revealed to Grace the passion
with which she had inspired him, but had been so rash and so im-
petuous as to make her a proposition of marriage.   Perhaps he
would not have proceeded so violently had her situation been different; but his anxiety to rescue her from her heartless relatives led
him to outstep the bounds of prudence, and of filial duty also.
Grace, upon her part, though grateful for his concern, and not indisposed to return his love, was too high-minded to involve him in a
connection which she had so much reason to think could not but be
highly objectionable in the eyes of his family.   He urged his suit
with ardor, but without shaking her resolution; still he persevered,
took every opportunity of meeting her, pressed her with every argument he could use, with all his rhetoric when they met, and with

letters when he could not otherwise address her; but nothing could overcome her determination; and the only result of a suit so fervent, which it was impossible for her to grant, was to increase her embarrassments, and suggest the idea of extricating herself from them by flight from Liverpool. This bold and perilous step, however, she did not resolve upon taking, until, one night, after experiencing particularly ungentle usage from Mrs. Narrowsmith, who, destitute of all motherly feelings, had the novercal instincts in perfection. Grace had to lock herself up in her room, and otherwise fortify the door, to save herself from personal violence; and even these measures of defense would not have been sufficient had not Mrs. Dorothea Potts, although not much of a cook, been something of a woman, and induced or obliged her barbarous mistress to abandon, for that time, her step-motherly designs. No sooner was the dreary house silent that night than Grace noiselessly removed the furniture with which she had barricaded her bed-room door, unlocked it with the same care, and crept to the neighboring attic occupied by Mrs. Potts. Dorothea was asleep, and not very easily awakened. When at length she awoke, Grace rapidly communicated her resolution to fly, and make her way to London by the express train at daybreak. In London she would easily obtain a livelihood as a teacher of music, or, at the worst, she would again have recourse to the good clergyman who had received her after the shipwreck, and throw herself, for a time, upon his protection.

She thought for a moment of the Spreads; but the unfortunate attachment of Philip was only an additional reason for adhering to the former plan. Mrs. Potts acted well; she proffered her aid with wonderful alacrity for a cook disturbed in her slumbers, and with the aid of a lucifer-box, lighted a candle, and proceeded to assist Grace in the few preparations she had to make for her dangerous expedition. Not until that moment did it occur to poor Miss Medlicott that she was totally unprovided with money! Here again Mrs. Potts behaved in a manner which no cook in a royal kitchen, which not Alexis Soyer himself, could have easily surpassed. She had hoarded a sum of seventeen pounds, seventeen shillings, and three-pence half-penny in the treasury of a worsted stocking; most of it was her honest earning, part of it the fruit, perhaps, of some little peculation in kitchen-stuff. Ten pounds of this treasure she insisted upon advancing to Grace, who reluctantly and gratefully received it, shedding a tear upon the coarse hand so ready to do a delicate service. They crept down stairs together. It was now approaching five o'clock. In the hall another difficulty encountered

them, which it was surprising had not been anticipated, at least by
Dorothea.   The street-door was locked, and the key in the miser's
bed-room, according to the custom of the house.   It was impossible
to escape with safety by any of the windows.   Mrs. Potts, however,
was not without a shift in this emergency.   Directing Grace to remain perfectly quiet, she ascended again, and knocked at Mr. Narrowsmith's door.   A venomous dog, between a terrier and a mastiff,
which always partook the miser's bed, started up and barked furiously.   The miser himself was at the door in an instant.   Dorothea informed him that she suspected that there were thieves upon
the roof, pilfering the lead, and desired him to light his candle.   The
light, as soon as it was kindled, revealed the keys of the house upon
a chair beside the bed, and the moment her master came forth, followed by his dog, and went up stairs to protect his property, Mrs.
Potts slipped into the room, and laid hands upon the keys of the
fortress.

The morning being bitterly cold, Mr. Narrowsmith did not un-
necessarily protract his observations, so that in less than a quarter
of an hour Mrs. Potts was enabled to rejoin Grace below stairs.
She now noiselessly unlocked the door, unbarred, unbolted, and un-
chained it, for it had as many fastenings as the gate of a jail; and,
followed by the agitated, but courageous girl, issued silently into the
dark street, and closing the door as much as it were possible to do
without shutting it (so as to be able to re-enter unperceived), took
the way to the terminus of the Liverpool and London rail-way.   In
half an hour Miss Medlicott was racing toward the metropolis with
the speed of a post-hurricane between Antigua and Barbadoes.
Mrs. Potts, having gone thus far in the affair, now felt that she
ought to go a step farther, and acquaint young Mr. Spread (of
whose passion she was aware) with the hazardous step that Grace
had taken.   It was in this way that Philip obtained that early news
of the poor girl's departure which enabled him to follow her the
same morning, by the next train that started for London.   The letter which he left behind him for his parents has been already mentioned; they lamented the impetuosity of his proceedings, but could
not but acknowledge that, in following the promptings of love, he
had also obeyed the dictates of humanity.   The dangers to which a
young, attractive, and inexperienced, girl would infallibly be exposed
in the "high-viced city" to which she had desperately committed
herself, were only too easily imagined.   But Philip's pursuit was
vain.   When he arrived in London he was much in the situation of
Antiphilus of Syracuse:

> "I to the world am like a drop of water,
>   That in the ocean seeks another drop;
>   And falling there, to find his fellow forth,
>   Unseen, inquisitive, confounds itself."

After a fortnight spent in unavailing researches, following twenty false scents, hunting all manner of places of refuge, probable and improbable, possible and impossible, offices for providing governesses, asylums for destitute females, boarding-schools, lodging-houses, even theaters, wherever he could trace any thing of the feminine gender, named Medlicott, he was just on the point of abandoning the chase, when he saw in a newspaper, among a list of passengers who had recently sailed for Ostend, in a packet called the *Fire-Fly*, the name of a Miss Medlicott, of whom, upon inquiry, he received a description, which left no doubt upon his mind but that it was Grace. He followed by the next packet, missed her at Antwerp, nearly came up with her at Aix-la-Chapelle, arrived at Cologne the very day she left it for Coblentz, and would have overtaken her at Coblentz if she had not just preceded him to Ems; from Ems she led him a dance to Schlangenbad, from Schlangenbad to Wiesbaden, from Wiesbaden to Mayence; there he almost had a hold of her, but she slipped out of his hands like a spirit, and hovered before him to Baden-Baden, where he at length overtook the fair fugitive, at the Bädischer-Hoof. It was evening; she was gone with her party to the Kur-Saal. Poor Grace!—what a change of scene was that for her! Philip ranged the rooms, scrutinized every face he met, and was just beginning to think that fortune was about to baffle him once more, when he heard the name of Miss Medlicott— "Unfortunate Miss Medlicott!"— pronounced at his elbow, and turning quick round, was just in time to see the lady thus unpleasantly alluded to lose fifty florins at *rouge-et-noir!* She was as like Grace as he was to Hercules.

This was but one of several unavailing efforts; it was the first research in which he had ever exhibited perseverance; at length, however, he abandoned all hope of recovering the lost lady, and pale and dispirited retraced his steps to England.

CHAPTER XX.

He asked the waves, and ask'd the felon winds,
What hard mishap hath doom'd this gentle swain ?
And question'd every gust of rugged wings
That blows from off each beaked promontory :
They knew not of his story !

Lycidas.

Fortune declares for a Moment in the Bachelor's Favor—The Nephew has found an Uncle, but the Uncle is not Mr. Barker—How well Barker behaved in the House, when the Weight was taken off his Mind—The Party at Far Niente—The Dean in his Glory—What Wines he produced to feast the Bachelor, who did not arrive to do them Honor—How Fortune deserted him again—The dangerous Trick she played him—How it broke up the Dean's Party—Portrait of Mrs. Lilly, the Nurse, and of Mr. Mooney, the pluralist Butler—Barker in the Doctor's Hands, and how he behaved in them.

WHEN the bachelor returned to the Albany, after his first visit to the Spreads at Richmond, and received from Reynolds the usual report of the proceedings in his absence, he found, to his annoyance, that his ancient writing-master, Matthew Quill, had been renewing his solicitations in person; but he was infinitely more chagrined to learn that his door had been twice besieged by a young man, in an enormous rough coat, who had displayed extreme anxiety to see him, and had made a statement to Reynolds to the alarming effect that he had very strong claims upon Mr. Barker, and was advised to press them. So the fox seems on the point of being unearthed at last! The bachelor had eluded his fell pursuer a long time, but he appears now fairly run down. His agitation was visible to his servant; his face grew livid, his hands quivered, his voice stuck in his throat, as he convulsively inquired if the young man had given his name?

Reynolds (who had his own suspicions) answered fearfully, that he believed his name was—Barker.

The bachelor did his best to hide the commotion of his mind, and cocking his hat more belligerently than he had ever cocked it before, strutted down to the House.   The first man he met in the lobby was Mr. Matthew Quill, the man of pothooks and hangers, who had posted himself in ambush behind a pillar, to pounce at the proper moment upon the honorable member for Boroughcross.   The seedy and dilapidated appearance of the old chirographer pleaded powerfully in his favor; he looked as if for a considerable time he had wanted a pot for his hooks, or, if he had the pot, wanted something substantial to put in it.

"But what can I do for you, Mr. Quill?—I have no interest.   I voted against the government last night.   An application of mine would hardly save a dog from being hanged."

"I presumed to hope, sir, that there might be something in your own department—"

Barker smiled, and merely said that he had not accepted the important and lucrative office of the Chiltern Hundreds, and did not intend to do so.

"Well, sir, I'm grateful to you all the same," said the subdued teacher; "perhaps there is some other way in which your honor might have it in your power to do something for my poor boy?"

Barker was touched by the humility, and the tone of real distress in which this was uttered, and could not help saying,

"You have a son, Mr. Quill?"

"A nephew, sir—a poor fellow thrown upon me by the death of a sister of mine abroad.   He writes a good round, free, legible hand, sir; and though he was giddy and wild when he first came over to England, and ran through a little money he had, he's an honest and deserving lad, is Alexander Parker."

Barker repeated the name, with an interest and emphasis which Matthew Quill attributed to his benevolent concern in his nephew's welfare.

"Parker's his name," said Mr. Quill.   "I was the only relation he had living—the only friend he had to look to in all England.   It's as good as a novel, sir, the way he ferreted me out."

"Well, Mr. Quill—"

"Stay a moment, pray, do, sir: I see Alexander yonder.   Alexander!—Parker!"

And the next moment the bachelor had the honor of having formally presented to him the "honest and deserving" youth, who had been for months an incubus on his spirits, and from whom, on several occasions, he had received such serious annoyance.

What a weight that introduction relieved him from!   Had he possessed the slightest influence, he would at that moment have

joyfully exercised it in behalf of the writing-master and his nephew.
As it was, he took the former aside, put a ten-pound note into his
hand, and ran into the House.

It was an early sitting. Barker was so elate that he made an inoffensive observation upon Irish affairs—omitted a fair occasion for a
snap at the home secretary—moved for a possible return—called
Mr. Buckram to order for calling another member a snake, and, in
the course of his speech, refrained from calling Mr. Buckram a
viper—then, with a bow to the speaker, and without a bow-wow at
the Treasury bench, he left the House, and went down to dine
with the Dean of Ormond, intending to sleep and spend the following day at the Spreads'. Seldom had the bachelor been in such
high spirits—never, certainly, since he entered parliament.

One of the friendliest parties that ever met was assembled that
day at Far Niente. The Spreads were there—all but Philip, who
shunned festive scenes ; the Smylys, incarnations of mirth and
laughter ; Dr. Borax, the local physician, a popular and clever man ;
Mrs. Martin, habited in green velvet, more like a countess than a
governess ; Mr. St. Leger, in tip-top spirits ; Sir Blundell and Lady
Trumbull, the baronet in great glee because he thought the squires
were coming in, and a *stable* government about to be formed ; Tom
Turner, preparing to veer about, and Will Whitebait, all anxiety
for dinner, having heard that the dean's *cuisine* was the most perfect
in England ; even Owlet was less abstract and monkish than usual,
perhaps because his union with Elizabeth was to take place in a
few weeks, perhaps because he had made some new convert to his
eremitical designs. As to Dr. Bedford himself, his radiance, his benevolence, his amenity, his fullness and fatness, are only to be illustrated by supposing that, by some marvelous alchemy, the spirit of good-
humor had been distilled, concentrated, and incorporated into a folio
body of divinity. The dean had brought forth from his cellar, for
the occasion, his oldest and finest wines : his very reverend port, his
right reverend claret, his episcopal champagne, and his archiepisco-
pal burgundy. He was particularly desirous of giving a noble reception to Barker, not only as the friend of Spread, but (what vexed
Mrs. Bedford greatly) as a prominent church-reformer. Seven was
the hour : it came and went ; so did half-past seven, without bringing the bachelor with it. It was unaccountable, especially as Reynolds had arrived, and it was therefore known that Barker had not
been detained on business. Dinner was ordered, and the party sat
down to dinner. It was strange that the absence of a single guest
and a guest, too, who did not always take pains to win the golden

opinions of the company, should have been felt as Barker's was.
There were twenty speculations on the cause of it, some serious,
some humorous.   Then his public character was discussed, and the
lords of the Treasury were very witty at his expense; but Mr.
Spread and Laura Smyly were more than a match for them.   Still,
however, the bachelor did not arrive.   At length, just before the
second course was removed, an express came for Dr. Borax, whose
services were immediately required for a gentleman who had been
almost drowned, by the upsetting of a wherry in the neighborhood.
It seemed most unlikely that Barker should have chosen such a mode
of conveyance; yet it was not impossible, and slight as the probability was, it put an end, for that day (sorely to the annoyance of Will
Whitebait), to the festivity at the dean's.   The doctor took the
messenger's horse and rode off at full speed.   It was soon ascertained that the sufferer had been carried to a cottage on the other
side of the river, directly opposite Far Niente.

The Far Niente boat was out of repair, or Mr. Spread would have
been soon at the spot; as it was, there was considerable delay, and
it was past ten o'clock before, accompanied by Mr. St. Leger and
Reynolds, he reached the spot, and discovered that it was indeed
the unfortunate bachelor to whom Fortune had played this rude
trick.   Mr. St. Leger returned almost instantly, to quiet the worst
apprehensions of the party, and reconduct the Spreads home.   As
to Spread himself, he never left the side of the bachelor's bed until
an advanced hour on the following morning, when, the usual reme-
dies having been at length successful, Dr. Borax pronounced his
patient out of immediate danger; not, however, venturing to express
himself confident of his ultimate recovery.   Mr. Spread then, after
discovering, to his great surprise, that the cottage belonged to Mrs.
Harry Farquhar, returned to the Rosary in his own boat, which had
been sent for him.   His first care was to send to London (which he
did with the cordial approval of the local physician) for the ablest
medical advice.   There was a consultation at the cottage in the
course of the day, and the case was pronounced to wear, upon the
whole, all things considered, and with the due number of provisions
and exceptions, a not very unfavorable appearance.

How the bachelor (who had never been given to aquatic sports) got
himself into so disagreeable a scrape as this will not take long to tell.
Having proceeded as far as Fulham in a hired Brougham, he there
had a dispute with the driver about something or nothing, which
ended in his discharging him, and taking a boat (the only resource
available) for the remainder of the journey.   Within a short distance

of Far Niente occurred one of those collisions which are not uncommon on the river; the wherry was overset; the bachelor was thrown into the water, and, being no swimmer, he would have certainly perished, had not one of the watermen rescued him; not, however, until he had sunk twice, and those who witnessed the accident believed that life was extinct.

Mrs. Farquhar had now an occasion for displaying the good points of her character, and she availed herself of it. When she heard of Barker's mishap, she evinced considerable concern, expressed herself happy that the accident had taken place where it did, and wrote instantly (in perhaps rather too dictatorial a tone), desiring that Mrs. Grace, the governess, would see that the bachelor wanted no attention which either she, the children, or the servants could pay him. This missive to Mrs. Grace was quite superfluous, for she had been all devotion to poor Mr. Barker from the moment he was brought into the house.

Mrs. Spread was wishing that Barker could have been brought to the Rosary, where she could have attended him herself.

"It would have been better," said Spread; "but he is not in bad hands in the care of the pretty little widow; if the house was her own, and if he was her father, I don't think she could do more than she does."

"Well, I dare say she *is* attentive," said Mrs. Spread; "but I shall, nevertheless, send Mrs. Lilly over to sit up with him for a few nights; the pretty little widow is too young, from what I hear, to have much experience in attending a sick-room."

Mrs. Lilly was the veteran nurse of the Spread family; she was a trusty and valuable domestic at all times, but in sickness she shone with transcendent luster. You knew little or nothing about her until you had a cold or a fever; then she almost ceased to be a mere old woman, and became transformed into a spirit of health and an angel of life. Like the thyme, burnet, and those other plants mentioned by Bacon, in his "Essay on Gardens," which "perfume the air most delightfully, when trodden upon and crushed," it was only when you occasioned Mrs. Lilly trouble, when you drew upon her energies all day, and kept her awake the livelong night, that you got at the virtue that was in her.

Spread visited his friend twice a-day; the recovery was a slow process, rendered still more tardy by the patient's irritability and nervousness. Care was taken not to let him know who was the proprietor of the cottage, and he continued under the impression that he was indebted to Mrs. Grace for the occupation of her house, as well as for her indefatigable personal attentions. Mrs. Spread took an early opportunity of visiting Mrs. Grace, being anxious to see the Farquhars, and also to apologize for the liberty she had taken in sending Mrs. Lilly to nurse the invalid.   If Mr. Spread had been fascinated by the young widow, Mrs. Spread was still more taken with her.   She was very young, to all appearance scarcely twenty, not handsome, yet very engaging; singularly modest and gentle, yet at the same time discharging all her duties, both as governess and as mistress of the house, in the absence of Mrs. Farquhar, with a discretion and a quiet firmness which, as Mr. Spread observed, would have been remarkable in a matron of twice her standing in the world. Far from being offended at the installation of the good Mrs. Lilly, it gave the little widow the liveliest satisfaction; there was so much to be done, particulary in attendance on a gentleman and a bachelor, which Mrs. Grace could only do by proxy, or could do but very imperfectly, without neglecting her other duties.   In short, Mrs. Spread was in raptures with her new acquaintance, and wrote to her sister the next day, expressly to let her know how fortunate she had been in the choice of such a governess for her children.

The Bedford family were almost as assiduous as the Spreads in their attentions to Mr. Barker.   When the dean was awake, he was always speaking of him, and longing for the period to arrive when it would be proper to fit out a barge, under the command of Mr. Mooney, his butler, and send it across the stream with a cargo of claret and burgundy, for he thought, after so much water, a little wine would do the bachelor no harm.   The boat was repaired, and Mooney made the voyage from Far Niente to the cottage and back again twice a-day, to report the progress of the patient and the latest opinion of the faculty.   Mooney was no light cargo himself for a Thames wherry, and had his voyages been round the world, he could not have set out upon them with more importance, or returned with more *éclat*.   The dean was never easy until he set out, and then he was never easy until he came back.   Mooney was a great man in his sphere, and almost as great a pluralist as his master. His largest benefice was his butlership; but he held several other little preferments, all the nicer and snugger for being Irish ones. He was verger of the cathedral church of St. Ormond, parish-clerk of Desert, in Tipperary, and sexton of Burnchurch, in the county of Cavan.   All these faculties he bore with surprising meekness, except in the servants' hall, where he was a far greater dignitary than the dean himself, drank his port like a prelate, and laid down the ecclesiastical law like Dr. Lushington.

Mr. Spread had great difficulty in making Barker tolerably amenable

H

to his medical advisers. The bachelor pronounced Chambers a quack, and Brodie a mountebank. Mr. Squills, the apothecary, he said, had more skill in his little finger than all the London doctors put together.

"The public is generally right," said Mr. Spread.

"The public is generally wrong," rejoined the sick bachelor.

"Efficaci do manus scientiæ," said Spread.

"What can any man know of the interior of my frame?" growled the patient.

"Physicians must know more about it than either you or I, Barker!"

"They either do or they do not," replied the bachelor, couching his sophistry in the form of his favorite dilemma. If they do, they should be able to cure all manner of disorders—there ought to be no such thing as a disease left in the world; if they do not, they prescribe in the dark—the system is downright humbug."

"Still, experience is something," said Spread, soothingly.

"But they have none, or not half as much as their patients. Plato observes very justly, that a physician ought himself to have gone through all the distempers he professes to heal. Was Brodie ever half-drowned as I was?"

"But tell me," said Spread, anxious to avoid further argument, "tell me, Barker, do you recollect your sensations when you were under the water!"

"Perfectly: I never passed a pleasanter quarter of an hour in my life."

Spread laughed, rose from the bed-side, carefully avoided counseling the bachelor either to do, or not to do any thing—(a discretion which people in general would do well to imitate, when they have cross-grained characters to deal with)—and rejoined his wife and his daughter Augusta, on the little lawn, between the cottage and the river; they had been anxious to see Mrs. Grace; but the pretty widow did not appear, to the great disappointment of Mrs. Spread. Indeed, it almost always happened, when the Spreads came over to Mrs. Farquhar's, that the young *gouvernante* was either not at home or so deeply engaged with her pupils or in her household affairs, as to be unable to receive them in person.

As to Philip, smitten as he was by Grace Medlicott, he was indifferent to all other women in the world. It was nothing to him whether the governess of his aunt's children was a wife or a widow, a maid or a matron, a beauty or a fright. He heard his mother and sisters highly commending some body of the feminine gender, but he never inquired who was the subject of their praises, and if he even heard her name, it went in at one ear only to go out at the other,

CHAPTER XXI.

You may take sarza to open the liver, steel to open the spleen, flower of sulphur for the lungs, castoreum for the brain, but no receipt openeth the heart but a true friend, to whom you may impart griefs, joys, fears, hopes, suspicions, counsels, and whatsoever lieth upon the heart to oppress it, in a kind of civil shrift or confession.

Bacon's *Essay on Friendship.*

Barker imitates Molière—A Session of the Court of Conscience—How the Bachelor tormented himself—Barker takes the Advice of a wise Man, and is much the better for it—Troubles of Mrs. Lilly—Her Interview with Mrs. Grace—Mrs. Lilly receives a Picture and undertakes a Commission—The Bachelor miserable again—How the Cuckoos and Swallows plagued him.

AFTER about a week's slow but steady progress, Barker had a relapse. He was too much given to collisions to "turn the corner" without knocking against it. Mr. Spread found one morning, on the small oval table at his bed-side an unopened vial, which Mrs. Lilly told him, in an emphatic and excited whisper, ought to have been shaken and taken the night before. Spread upbraided the patient mildly with this rash neglect of the doctor's prescriptions.

"Do you remember," growled Barker, "what Molière said of his physicians ?—'*Ils m'ordonne des remèdes ; je ne les prends pas, et je guéris.*'"

Barker, however, was not as successful as Molière in this humorous way of profiting by medical advice, for he became seriously ill in the course of the afternoon, and an express had to be sent for Dr. Chambers. This second crisis not only alarmed the bachelor, and made him less difficult to manage, but it also led him to summon his thoughts to council upon his temporal affairs, and hold a session of the court of conscience. Again and again his mind recurred to those repeated and earnest notices which he had seen in the public journals, not appealing to his interest (which a man is at liberty to slight, if he pleases), but rather implying that others were concerned as deeply as himself, assuming that he was in reality the Mr. Barker to whom the advertisements referred. He had hitherto ascribed these notices to a quarter from which it was now certain that they had not proceeded. Some mysterious connection or relationship was possibly, therefore, still impending over him. His brother *might* have left a son or a daughter, who would, of course, by the laws of nature, have the best title to their uncle's property. He now began to reproach himself for not having made the proper inquiries while he was in a condition to do so. It would be monstrous to leave his property to strangers, while there were claims of kindred to be satisfied, or while there remained a probability, ever so slight, that claims of such a nature were in existence. Barker shrunk from the idea of doing posthumous injustice as instinctively as he did from the risk of incurring living responsibility. But what was to be done? He tortured himself thinking; resolved to dispatch Reynolds to Mr. Ramsay, of Chancery-lane; resolved not to do so; decided upon consulting Spread; reversed his decision, and determined to write upon the subject; changed that resolution again; adopted twenty others in its place; but ended by making up his mind finally to consult the oracle of friendship.

Then he racked himself also about things of less moment. What obligations was he not incurring to the proprietor of the cottage? He imagined what his own situation and feelings would be if a stranger, who had tumbled into the Serpentine, were brought to his chambers at the Albany, and were to use them as a hospital for several weeks, attended by doctors, apothecaries, and nurses, and visited there by all his friends and acquaintances. If the trouble he was giving, and the attentions he received, had been such as he could make a pecuniary return for, the case would have been different; but he was under the roof of a person whom he could only thank for her kind offices, and that person (to make matters worse) was a young and a pretty widow. Another man in his circumstances would have derived satisfaction from the feeling that the widow was young and pretty, instead of old and ugly; but Barker was unrivaled at extracting bitter out of sweets, and what would have gratified any body else only vexed and exasperated him. Mrs. Lilly was so conversable a woman, that she was in the habit of talking to herself when she had no one else to talk to; and as she mumbled the praises of Mrs. Grace from morning to night, and often so that the bachelor could hear well enough what she said, a suspicion at length flashed across his mind that Mrs. Grace (doubtless a crafty widow) had a sinister design in her attentions, and that Mrs. Lilly was a tool in her hands to victimize an ill-starred bachelor with twelve hundred a-year, and catch a lover or a legacy, accord-

ing as he might or might not recover. A whimsical brain is never
so whimsical as in sickness. This absurd crotchet took so fast a
hold of Mr. Barker's fancy, that at last he began to persuade
himself, not only that the doctors were engaged in the plot, but that
there was something not purely accidental in the circumstance of
the boat being overset close to the widow's cottage. In short, it
would have been just as well for the bachelor's ease of mind to
have informed him from the first that the cottage belonged to Mrs.
Harry Farquhar.

As to poor little Mrs. Grace, she was the farthest person in all
the world from harboring any sinister design against the heart of
any man living. She was certainly all anxiety, even to devotedness,
for the sick gentleman; but was there any thing more in this than
ordinary good-nature, not to mention the directions she had received
from Mrs. Farquhar to pay Mr. Barker every possible attention?
It was certainly not for him that she looked so very piquant and
wore her mourning weeds so smartly, for she never so much as
came to his door to ask him how he passed the night, although now
and then, when the door was ajar, he heard a musical whisper on
the stairs, which he concluded was the voice of the wily widow, for
it was very different from the mumbling of Mrs. Lilly.

When Spread visited him next, the bachelor alluded to the subject
now uppermost in his thoughts, and gave the conversation such a
turn that his friend was under the necessity of observing—

" You had a brother, Barker, I think.".

" Yes—he died at Bermudas."

" Did he leave a family ?"

" I never heard that he did."

" Are you sure that he did not ?"

" I can not exactly say that ;" and Barker then, after some little
hesitation, informed Mr. Spread of the advertisements which had
been so often repeated in the leading journal of England.

" Ha !—how long since did the first advertisement appear ?" cried
Spread.

" About two months—two or three."

" Well, and what did you learn from Mr. Ramsay ?"

" Nothing—I never applied to him."

" Never applied to him !   That was wrong, Barker, very wrong,"
said Spread, his countenance suddenly assuming its gravest expression.

" You think so ?"

" Of course I do. You may have been injuring others. Sup-

pose, for a moment, the truth to be, that your brother died, leaving
a child, or children, behind him, you would be their natural guardian
in the place of their father; then suppose, further, that he left his
offspring unprovided for, or suppose that he had property involved
in litigation, or died intestate, in which case it would be your duty
to take out administration—I can imagine twenty cases in which
the services of a brother would be invaluable—excuse my freedom,
Barker, but I must frankly tell you that you have, in this instance,
indulged your aversion to business and responsibility to a most
blamable extent."

This was a pleasant panorama of contingencies to present to poor
Mr. Barker's view.

"But the chances," he replied, peevishly, "are a thousand to
one that my brother left no family—I never heard that he was
married."

"He may have left children, nevertheless; legitimate or not, they
would naturally look to their father's brother for advice, countenance, and protection."

The sigh which here escaped the bachelor was so comic, that it
was with no little difficulty Spread refrained from smiling.

"How coolly you talk of protectorships and guardianships—going to law and taking out administrations!" said Barker, languidly,
and falling back upon his pillow.

"It is a great pity, my dear friend, that the path of duty should
not be always strewn with flowers; but we must tread it, be it ever
so thorny."

"What would you have me do? I am prepared to take your advice."

"What you ought to have done three months ago."

"Reply to that trumpery advertisement?"

"Undoubtedly—how do you know whether it be trumpery or
not, until you have made inquiries? If there is nothing in it, you
are no loser; if it should really concern you, you have only to hope
that you have not deferred answering it too long."

"In what this may involve me, Heaven only knows!"

"True; duty is *sometimes* very embarrassing; but I have uniformly observed—and I know something of the business of life—that to
neglect or think to shirk it, is embarrassing *always*, ten times more
embarrassing in the long run than to discharge it in the first instance."

"Perhaps you are right. Will it suffice to send Reynolds to ask
the necessary questions?"

"No. I am going to town to-day; I will call myself in Chancery-lane, and acquaint you with the result on my return in the evening. Meantime, my dear Barker, keep your mind tranquil—take the advice of the lady in 'Comus,' and

'Be not overexquisite
To cast the fashion of uncertain evils.'"

"It is easy, Spread, to say, 'be tranquil.' I believe I am the most unlucky dog in the empire."

"You forget you were not drowned," said Spread, moving to the door.

Barker muttered something to the effect that it was too soon to decide whether his escape from a watery grave was a blessing or the contrary.

"And," added Spread, rolling his benevolent and pleasant eye round the neat little chamber, with its white curtains and open casement, admitting all the sweet sounds and perfumes of the season, "here I find you in the nicest hospital in the world, and under the care of such a charming little widow—by Jove, Barker, it is when you are on your legs again you will have to take care of yourself in earnest."

A low growl was the answer to this speech, and Spread retired, without pressing his joke further at that time.

. At the foot of the stair-case he met Mrs. Lilly, and had a short colloquy with her, as usual.

"Well, Mrs. Lilly, what do you think of your patient? He seems making way, at last."

"He's the fretfullest gentleman I ever see'd," said Mrs. Lilly, "and the hardest to please; only think, sir, he won't look at chicken broth."

"Ah! prefers giblet soup—strange man, Mrs. Lilly."

"And he ordered me not to think of tapioca and sago."

"Odd fellow!"

"'Deed, sir, it's hard to know what he likes—what to give him; he'll take a pill as if he was paying you the greatest compliment in life, but he don't fancy powders."

"A most eccentric character!" said Spread, with the profoundest gravity, puffing his cheeks and shaking his head.

"Oh, sir, 'deed, he's very centric," rejoined the worthy nurse; "I'm going up to him now to try will he relish some nice thin gruel, with sugar and nutmeg; Mrs. Grace made it herself, but I wouldn't tell him so for thousands of pounds."

"Why so?" asked Mr. Spread, surprised.

"Because he always frowns so, and looks black when I talk of the dear, good young woman, and say how thoughtful she is, and how pretty and ladylike."

"Well, that's the oddest thing you have told me yet, Mrs. Lilly."

"Isn't it, sir."

"But I hope Mr. Barker still thinks she is the mistress of the house—not a word, you know, of Mrs. Harry, no more than of tapioca and sago."

"Oh, not a word, sir, not a word—of course not; but you know, sir, I suppose, that Mrs. Farquhar is expected here the day after to-morrow to see the children."

"No, Mrs. Lilly, I did not know; but she won't think of visiting Mr. Barker, so he need hear nothing about her. You must be particularly careful, however, while she remains; dont leave the door of his room open for a moment."

"No, no, sir, I'll take care."

"Very well, Mrs. Lilly, I'll see you again in the evening; give my compliments to Mrs. Grace."

Spread went his way, and Mrs. Lilly proceeded with her nice thin gruel to the chamber of the peevish invalid, resolving in her worthy mind to be silent as the grave on the two subjects of tapioca and Mrs. Farquhar.

But the bachelor had followed Bacon's admirable prescription for congestion of the heart, and had derived inexpressible benefit from it. It was, indeed, as if Spread had shriven him. Mrs. Lilly was astonished to find him as bland and submissive as he had hitherto been morose and obstinate. He took a small silvered pill without a murmur; looked at the gruel without turning it sour; and modified his high opinion of the quantity of skill in the little finger of Mr. Squills. In a short time he evinced a disposition to sleep; and Mrs. Lilly thought it a good opportunity to go in quest of Mrs. Grace, to report the visible improvement of her patient.

She found the attractive little governess writing in a small apartment, opening into a flower-garden, where her pupils were disporting themselves, chasing butterflies, and collecting heaps of minute snails from the leaves of the lily of the valley.

When Mrs. Grace looked up from the table at which she sat, apparently examining a picture, Mrs. Lilly at once perceived that she had been crying, and the good nurse was the more struck by the circumstance, as in the house where she had spent the greater part of her life she had never once seen a governess in tears, with the

exception of Miss Pickering, when her peculations were detected.
Mrs. Grace rose hastily when the nurse entered, wiped the evidences of grief quickly from her eyes, and returned the picture,
which was a miniature portrait of a gentleman, to the case belonging to it, while, with a countenance beaming with satisfaction, she listened to the good news which Mrs. Lilly brought her.   Then she
expressed her hope for the twentieth time that Mr. Barker wanted
nothing which the house could supply, that the voices of the children
playing did not reach him, and that the nurse herself was properly
taken care of.

"Poor lady!" said Mrs. Lilly to herself, as she retired; "she
was crying over the picture of her husband.   Poor lady! how sorely she has been visited.   Her heart is with him in the grave; but
sorrow won't bring him back to you, poor thing! More's the pity."

She had scarcely made this short soliloquy, when she heard
the voice of Mrs. Grace calling her back.   She obeyed, and found
the young widow standing beside the table, with the miniature in
her hand again; she had again taken it from the case, and the nurse
concluded it was with the intention of showing it to her; but that
was not Mrs. Grace's object.

"Mrs. Lilly," she said, "I am going to request you to do me a
favor.   It will appear strange, but you will be kind enough not to
ask me for an explanation at present.   Take this picture, and as
soon as Mr. Barker is considered by the physicians so far recovered
that a little surprise—perhaps even a little agitation—would not injure him, take an opportunity of letting him see it.   Perhaps the
best way would be to hang it somewhere in the room, where it
could not fail to catch his eye.   May I depend on your doing me
this—service?"

Mrs. Lilly promised: it was impossible, indeed, to do otherwise,
the request was made in accents so very sweet and earnest; there
appeared, too, so very simple an explanation of the mystery, namely, that the widowed governess had discovered in Mr. Barker a
friend or relative of her deceased husband, and desired to introduce
herself at the proper time, through the medium of his portrait.

When Mrs. Lilly returned to the bachelor's room, he was wide
awake, and as fretful and fidgety as ever.   The time was drawing
near when he might expect Spread back from town.   In what a
sea of troubles might he not be involved before nightfall!   The setting sun might see him the guardian of a minor, the committee of a
lunatic, a plaintiff in a chancery suit, or a kind of dry nurse, like Mr.
Farquhar, to a pack of obstreperous children.   Poor Barker felt as

H*

embarrassed as the celebrated Sir Boyle Roche, who knew not
" whether he was an uncle or an aunt." All sorts of duties, obligations, involvements, perplexities, liabilities, and accountabilities,
thronged and fluttered about him, like a swarm of gnats or mosqui-
toes. The very least misery he anticipated was to find himself the
executor of a disputed will, the center of a group of impatient creditors and grasping legatees.

But he was harassed from without as well as from within.
The various rural sounds which reached his ear from the surrounding meadows aggrieved him exceedingly, particularly the
cuckoo, which, though supposed in general to " mock married men,"
seemed bent that day on mocking a single one. The swallows,
too, were inclined to be impertinent; they went on twittering just
as if there was nobody in the cottage but Mrs. Lilly, or as if every
body was as fond of them as Anacreon, or Mr. Spread.

Mrs. Lilly was ordered to close the windows. In doing so, she
inadvertently laid the picture down on the small table at the side of
the bed; however, as the patient's head was turned the other way,
he did not notice the circumstance; but it led, as we shall see, to a
premature accomplishment of Mrs. Grace's purpose. Poor Mrs.
Lilly! She surely had enough to do, to manage a crusty bachelor,
without being also the diplomatic agent of a manœuvering widow.

CHAPTER XXII.

For we were nursed upon the self-same hill,
Fed the same flock by fountain, shade, and rill,
Together both, ere the high lawns appeared
Under the op'ning eyelids of the morn,
We drove a-field, and both together heard,
What time the gray-fly winds her sultry horn.

Lycidas.

Historiette of a literary Friendship—The Quarrel—The Reconcilement—
The Exchange of Rings—The Rosary on a May Evening—A Clew to the
Discovery of Miss Medlicott—Dinner of the Icthyological Society—Philip
Spread flies on the Wings of Love to the Cornish Coast—Arrival of Mrs.
Briscoe and Letty—Mrs. Spread's Domestic Troubles—Mrs. Martin grows
troublesome—Threatens to lecture Mr. Barker—Ends with lecturing
Elizabeth Spread—Library for the Sick-Room—A Parcel of Books is made
up for the Bachelor.

IT was late in the evening when Spread returned from town.
He had not seen the gentleman named in the advertisements (for he
happened to be in the country), but he had learned from one of his
clerks that Mr. Ramsay of Chancery-lane only represented his
brother, a clergyman in Cornwall, who was the proper party to
apply to. The clerk, in fact, knew no more about the matter, than
that the person chiefly interested in the inquiry was young, an
orphan, and a female. Mr. Spread could do no more than note
down the name and address of the Cornish clergyman, and return
to report the very little progress he had made.

As he rose to take leave of his friend, after a visit, the duration of
which was proportioned to the news he had to communicate, the
case containing the miniature caught his eye, and he took it up and
opened it almost unconsciously.

"What is that?" asked Barker, seeing a picture in Spread's
hands.

"I ought to ask *you*," said Spread; "is it not yours?"

"Mine?   No—how did it come there?"

"More than I can explain," said Spread, handing the miniature

to the bachelor, who no sooner glanced at it, than he started, and
exclaimed,

"Raymond!"

"Then you know whose it is," said Spread.   .

Barker made no reply, but continued to gaze intently and affectionately upon the picture, again murmuring—"Raymond!"

Spread saw he was affected and remained silent.

"It is like, very like an old friend of mine—I do not think, Spread,
you ever saw him."

"No," said Spread; "if I had, I should have recognized the likeness; I have a retentive memory for faces, and that is a remarkable
one."

"Doubtless an accidental resemblance," said Barker.

"Shall I question Mrs. Lilly about it?" said Spread.

"I'll question her myself," said the bachelor; and having once
more scrutinized the picture, he restored it to the case, and replaced it on the table.

Spread left the cottage that evening without seeing Mrs. Lilly;
but Barker seized the first opportunity of interrogating her on the
subject; and the worthy dame, being confused by the suddenness
of the inquiry, and the consciousness of having acted the part she
had undertaken with *maladresse*, gave a very unsatisfactory account
of how the picture found its way to the bachelor's bed-side; but said
that, of course, she presumed it belonged to Mrs. Grace.   Mr. Barker made no remark, and the nurse having arranged his chamber
(an office which she discharged with a tedious minuteness that invariably elicited sundry small growls from the impatient patient)
retired, much discontented with herself, to an adjacent room.

Raymond—Raymond.   Barker had for many years almost forgotten the name, but now that accident recalled it: a hundred recollec-
tions of scenes and places, of pleasures and pursuits connected with
that name, came tumbling in quick succession from the long unvisit-
ed nook in the cave of memory, as moldy papers or old coins roll
out of the recesses of some cabinet unlocked for three generations.
He had met Raymond in his fresh youth, before his cynical character
had been formed, and they had contracted an ardent friendship, like
that of Cowley and Hervey, or Milton and his Lycidas, upon the
basis of a common passion for the pursuits of literature.   Hand in
hand they had roamed the flowery tracts of Greek and Roman learning, more thoughtful of wit and philosophy than of prosody and syntax
—not in the steps of the Bentleys and Bloomfields, to discuss the
digamma, or wrangle about accents; but to gather the sweet fancies,

the deep maxims, and the glorious sentiment of the bard, the historian, and the orator.   Together they had lingered over Livy's pictured page; listened, enchanted, to the notes of "sweet Electra's
poet;" laughed (especially Barker) with Aristophanes and Lucian,
at the perennial follies and impostures of the world; and thence repaired to the famous orators—

> " Those ancient, whose resistless eloquence
>   Wielded at will the fierce democratie—"

to learn how the thunderbolts of speech were forged by the Cy-
clopean hands of old.   Descending the stream of time, the young
fellow-travelers through the commonwealth of letters rapidly visited
all that is most worthy of note or cultivation in the literature of
Italy and France, but lingered over that of their own country,
traced and retraced its highways and its byways, "in prose and
rhyme," until, like the old swain, they

> " Knew each lane, and every alley green,
>   Dingle and bushy dell in that wild wood,
>   And every bosky bourn from side to side."

It is in haunts like these that the fastest friendships are formed;
in the common adoration of Milton, or the common joy in Shakspeare.   Barker recalled the very places where he and his friend
made their first acquaintance with the master-pieces of the English
language; there was a path through some meadows, not far from the
spot where he was now confined, hallowed in his mind by association
with the fables of Dryden; under the ruin of a great tree in Ken-
sington Gardens he had listened to Raymond reading Lycidas; and
he particularly remembered his own raptures at the invective upon
the clergy of the Church of England, which the republican poet
puts into the mouth of St. Peter, in the course of that noble pastoral
dirge.   Raymond's tastes were softer than Barker's; his temperament was melancholy, without being morose.   There was something
mysterious about his family and position in life, which, with all his
intimacy, the bachelor recollected that he had never been able to
fathom.   He was limited in his circumstances, and careless about
making them better.   He seemed perfectly isolated in the world,
and likely always to remain so.   Though his manners were gentle
and his tastes refined, Barker was rather disposed to think that his
origin was humble.   After the first year of their acquaintance, Raymond's small income must have been considerably reduced, for
he sought to turn his literary talents to account, and became a re-

porter to a weekly newspaper, and a contributor to several reviews
and magazines.   He would have risen in that path, thorny and tedious
as it is, had he persevered; but he had little ambition, and less avarice.   Many an empty coxcomb strutted about town in Raymond's
literary feathers; many an editor regaled himself at Blackwall with
the remuneration which Raymond neglected to claim for his brilliant
papers.   Barker pointed out in vain the folly of working hard for
neither fame nor money.   Raymond was easily convinced, but never
reformed.   He was thoughtless and reckless of himself, as improvi-
dent as if he expected to be fed by the ravens, or by manna dropping
from the skies.   He made friends, but made no use of them when
made.   He lost friends, and took no pains to recover them.   Now
and then some high-minded man, with social or political influence,
aware of his worth, or charmed by some production of his pen, would
make an effort to raise him to his proper place in society; but he
commonly repelled such services, and seemed perversely to prefer a
precarious to a certain revenue.   At length he wrote a tragedy; it was
printed, and pronounced not only a fine piece of dramatic writing, but
eminently adapted to the stage.   The managers of two theaters
offered large terms to secure it, but Raymond had not written it for
representation, and obstinately refused both proposals.   This was
the occasion of the only disagreement (save on points of criticism)
that had ever occurred between him and Barker, who could not see,
without extreme impatience, the road to reputation and independence opened to his friend in vain.   He urged him vehemently to
take the prudent course, and censured him harshly when he proved
inaccessible to reason.   The sensitive author was offended, and the
intercourse of friendship was suspended for some weeks.   But Barker was seized with a malignant fever, and instantly Raymond was
at his side.   When the bachelor rose from his couch, a stranger
would have been at a loss to decide whether he or his friend had
been the victim of disease.   Their final separation was then near at
hand.   Raymond had at last been induced to accept a small colonial appointment.   Barker was grieved to lose him, but glad to see
uncertainties at length exchanged for certainties.   When the heavy
hour arrived, the young men (neither had reached his three-and-
twentieth year) embraced with more than brotherly affection, and
with a sentiment becoming their age, exchanged their rings.   Raymond's was a carbuncle, with a head of Shakspeare: Barker's a
topaz, with his heraldic emblem, a mastiff.   The Atlantic soon divided them, a few letters were interchanged, and then poor Raymond was no more heard of.

All these, and many other incidents connected with the same passage of his early life, floated in quick succession through Barker's awakened memory; while the deepening shadows of evening suited the strain of melancholy thought, and induced a dreaminess of mind which, spanning like an arch the gulf of years, reunited the present with the past, and almost restored his friend to his bosom. He raised his finger to his eye to contemplate the gem which had once been Raymond's, but scarcely could distinguish the work of the sculptor. The bats were flitting in the twilight, but they gave him no molestation. He fell back upon the pillows, sighed, and slept.

Meanwhile, Spread had returned to his ever-smiling home. How beautiful the Rosary looked that sweet evening! To the eyes of Spread, at least, it seemed a paradise; and it was a paradise, for it was the residence of tranquillity and love, those spirits that make an Eden wherever they fix their seat. The fondest of wives and daughters were impatiently waiting his return; he saw their fair forms at a distance, moving to and fro among the flowers, and thought of the sweet words of Martial—"*in eternâ vivere digna rosâ.*" Mrs. Spread and Augusta were side by side, speculating upon the profusion of roses which promised to make the villa, in another week, a rival of old Pæstum; Elizabeth was at some distance, hearkening to her lover, who was descanting on the ceremony of baptizing church-bells, while his auditress was internally wishing him to speak of another rite, in which she felt just then an infinitely deeper interest.

At dinner Spread related the proceedings of the day, particularly the affair in which he had been engaged on the part of the Bachelor of the Albany.

No sooner did he mention the Rev. Edward Ramsay, vicar of the marine parish of Sandholme, than his wife recollected that it was a clergyman of that name who had shown kindness to the ill-fated Grace Medlicott, after her shipwreck on the coast of Cornwall.

"How strange, if it should turn out," she exclaimed, "that poor Grace is related to Mr. Barker!"

"Not very probable," said Spread; "but, at all events, there is a twofold reason for communicating with Mr. Ramsay at once: we may hear something of Miss Medlicott, while prosecuting the other inquiry."

"Really," said Adelaide Smyly, "it seems very lucky that Mr. Barker fell into the river. Only think of his leaving such an advertisement as that so long unanswered!"

"You forget," said Laura, slightly coloring, "how much occupied he has been by his parliamentary duties."

"It was monstrously selfish, Miss Smyly," said Mrs. Martin, in such a legislative tone that Laura ventured no replication.

"Sweet," said Spread, "are the uses of adversity."

"A decided case of the water-cure," said Adelaide.

Philip was not present; he had been prevailed on to attend a festive meeting of the Ichthyological Society, of which Mr. Periwinkle was president. It was the first appearance of the philosophical amoroso in public since his return from the Rhine; and the assembled ichthyologists attributed his pale features and languid air to the enthusiasm with which he had devoted himself to the objects of the association. Mr. Periwinkle made a speech less scientific than usual upon the occasion, introducing in the course of it some pleasant observations upon the influence of fish, politically and religiously considered; the consequence, for instance, of whitebait in a parliamentary crisis, and the virtue of the herring and the cod in times of famine or pestilence, to appease the wrath of offended Heaven. He concluded by proposing Mr. Lovegrove (for the dinner was at Blackwall) an honorary member of the association, a motion which was received with cheers by the company, who grew so exceedingly jovial, that, when Philip left them at ten o'clock, three ichthyologists were half-seas over, and a professor of conchology under the table.

His joy may be imagined, when he learned the next morning that a clew had been found which might possibly lead to the discovery of Grace Medlicott. Propose to him, indeed, to wait for the slow operations of the post-office, the tedious dispatch and receipt of letters! You would have supposed, to hear him talk, that her majesty's mails were carried by snail-posts, or on the backs of tortoises. Before the dew was well dry upon the grass he had started for London, and before the sun crossed the meridian he was far on his way to Cornwall.

> A true-devoted pilgrim is not weary
> To measure kingdoms with his feeble steps;
> Much less shall he that hath Love's wings to fly.

Nothing that tenderness, directed by sound judgment, could do to cure a lover of a passion, not only imprudent, but seemingly hopeless, had been neglected in Philip's case. When it was evident that love was seated too deep to be reached by counsel and remonstrance, his parents interfered no longer, but left the disease to the slow but sure operation of the old surgeon with the scythe and hour-glass.

This was indeed the only chance of recovery, for the missing girl had more than captivated the affections of young Spread—she had changed his character: he was no longer "the fickle Philip," or "Philip the Inconstant;" the present was none of the slight, sentimental attachments that evaporate in a sigh or go off in a sonnet; it was "an inward bruise" and serious affection of the heart, which you might as well hope to cure with "parmaceti" as dream of healing with philosophy. His father fancied for a while that mathematics might restore him to reason, as if triangles, which have their loves themselves, were capable of restraining the amorous inclinations. At all events they had no such effect on Philip. His essay on insect-geometry lay unfinished on his table; the bees constructed their golden halls, and the spiders threw their suspension bridges across the walks, unstudied and unobserved by our enamored *savant*.

The party at the Rosary was re-enforced before dinner, by the arrival of the vigilant Mrs. Briscoe and her lazy, fat maid. Poor Mrs. Briscoe still harbored a grateful reminiscence of the attention paid her by Mr. Barker at the rail-way station, when the bachelor insisted upon carrying her *sac de nuit*; she instantly proffered her services to go over and nurse him, and being with great difficulty dissuaded from that design, set her heart just as intently upon nursing Pico, who happened at the time to be slightly indisposed. Mrs. Spread had never been so full of affairs since her wedding-day. There was the attention due to her husband's friend, the preparations for her daughter's nuptials, her anxieties about Grace Medlicott, and the difficulty of keeping, not only Mrs. Briscoe quiet, but Mrs. Martin also. Mrs. Martin began to be troublesome just now in her own way. She expressed much surprise and displeasure when she learned that Mrs. Grace had never visited Mr. Barker at a period so favorable for serious and improving conversation. It was throwing away the time, she said, for making a lasting impression. In short, she announced her intention of giving the ascetic bachelor a course of clinical lectures, as soon as he was sufficiently restored to admit visitors.

"Why, the woman must be mad," said Mr. Spread. "Barker would just jump out of the window, were she to enter his room for any such purpose."

"I'll positively forbid it," said Mrs. Spread; and, as she knew how to be decided and peremptory at the proper time, Mrs. Martin was compelled to abandon her didactic designs; which, however, she did not do, without turning her artillery, as usual, upon poor Elizabeth Spread.

" The-sick room, my dear Elizabeth," said this notable mistress
of arts, beginning her second lecture upon the causeuse in her
dressing-room, " the sick-room is the place where a woman ought
most to shine.   You will feel the truth of what I say as soon as you
are married, and have your husband in a fever, or a fit of the gout,
my love, which, when he is a beneficed clergyman, will probably be
once or twice in the year."

" I hope not, Mrs. Martin," said the still Elizabeth, very gravely.

" I hope so too, my dear—of course I do ; but allow me to proceed.   If the conversation of a woman ought to be edifying at all
times, how much more, Elizabeth, when a brother, a friend, or a
husband is confined to a sick-bed.   Then is the time, believe me, for
elevating a man's moral standard, leading him to enjoy intellectual
pleasures, and curing him of that besetting sin of men—of all the
men I ever knew—selfishness."

" Surely my father is not selfish," said Elizabeth.

" I only lay down general propositions, my dear—your father is
the *least* selfish man I ever met with—but now do follow me.   I *do*
think I should have been of great service, *morally*, to Mr. Barker, if
your mother had consented to my visiting him a few times.   The
advantages the sick-room affords are immense.   I have seen men in
health take up their hats, and walk out of rooms, when a sensible
woman was trying to engage them in improving conversation.   I
have known others whistle tunes, or play with a child, or a greyhound.   They can't do such things when they are confined to their
beds.   They *can*, of course, and they *will*, as often as they can, my
dear, try to divert the conversation to the news of the day, or the
gossip of the neighborhood—but this you must never condescend to.
It is much better, Elizabeth, not to amuse at all, than to be amusing
without being at the same time instructive.   But to return to the
sick-room.   I have taken the trouble to classify the disorders and
accidents to which men are most liable, and the topics of conversation suitable to each case.   You will find them arranged in this
paper, for convenience sake, in a tabular form.   Take it, my dear,
copy it, and keep it always by you.   There is also subjoined a list
of books adapted to invalids.   I call it my Library for the Sick-Room.
Now go, Elizabeth, my dear, and by way of an exercise upon what
I have been saying to you, select from your father's library the books
you think fittest for poor Mr. Barker's case ; I will revise it, and the
books can be sent to the cottage in the course of the day."

The parcel of books which Elizabeth, aided and abetted by Adelaide Smyly, prepared for the bachelor's amusement, subject to the

approbation of Mrs. Martin, consisted of the following works, all appropriate, certainly, either to his character or his recent misadventure : " Falconer's Shipwreck," " The Loss of the Medusa," " Lycidas," " The Triumphs of Temper," " The Bachelor of Salamanca," " Crotchet Castle," and Sir Edward Bulwer Lytton's " Essay on the Water-Cure."   Mrs. Martin took out " The Bachelor of Salamanca," and judiciously replaced it with " Cœlebs in Search of a Wife;" she then added her own treatise on " The Prerogatives and Dignity of Woman ;" and Owlet insisted on stuffing in " Ward's Idea of a Christian Church," and a couple of dozen of the Oxford tracts.   But it fortunately happened that Mrs. Spread revised the entire collection, before it sailed for the cottage, abstracted nine tenths of the lot, and supplied their places with publications which she thought would be more agreeable to Mr. Barker.

CHAPTER XXIII.

There be land-rats and water-rats, water-thieves and land-thieves—I mean pirates.
Merchant of Venice.

Doings of Mrs. Harry Farquhar—How the Swallows maltreated the Bachelor—He hears a Dialogue not meant for his Ear—Character of the Hon. Mr. Saunter—Dean Bedford's Present to Mr. Barker—The Risk that it ran of being carried off by Pirates on the River—A Lord of the Treasury gets a Ducking—How the Piracy was prevented, and who arrested the Pirates —Mr. Farquhar prefers a quiet Dinner at the Cottage to a gay one at the Star and Garter.

MRS. HARRY FARQUHAR was a woman of pleasure every inch; she lived only for it, and was ready to die for it, too, the victim of a *fête*, or the martyr of a ball. She was not only a rake at heart, but rakish in her heart's core. In the merry month of May she always began to feel pic-nickish; and her's were generally the earliest expeditions to Eel-pie Island, and parties at the Star and Garter. Maternal cares sat as lightly on her as diocesan duties on absentee prelates. She kept governesses for her children, just as heads of departments keep secretaries or deputies, to shift the burden of office from their own shoulders; and where a little parental superintendence was indispensable, she devolved it on Mr. Farquhar, who, by dint of practice, was grown a capital children's maid, and a very useful and tidy person in a nursery.

Mrs. Harry came thundering down in her pony-phaeton and a cloud of dust on the day which she had affectionately fixed for paying her little ones a visit. Perhaps this was her primary object; if so, it was only incidentally that she had named the same day for a gay dinner at the Star and Garter, where she usually opened her summer campaign.

It had been arranged that Tom Turner, Will Whitebait, and the Honorable Mr. Saunter, should meet her at the cottage at four o'clock, and from thence, "launched on the bosom of the silver Thames," proceed to join the rest of the party at the festive place and hour.

The day was brilliant and warm, as if the sun was as much Mrs. Harry's devoted servant as the lords of the Treasury. The cuckoo was indefatigable; the swallow clamorous; the cloudless sky was full of pleasing sounds and sweet odors; and the river ran smooth, splendid, and harmonious, as the immortal verse of the bard of Twickenham. Barker's windows were again open, and the soft south wind that ventilated his chamber was more salubrious than all the medicines in the pharmacopœia. He felt its influence—the "healing on its wings"—and sat up in the bed, to take larger draughts of the delicious air that floated about him. The next moment something struck the white curtains of his bed, and there was a loud twitter just at his ear. It was a swallow, more presumptuous than his fellows, which had actually dared to penetrate the bachelor's bed-room.

"Shut the window, Mrs. Lilly."

Poor swallow! had you been a cormorant, or a vulture, Barker could not have looked fiercer, or spoken in a surlier key.

Mrs. Lilly obeyed, but not without a mumbled remonstrance in behalf of the fresh air, in whose virtues her belief was potent; nor without muttering a series of low, inarticulate, benevolent noises, as much as to say (as far as the language was translatable into the vernacular) she was extremely sorry the birds were so ill-mannered, but that at the same time she had never heard, in tale or song, of a swallow eating any body up, much less a member of the imperial parliament. The day was so hot, however, and the room so small, that Barker was soon obliged to recall Mrs. Lilly, and have the window reopened. But he thanked her this time for her services, and then said she might go down stairs: he would signify by pulling the bell when he next required her attendance.

Meanwhile a little group of personages had assembled in front of the cottage, immediately under the bachelor's apartment, and he soon had his attention diverted from the twittering of the swallows by the chatter of human voices.

"It's a wonderful recovery," drawled the Honorable Mr. Saunter, who spoke at the rate of a syllable a minute.

"Not at all wonderful," said Will Whitebait; "the doctors pronounced the case hopeless, and he recovered out of pure opposition."

"How did the accident happen?"

"There are various accounts; the truth is, he overset the boat himself."

"He was near oversetting the government more than once," said Turner.

Barker overheard every word, and very speedily discovered that he was himself the subject of the conversation.

"What a capital nickname Mrs. Harry has for him!"

"What?"

"Peter the Hermit."

"Capital!"

"I lost one of the best dinners in England by the accident, at that villa yonder," said Whitebait; "it broke up the party."

"The party you love best, Will—the dinner-party."

"I own the soft impeachment," said Whitebait, "that's the party for me. Talk of able governments, and stable governments, the best government of all is the table government. By-the-by, it is half-past five, and Mrs. Harry not arrived. I shall eat enormously to-day; that I foresee, Tom."

"So shall I," said the Honorable Mr. Saunter.

"You eat enormously every day, I think," said Turner.

"No," replied Saunter; "I have had no appetite for some days back. I do not feel quite well."

"How do you feel?" asked Turner.

"Wakeful—a most distressing sensation; but I think I know the cause of it—taking tea at breakfast."

"Tea!" cried Whitebait, "I have not taken tea for breakfast for several years—when I did, it used to keep me awake all day."

"Precisely—that's the effect it has on me; I'll take chocolate in future."

Instead of feeling, with Sallust, that the body is a clog on the mind, the Honorable Mr. Saunter rather felt that the mind, the little mind that he had, was a clog on the body. He actually wished himself more of a mere animal than he actually was. When his brain was in the least degree active, he thought himself out of order; indeed, his intellect seldom evinced the slightest vivacity, except under the influence of champagne, or the excitement of cigars and brandy.

"I hope and trust we shall not have Farquhar," said Will Whitebait.

"The idea of Mrs. Harry having her husband at one of her dinners! No—Farquhar will stay at home and dine with the children on mutton chops."

"The children are here with their governess," said Tom Turner; "but, hurrah! here comes Mrs. Harry—here comes my Færy Queen—her ponies *ventre-à-terre*—by Jove, she's the best whip and the best fellow in England."

"She is what I call a brick," drawled the Honorable Mr. Saunter.

At the mention of the name of Farquhar, Barker had raised his night-cap and cocked his ears; but now, no longer able to restrain his curiosity, he scrambled out of bed, weak as he was, donned his *robe-de-chambre*, wrapped himself in the counterpane, thrust his feet into his slippers, and he had just crept over to the window as the pony-phaeton, turning a sharp angle in the little plantation that intersected the lawn, drove smoking up to the door; and the astonished bachelor beheld Mrs. Harry, in all her noonday splendor (green silk dress, pink crape bonnet, and marabout feathers), receiving the homage of the three political butterflies, whose faces he was perfectly familiar with in the House. He had already heard quite enough to settle who was the true owner of the cottage; but all doubt on the subject was removed when he saw a modest and elegant young woman, in widow's weeds, appear to present her pupils to their dashing and dissipated mother.

Mrs. Harry merely nodded to Mrs. Grace, hastily caressed her children, and desired one of the gentlemen to see that the boat was ready. Whitebait proceeded on this mission, and Mrs. Harry, nodding again to Mrs. Grace, strutted down to the water-edge, followed by Saunter and Tom Turner; Tom playing with her tiny parasol, and Saunter crawling after, oppressed with the weight of her cashmere shawl.

Just at this moment Mr. Mooney (the pluralist butler) arrived, on his dayly cruise with Dr. Bedford's kind messages to Mr. Barker; and upon this occasion he was also the bearer of a small hamper containing some bottles of the dean's episcopal Madeira, well worth all the drugs that Mr. Squills ever brayed in a mortar. Mooney looked so round and so reverend, that Turner and Saunter thought he was the great dignitary himself. Saunter was on the point of taking off his hat and making him a low obeisance.

"What's in the basket?" demanded Mrs. Harry, in her sharp, imperious way.

"Half a dozen of Madeira, madam," replied the buxom butler, quailing under her vixenish eye.

Will Whitebait had tasted the dean's Madeira, and knew how marvelous it was; he whispered something to Mrs. Harry, who instantly called to the governess—

"By-the-by, Mrs. Grace, I forgot to ask for Mr. Barker. What do the doctors say? Will he recover?" Had she been talking of her sister's lapdog, she could not have asked the question in a more unconcerned tone.

The bachelor heard every syllable; Mrs. Harry's voice was clear and shrill, and there was not more than twenty yards between them.   .

"He is much better—nearly well," answered Mrs. Grace, shocked at the levity of the inquiry; and glancing anxiously behind her, she was still more horrified to observe the windows of Mr. Barker's room wide open, and standing at one of them a strange spectral figure, imperfectly shrouded by the curtain, which could be no other but the sick gentleman himself, although it might well have been taken for the apparition of Menippus, or the ghost of Piron.

"But is he allowed to take wine yet?" cried the little conscienceless Amazon again.

"Not yet, I believe," replied the agitated young widow.

"Then we may as well have the Madeira up to the Star and Garter," cried Tom Turner, looking at Mrs. Harry, who winked and nodded her perfect concurrence in a step she had already resolved on; and in another moment (to the amazement of Mr. Mooney), the hamper was in the grasp of the larcenous lord of the Treasury.

Instantly the furious ringing of a bell was heard from the house. Mrs. Grace alone knew what it imported.   Barker would have freely made a present of the wine, and thought it a very small return for the attentions he had received in Mrs. Farquhar's house; but he had no notion of allowing himself to be openly pillaged and imposed on.

"Push off!" cried Mrs. Harry.

The boatman obeyed; and Turner, who was just at the moment engaged with both his hands, depositing the confiscated wine in the bottom of the boat, was dragged into the water and ducked up to his waist.   Tom was a dandy, and attached enormous importance to spotless trowsers and dazzling boots, which made the disaster, in his case, doubly disagreeable.

Mrs. Grace was silent, but she looked pleased; the little Farquhars set up a cheer, and even Mrs. Harry herself could not help smiling at the ridiculous plight of her *cavaliere servante*.   Another laugh was heard at the same instant—it was that of a woman certainly, and a woman not far off; but nobody was visible; perhaps it was only an echo.   Tom bore both the ducking and the ridicule exceedingly well; with a single but very tragical glance at his boots, he jumped into the boat, dripping like a water-god, and the piratical crew was just making off with their prize (heedless of Mrs. Lilly, who was hurrying to the water-side, with the proverbial expedition of her age and office) when a young lady, graceful and spirited as one of Diana's maids of honor, sprung from behind a clump of lilacs and acacias, caught the boat-chain which still trailed on the ground, and, with a ringing laugh, the exact counterpart of that which had just been noticed, attached the whole part of piracy in the name of her majesty, Queen Victoria.

The merry officer of justice upon this occasion was instantly recognized, not only by the crew of the "jolly boat" but by Mr. Barker, from his observatory, as one of the Smyly girls. Indeed, the bachelor, who had a quick eye and a retentive memory, decided at a glance that it was Laura. She had been visiting at a house at no great distance, and intending to cross over to Far Niente, her headquarters, she had come down to the cottage, where she knew that at four o'clock she would be sure to catch the dean's boat.

Mrs. Harry made a joke of the Madeira affair—the only thing to be made of it.

"We must give you an office in the Preventive Service, Miss Smyly," said Mr. Saunter.

"I should be too active to please you," said Laura.

"A place would cure you of that fault," said Mrs. Harry.

"A place in the Treasury certainly would," said Laura, looking at the Honorable Mr. Saunter.

"Push off—we shall be late," cried Mrs. Harry; good-by, Miss Smyly. Mrs. Grace, tell Mr. Barker I am glad to hear so good an account of him. He may stay here as long as he likes, but I advise him not to make too free."

Miss Smyly chatted awhile with Mrs. Grace, to make up for the insolent neglect of Mrs. Harry, and then embarked with Mooney for Far Niente.

About an hour later, there arrived at the cottage a gentleman of very respectable appearance and inoffensive demeanor. It was Mr. Harry Farquhar. He merely wished to learn where his wife dined; and having heard that it was at the Star and Garter, with a party, he serenely observed that if Mrs. Grace would order him a chop he would prefer taking a quiet dinner at the cottage.

I

CHAPTER XXIV.

And either tropic now
'Gan thunder, and both ends of heaven; the clouds
From many a horrid rift abortive pour'd
Fierce rain with lightning mix'd, water with fire
In ruin reconciled.
Paradise Regained.

A Change of Weather—Its Effects—Who remained at Richmond during the Night, and who passed the Night at the Cottage—Mr. Whitebait on the Fine Arts—How Barker's Sleep was broken, and who broke it—The Cottage on Fire—How Barker was saved, and how and where Mr. Saunter was roasted—Vigilance and Bravery of the Smyly Girls—Mr. Mooney's balmy Slumbers and golden Dreams—The Escape of the real Incendiaries, and who suffered in their stead—How Mr. Barker looked in the Boat—His Soliloquy.

THE night proved wet and tempestuous; at ten o'clock the rain fell in cataracts, and a magnificent storm of thunder and lightning was witnessed on the river by those who were sufficiently indifferent to their personal comforts to relish the elemental war. Many affect to enjoy such scenes, while in their hearts they wish themselves snug in their beds, or in any mouse-hole; it is so romantic and Byronish to talk familiarly of thunder, and affect a friendship with tornados! Mr. Farquhar had more sense, for he gladly accepted Mrs. Grace's proposal to have the only spare bed-room prepared for him; and, in truth, as he paid the rent of the cottage, and was its proprietor and master in point of law, his title to the accommodation of a night's lodging was not a very bad one. The carouses at the Star and Garter were also disconcerted by the change of weather. After spending a jovial evening, even without the help of Dean Bedford's Madeira, the hour of reckoning came, that serious moment, which the old French proverb calls *le quart-d'-heure de Rabelais*; and while Tom Turner, a little unsteady on the legs, was discharging the bill, and making a multitude of fiscal blunders, particularly disgraceful in a lord of the Treasury, Will Whitebait, the Hon. Mr. Saunter, and one or two more of the revelers, strolled, or, rather, rolled, out into the gardens, to cool the flames of the wine of which they had drank like mitered abbots.

Will Whitebait was chattering on the fine arts, as he invariably did when he was boozy. It was highly amusing to listen to him, for the few ideas with which he commenced soon got jumbled with the fumes of the claret, into the most extraordinary medley imaginable; he prattled of pictures and engravings, cartoons and frescoes, statues and statuettes, until the subjects were quite confounded in his brain, and he ended with extolling Hogarth's "Last Supper," and Poussin's "Rake's Progress," or talked of Raphael's chisel, and the pencil of Canova. He was now drawing nigh this last stage of mental aberration, and earnestly lamenting that Sir Christopher Wren had not been employed to erect the new Houses of Parliament, when a vivid flash of lightning, followed by the roar of a whole park of aerial artillery, silenced, if it did not sober him for the evening. There was scarcely time to retreat into the hotel before the storm raged as we have already described; the party was assembled ready to depart, some by water, others by land, but only those who had close carriages, and they were few, were venturous enough to move. At last Mrs. Harry Farquhar and a few more, among whom was the assiduous Tom Turner, made up their minds to remain all night; but as to Will Whitebait, who was always fool-hardy after dinner, as well as foolish in other ways, he determined to return to town, and by the river, too, as he came; and all that the rest of the company could urge to dissuade him from such a mad proceeding was urged to no purpose. Indeed, he would even have started alone, had not one of the party (a young M.P., who would have had no objection to fill a vacant place in the Treasury), offered the Honorable Mr. Saunter a wager that he would not bear Will Whitebait company. Had Saunter been sober, he would as soon have jumped from the top of the Monument; but, as he was, he booked the wager, and set off with his discreet friend. Mrs. Harry, however, had the charity previously to remind them both that there was a spare bed at her cottage, should they change their minds, or find it impossible to proceed farther. She had, as we have said, her good points, like the rest of the world.

> "Narcissa's nature, tolerably mild,
>   To make a wash, would hardly stew a child."

Such was precisely the amount of humane feeling which Mrs. Harry had for Saunter and Will Whitebait. But it was very fortunate for them she was even so considerate, for the unruliness of the night soon cooled an ardor for enterprise which was merely the effect of too liberal potations.   They were only too glad to put in at the cottage; and their vexation may easily be imagined when, on landing there, which they accomplished with great difficulty, considerably after midnight, they found the spare bed-room already engaged, and, of all people in the world, by Mr. Farquhar, who was only the owner of the house!

Mrs. Grace had retired to rest; but, on learning that two gentlemen, friends of Mrs. Harry, had arrived under such circumstances, she got up, dressed herself hurriedly, and hastened to make the best arrangements in her power for their reception.   On the whole, perhaps, considering the wine they had taken, that they were young men, and that Mrs. Grace was a fascinating woman, they did not behave *extremely* ill; but she was not sorry, nevertheless, to escape to her room, after having first provided them with some excellent cogniac which Mr. Farquhar had brought down with him. It was an unfortunate concession, for, having kindled a huge fire, and lighted all the candles they could find, they commenced smoking cigars, drinking brandy and water, singing snatches of humorous songs, and practicing all sorts of parliamentary noises, coughing, groaning, cheering, braying, and crowing, by which latter performances poor Barker, whose room was almost immediately over them, was not long in divining who the murderers of his sleep were.   At length, however, there was silence; the rioters were evidently asleep, and at the same time the gale ceased, and the night was profoundly still.   Suddenly there was a smell of fire in the cottage. Mrs. Grace was the first to notice it; she sprung up, ran down stairs; the room occupied by the disorderly young men was in flames.   She screamed, and ran to the children's apartment.   The alarm was soon general.   The flames advanced rapidly, and it was not without difficulty that Mr. Farquhar and Mrs. Grace succeeded by their united efforts in rescuing those who naturally were their first care.   The servants were in but little danger, as their rooms were in a remote and almost detached part of the cottage.   Mrs. Grace no sooner saw the little Farquhars safe, than her next thought was of Mr. Barker.   To return up-stairs was impossible; she ran round to the front of the cottage, and the first sight that presented itself was Mr. Saunter and Will Whitebait forcing their way out of the parlor windows, followed by the flames, which seemed doing their best to overtake them.   The Honorable Mr. Saunter was hindmost, and his bellowing clearly indicated that he was already partially roasted.

"Oh, gentlemen, save Mr. Barker—for the love of Heaven, save Mr. Barker; he is ill, and unable to save himself," she cried, passionately, raising her clasped hands in earnest supplication.

At the same moment the bachelor's windows were thrown open, and Mrs. Lilly appeared despairing in dimity, and screaming for succor. Turner called for a ladder; the servants ran in all directions to seek one, but there was no ladder to be found, as generally happens when ladders are wanting to save human lives.

"There is nothing for it but to jump out," cried Whitebait.

"It's only twenty feet from the ground," said Saunter, rubbing himself in a manner which, at any other time, would have been highly comic, for he had got such a scorching that night that it was a fortnight before he found it convenient to resume his seat in the House.

A ladder, however, arrived in time to obviate the necessity of jumping twenty feet, which would probably have been as fatal as the fire both to Barker and Mrs. Lilly. To learn how this relief was procured, we must cross the river for a moment to Far Niente. The fire was first discovered there by the Smylys, whose chamber looked on the Thames, and who were the only inhabitants of the villa who slept lightly and intermittently. Curiously enough, Adelaide had that very night been pleasanting with Laura on the subject of the bachelor, teasing her with silly predictions that she was certainly destined to be Mrs. Peter Barker, on no better ground than that they had once accidentally exchanged watches, and that Laura, the day before, had prevented the robbery of the bachelor's Madeira.

"What nonsense you do talk," said Laura.

"Love often begins with gratitude," said Adelaide.

"Gratitude!" cried her sister. "One would think I had saved his life."

"That may be in the fates, too," said Adelaide.

The storm was raging, and the lightning was flashing vividly, when the merry sisters went to sleep. In about two hours they were both awake again, and found the storm entirely abated, and their chamber utterly dark, save the perpendicular thread of gray light that marked through the curtains where the shutters of the windows had been designedly left imperfectly closed.

Suddenly the room was illuminated.

"The storm is re-commencing," said Adelaide: "did you see the lightning?"

"It can't be lightning," said Laura; "you see the light continues."

"What can it be, then?" said the other.

"It must be fire," said Laura; and she was instantly out of bed and at the window.

"Oh, Adelaide!" she cried, "it is fire, indeed; and it must be Mrs. Farquhar's cottage."

There was soon no doubt upon the subject.

"Shall we inform my uncle?" said Adelaide.

"What use?" said her sister. "No; but let us call up Mr. Mooney—he has the key of the boat-house. The best thing to be done is to send some of the servants over to give their assistance."

The girls dressed hastily; but as to calling up Mr. Mooney, they might as well have called up "thrice great Hermes." Call up Mr. Mooney! There are ten thousand things easier said than done, and calling up Mr. Mooney was of the number. Call up Mr. Mooney! Call up the Pharaohs from under the pyramids! He slept as if his bed was of poppies and his pillow steeped in mandragora. He slept as if he were descended from a thousand watchmen. Mab was at that very hour tickling his acquisitive organ with other vergerships, sextonships, clerkships, and sundry snug little lay benefices —sinecures all of them; for not even into Mooney's visions did the notion of personal service once enter: his fancy was too Irish for that. He rung imaginary bells by deputy, and dug graves for shadows by proxy. The idea of calling up Mooney from such slumbers and such dreams!

However, they succeeded better with the groom and one of the footmen; and, the key of the boat-house having been easily found, the gallant sisters, followed by the men, hurried to the water-side, resolved to see the boat on its way before they returned to their room. As they issued from the house, Laura observed a ladder lying in a passage, which a bell-hanger had been using the day before. It immediately struck her that it might be of service, and the groom, by her directions, carried it down. But an unforeseen difficulty occurred the moment the boat was launched. The footman knew as much about handling an oar as he did about cooking a dinner; and the groom was just as capable of steering a boat as he was of piloting the nation. This was just the emergency to prove a girl's mettle. Adelaide took the tiller; Laura took one of the oars, and the groom the other; the footman sat, like a fine gentleman, gaping at the fire, and doing nothing; and by this division of labor the party gained the scene of distress—critically in time to rescue Mr. Barker and the excellent Mrs. Lilly.

The awkwardest personage in the world at escaping by a ladder

from a house on fire is a sexagenarian nurse. It took full ten minutes to save Mrs. Lilly; and when she got within four feet of the
ground, instead of taking the rest of the descent quietly, she thought
proper to fling herself into the arms of the Honorable Mr. Saunter,
who was instantly rolling on the ground, with the old lady in dimity
sprawling and screaming over him. Barker, notwithstanding his
reduced strength, showed the greatest composure and firmness, for,
foreseeing the time it would take to rescue Mrs. Lilly, he took advantage of the unavoidable delay to throw every thing of any value
on which he could lay his hands out of the window, beside thrusting
many small articles into the pockets of his night-gown. When his
turn came to take advantage of the means of escape, the flames were
bursting in at the door, and, as he turned his face toward the house,
after planting his feet firmly upon the ladder, they showed him the
miniature of his friend Raymond lying on the carpet. He deliberately went back to seize it, and, had the return occupied a minute
more than it did, he would probably have been lost. Every body
was now safe, and Mrs. Lilly thought she never could be grateful
enough to Whitebait and Saunter, who had raised the ladder to the
windows.

"Dear, brave gentlemen; we owe them our lives," cried the good
woman, over and over again.

"Fool," growled the bachelor, audibly, without vouchsafing so
much as to look at the personages alluded to, "we owe them *the risk*
of our lives—that's the amount of the obligation." And he pushed
his way to the dean's boat as fast as an invalid could move, wrapped
in a quilt and two pair of blankets over his ordinary nocturnal wear.

"What a cross fellow!" drawled Saunter, still using the comic
action above described, which, it is to be supposed, was some relief
to his wounded feelings.

"We have made a pretty night of it," said Will Whitebait; and
the worthy pair of officials made the best of their way on foot to
Richmond, and from thence took a fly, and returned to London,
without stopping to acquaint Mrs. Harry how they had burned down
her house. That agreeable task was left to poor Mr. Farquhar,
who was pronounced the only person to blame in the transaction,
for presuming to sleep in his own cottage without express permis-
sion from his wife.

The rosy light of morning was mingling with the ruddy glare of
the yet unextinguished flames when the boat of the Irish dean,
manned (to use an Irish bull) by two young ladies, returned to Far
Niente bearing with it, in safety, not only the member for Borough-

cross (against whom all the elements seemed to have conspired), but also Mrs. Grace, the little Farquhars, and the excellent Mrs. Lilly, who still persisted to irritate the bachelor by her thanksgivings to Messieurs Whitebait and Saunter.   Mr. Barker was amazed (as well he might) to meet the Smyly girls at such a moment and in such a situation.   The servants were not slow to inform him that, in all human probability, he owed his life to the vigilance, address, and forethought of Laura in particular.   He could not but express his grateful sense of so signal a service; nor could Adelaide help reminding her sister of the prophecy she had hazarded only a few hours before, little dreaming how very soon it was destined to be so strangely fulfilled.   Barker was seated between Laura and Mrs. Grace; he certainly cut a most grotesque figure in his counterpane and blankets, looking excessively like a decrepit old nurse; while Mrs. Lilly, on the other hand, having snatched up the bachelor's blue cloak in her trepidation, and at the same time lost her cap, had assumed quite a manly appearance.   It was a scene not to be caricatured, for its humor was incapable of exaggeration.   Adelaide made a colored sketch of it the next day from her memory, and the time came when she was not afraid to show it to the principal personage himself.

Barker was morbidly sensitive to ridicule, and felt as sore when he thought of his costume as if he had been on an ordinary aquatic excursion.   Then to think of a man of his stamp, a man of the Albany, being huddled into a small boat with a parcel of girls, infants, and old women—he, too, the most helpless of them all—was it not as cruel a practical a joke as ever Fortune played on a wretched mortal.   "In vain," he rationally soliloquized, "do we lay down rules of life and propose systems of conduct.   We are overruled by chance or providence—call it what you will; our systems are knocked down with as little scruple as the houses which children build of cards; my cherished scheme of isolation and no-responsibility ended with that fatal visit to Liverpool; in truth, I begin to think that Spread had reason when he said that there was no living among men uninvolved in human ties and obligations.   But six months ago I was as free and unfettered as any man in existence, and here I am now, a member of parliament, probably an uncle or a guardian, under obligations to friends and enemies, a burden upon all who know me, and indebted for my life to a couple of young women.   But for the care of one, I should have died by water, and but for the bravery of another, I should have perished in the flames."

Fortune, indeed, had now very nearly demolished the Albany system. No! it was not Fortune: it was but the common action of the stream of human events against the life of an individual member of society. We may dwell in cities without taking municipal offices, accepting mayoralties, or sitting in town-councils; but there is no existing in the great assemblage of the world without taking our share of social duties and liabilities—without being *of the corporation!*

I*

CHAPTER XXV.

How am I changed! by what alchemy
Of love, or language, am I thus translated!
Her tongue is tipt with the philosopher's stone,
And that hath touch'd me through every vein!
I feel that transmutation of my blood,
As I were quite become another creature,
And all she speaks it is projection.

JONSON'S *New Inn.*

Dean Bedford visits the Sick—The Bachelor's rapid Recovery—Explanations of it—The Magic Ring—The Discovery made with it—Mr. Barker promises his Friendship and Protection to a young Widow—Conversation at Tea—Extent of an Irish Parish—The Bachelor chats with two charming Girls by Moonlight.

THE reputation of Irish hospitality was nobly sustained by Dean Bedford. With open house and heart he received and welcomed the refugees, and at an early hour the next morning—an early hour for him—he proceeded, supported by Mr. Mooney (who was nearly as much in need of support himself) to discharge his pastoral duty, by visiting the sick bachelor. Any other man would have had his recovery seriously retarded by the shocks his nervous system had recently sustained; Barker, however, was an exception to common rules; excitement and danger seemed to have benefited him; the weather, perhaps, contributed; the Spreads thought the Smyly girls had something to do with it; but certainly, he grew so rapidly better, that on the third day of his sojourn at Far Niente he dined on a boiled chicken, with a glass of that episcopal Madeira, and on the fourth he made one of the family party at their usual six-o'clock dinner, and answered in the affirmative Mrs. Spread's invitation to assist at her daughter's wedding on that day week.

The interval was filled with events of interest. The bachelor, it will be recollected, had, at his imminent risk, saved the picture in which he had recognized the likeness of an old friend. On reflection, however, he made up his mind that probably the resemblance was merely casual; and still fearful of involving himself with woman-

kind, he restored the miniature of Mrs. Grace without making a
single remark. She was rejoiced to recover it, but disappointed at
its not having produced the effect she anticipated. The *denouement*,
however, was not fated to be long deferred. At dinner, the following day, Barker sat beside the young widow. The conversation
turned upon heraldry, supporters, mottos, crests, and blazons, azure,
gules, and argent. The dean's crest was a porpoise couchant; his
motto *Dormio*.

   "Two good hits, Mr. Barker, are they not?" said the good-humored ecclesiastic, with his jolly laugh, worthy of the merry days of
the monasteries.

   Mrs. Bedford had prodigious respect for the porpoise on her
spoons: the Established Church and the Heralds' College were, in
her eyes, institutions of equal sanctity: so she checked what she
considered her husband's unbecoming levity.

   "Too bad, Mr. Barker," continued the jovial dean, "not to be allowed to pick a hole in one's own coat."

   "Three fourths of the art of blazonry," said the bachelor, "con-
sists in painting puns—what the heralds call 'canting arms'—the
French, '*armes parlantes*'—a system of vile puns upon family
names."

   "Your crest, I presume, is a dog?" said the dignitary.

   "A mastiff—and the mastiff is, of course, *latrant*."

   Had any body been observing Mrs. Grace, he would have seen
that what Mr. Barker said affected her.

   "That's the device upon your ring, I think, Mrs. Grace?" said
one of the Smyly girls.

   Mrs. Grace, now visibly disconcerted, looked nervously at the
ring on her finger, and grew white and red alternately, in the space
of an instant. The bachelor seemed disconcerted also, but con-
trolled his feelings better. A glance at the ring on his fair neighbor's finger showed him that it was a topaz—the identical ring which
he had given, twenty years before, to his friend Raymond, as a
pledge of his affection, when he parted with him on the quay at
Bristol.

   Dean Bedford twice invited Barker to taste his imperial burgundy before the bachelor heard the hospitable challenge. He drank
the wine almost unconsciously, and spoke no more during the repast. All the company but one ascribed the collapse of his spirits to
the yet unconfirmed state of his health. Mrs. Grace knew it was
the magic of the ring.

   An invalid was not expected to sit long over his wine. The bach-

elor left the dining-room in ten minutes after the ladies, approached Mrs. Grace as soon as he could without attracting attention, and
begged her to favor him with a moment's conference in the conservatory.   When they were separated from the rest of the company by
a grove of balsams and pelargoniums, Barker addressed the young
widow, not without some nervousness of manner, and said: .

"Excuse me, madam, but I recognized that ring upon your hand
—you will probably be surprised when I tell you that it was once
mine."

"Sir," said the widow, with charming frankness, and with a voice
of extreme sweetness, "it was my father's ring."

"You are the daughter, then, of my friend Raymond.   I loved
him, madam," said Barker, tremulous with unaccustomed emotion,
"I loved him as a brother, and his daughter may reckon upon any
service which it may be in the power of a man who is neither influential nor wealthy to render her."

Here a projecting shoot of a geranium, loaded with scarlet flowers, had the presumption to tickle Mr. Barker just under the right
ear, and he changed his position abruptly, with a vindictive glance at
all the plants in the green-house.

"Your friendship, dear sir, will indeed be valuable—invaluable;
I have no other friend."

"Had you any knowledge of the friendship that existed between
your father and me."

"Yes—yes, I had; that is, I knew he had a friend in England of
your name: I made inquiries to no purpose."

"Inquiries! through what channels?" asked the bachelor, with
some eagerness.

"Through the newspapers," she replied.   "I put several advertisements in the *Times*, and as I did not know the Christian
name—"

"You alluded to my brother's death—you knew him?"

"No, the allusion was merely for the purpose of catching the eye
of the Mr. Barker I wanted to discover.   The picture, too—"

"I recognized the picture directly I saw it, but concluded that it
was an accidental likeness."

"And I, sir, when you restored it to me without a remark, concluded that you could not be my Mr. Barker."

Though the words "*my* Mr. Barker" were so natural, they gave
the bachelor a twitch, just as the geranium had done a moment before, and grated on his sensitive ear displeasingly.   It was the first
time in his existence (for he did not remember a mother) that any

thing in woman's form had presumed to claim an interest, a sort of property in him. The pronouncing of that possessive pronoun was an epoch in his life, another blow to the selfish system. She stood before him so modest, and looked so filial, that in an instant he more than pardoned her; the words "my Mr. Barker" lingered agreeably in his ear. Had it been a stroke of art in the little widow, it would have been quite masterly; yet, had she known the bachelor all her life, she would hardly have tried it.

Barker was the first to move; he was fearful of exciting attention by protracting the *tête-à-tête*, but as he returned to the drawing-room with Mrs. Grace by his side, he could not but allude to her widowhood, or avoid inquiring how long it was since so great an affliction had befallen her. The young woman averted her face, and suddenly disappeared by a side-door which led out into the grounds. "Ah!" thought the bachelor, "the wound is yet too recent; I ought not to have touched upon the subject." Then, on a little reflection, he thought it not unlikely that, being so very young, she had made some imprudent marriage, probably with the ensign of a marching regiment, or a friendless lieutenant in the navy, who had died of blue cholera at Madras, or yellow fever in Jamaica, and left her in the capacity of a governess, to envy the lot of a maid-of-all-work.

In the drawing-room he found the Spread girls, escorted by their father, the Rev. Mr. Owlet, and Mr. St. Leger. Mr. St. Leger had suddenly come into the possession of a nice property in Ireland, by the death of a distant relative; and he had just arrived at the Rosary to prosecute an old design of his upon the heart of Augusta Spread.

"I am acquainted," said the dean, "with that property; it lies entirely, I think, in one of my parishes. What's the name, Letty, of my benefice in Kilkenny?"

"Desartmore," said Mrs. Bedford, peevishly, for she was vexed, not so much at the dean's ignorance of the very mines from which he derived his opulence, as at the frankness with which he owned it.

"I hardly think it can all be in Desartmore, sir," said St. Leger, "for it is a straggling property; scattered over a district sixty miles in length."

"Desartmore is sixty miles long—is it not, sir?" said Laura Smyly to the dean.

"I only wish, my dear, it was as broad as it was long," said the hearty dignitary, with that exceeding pleasantry which made the colossal abuses of his church attractive and comely in his person.

Mr. Spread had walked over to Far Niente expressly to see the
bachelor. A letter which he had received from Philip, written at
the house of the Reverend Mr. Ramsay, in Cornwall, contained information which he was anxious to communicate to his friend without loss of time. Drawing him to some distance from the rest of
the company, Spread asked him had he forgotten the subject which
he had commissioned him, about a week before, to investigate on his
behalf.

"No," said the bachelor.

"Well, we have not been idle. Do you happen to recollect a
young lady who was at our house at Liverpool when you were with
us last Christmas—a niece of Narrowsmith's?"

"The little girl who was brought in to make a fourteenth at dinner?"

"The same; we have ascertained that it was upon her part the
advertisements addressed to a person of your name were inserted in
the *Times*."

"You have!" said Barker, ironically.

"You are not related to the Narrowsmiths, I believe," continued
Spread, not taking notice of Barker's manner.

"I should think not," said the bachelor, contemptuously.

"The fact is," continued the ex-merchant, "I thought it very
unlikely that such could be the case; at the same time, there is no
doubt of what I tell you; the advertiser is Miss Narrowsmith—of
course it does not necessarily follow that you are the Mr. Barker
she is in search of."

"Spread, you have discovered a mare's nest," replied the bachelor,
triumphantly. "I know more of the matter than you do; I *am* the
Mr. Barker referred to in the newspapers, and the advertiser is not
Miss Narrowsmith, nor any relation of the Narrowsmiths, nor a
miss at all—you are wrong in every particular, totally and accurately
wrong."

"But I have it from my son, who, I regret to say, has formed a
most imprudent attachment to the young lady."

"But I have it from the young lady herself, and I am positive she
never saw your son in her life."

"Passing strange!" said Spread; "there is some mystery in all
this. Who is the lady you speak of?"

"Mrs. Grace—the little widow—your sister-in-law's governess;
she turns out to be the daughter of an old friend of mine; by-the-by,
it was his picture which you saw one evening while I was confined
to my bed."

" What was his name ?"

" Medlicott."

" Good Heaven !" cried Spread ; " Medlicott was the name assumed by my partner's brother ; Mrs. Grace must be Grace Narrowsmith in disguise !"

Barker scoffed at the notion, ridiculed it, ridiculed Spread for conceiving it, called it nonsense, said it was not only improbable, but impossible, declared the question lay in a nut-shell, and was so positive and pugnacious, that his friend was not sorry when his daughter approached to remind him that it grew late, and that they had to walk home.

Of course, a moment's further conference that same evening with the daughter of his friend Raymond sufficed to convince even so skeptical a person as the bachelor that Spread was right, and that she was indeed the niece of the miserly merchant, and the lady with whom Philip Spread was in love.   He was vexed at finding that he ran the risk of being entangled ever so slightly with a family which he abhorred so utterly as he did the Narrowsmiths ; but what can't be cured must be endured, as the old proverb has it, and besides, he was now in a situation which did not long permit his thoughts to flow in a disagreeable channel.

The Spread party returned by moonlight along the banks of the sparkling river, by a meadow-path which led from Far Niente to the Rosary ; and the population of the latter villa speedily separated and sought their respective dormitories, up the noiseless stairs, and through the unresounding corridors.

There was a bay-window commanding a lovely view of the Thames, and the woods beyond it, which on summer evenings the Smyly girls seldom passed without lingering awhile, sometimes for half an hour, upon a small *causeuse* placed in its recess, as it were expressly to invite you to revery, or predispose you to slumber. The prospect, however, was what generally enticed the Smylys to tarry there.   It was especially beautiful when a May moon was beaming ; the difficulty then was to tear yourself from the spot. With such a scene before your eyes, such a couch to rest on, such carpeting under your feet, such repose all around you, it was impossible to conceive a pleasanter halting-place on your pilgrimage to the land of Nod, particularly with an Adelaide and Laura to whisper and titter with, ten times pleasanter company, both, or either, than half your regular beauties entered at Almacks.

When they reached this favorite point on the night in question, Adelaide remarked that she did not feel sleepy.

" Neither do I," said Laura.

The words were scarcely uttered before they were both on the *causeuse*, and sat gazing upon the silvered landscape and listening to the music of the stream.

" We are neither of us sleepy to-night," said Adelaide, " because we have not walked to-day.   I only walked round the garden with that dear little Mrs. Grace."

" I had nearly as long a walk as that," said Laura; " I walked round my uncle."

Adelaide's laugh, though not much louder than the genius of the place licensed, was loud enough to prevent either girl from hearing the approach of Mr. Barker, who had also to pass the bay-window on his route bedward.   He might have passed on undiscovered, but he paused to consider the *tableau vivant* before him.   Laura was sitting erect; Adelaide was partially recumbent, her head reclining on Laura's shoulder, while one arm of the latter encircled her sister's waist.   Their bright tresses were interwoven; their faces almost touched, and seemed to prattle together, even when their lips were still.

What was all this to the Bachelor of the Albany?   Why did he pause to contemplate it?   Was it that the power, which the poet describes as the delight of gods and men, was beginning to cast her dazzling spell over him?   He moved again; and either his step or his breathing was audible, for Adelaide glanced back over her shoulder, and detected his presence.   The sisters rose together, smiled and courtesied; Mr. Barker bowed formally; but why did he not then pursue his way to his chamber?   Ask the moon why she shone that night so mischievously brilliant?   Ask the river why it rolled so musically?   Ask the *causeuse* before the window, why it was large enough for three?   Ask the sisters why they were both so fascinating?   Ask Laura Smyly, in particular, why she could not just as well, that evening, have enjoyed a moonlight on the Thames from the casement of her own bower, as from the bay-window on the corridor?

However, it is matter of history; the bachelor sat down, and passed with the two Smylys thirty of the most agreeable minutes of his life.   Adelaide spoke little; the conversation was chiefly supported by Laura and the bachelor.   It was sparkling and fanciful on her side, and shrewd and sensible on his; they amused and pleased one another equally; and when the clock of Twickenham church, striking the witching hour, gave them a broad hint that they had protracted their sitting too long for the health of an invalid, and the habits of the cottage of indolence, Barker retired to his chamber, and remembered, before sleep sealed his eyelids, an energetic expression which Mr. Spread had used one day in his chambers at the Albany, to the effect, that *a single love is worth a thousand friendships*.

The next morning he rose early, wrote a note to the dean, pleading the calls of his parliamentary duties, and departed abruptly for town. He took personal leave of nobody; as to Mrs. Grace, there is good reason to think that he never once thought of her, so much did either the cares of legislation, or some more interesting subject, preoccupy his mind. Mrs. Grace, however, had other friends who were not so negligent. The delight of the Spreads, when they ascertained her identity with Grace Medlicott, was only equaled by their curiosity to learn her motives for disguising herself as she had done. This was easily explained. Compelled to rely upon her talents to obtain a livelihood, she had found upon several occasions that her youth was an obstacle to her success as a teacher; and it had occurred to her to assume the garb of a widow, as being the demurest she could adopt, and that which was best calculated to produce an impression of some matronly experience and standing in the world. Disguise was not her object in the first instance, although she had been gratified to find that her borrowed weeds answered that purpose, too, in the most efficient manner. Her entrance into a family closely connected with the Spreads was purely accidental; it was, however, a fortunate accident, as it proved the means of discovering what she wanted so much—a friend and a protector.

CHAPTER XXVI.

I thank thee for't ; my shipwreck's now no ill,
Since I have here my father's gift by will.

                              Pericles, Prince of Tyre.

The Bachelor arrives at the Rosary—Conversation of Spread and Barker in a
Tent—How Barker execrated the Grasshoppers—An important Arrival
and a momentous Disclosure—Mr. Upton's Opinion of colonial Judges,
and Mr. St. Leger's Remark on the Distribution of colonial Patronage—
The Bachelor is thrust into three Situations of Trust and Difficulty by one
Revolution of the Wheel of Fortune.

As the time approached that had been fixed for the marriage of
Elizabeth Spread, the probabilities of other marriages began to be
much talked of; the Rosary was thronged with guests full as a bee-
hive ; and the arrival of the Smyly girls in the dean's phaeton, closely
followed by the bachelor, gave employment to twenty idle and merry
tongues.

" His name ought to be Petrarch Barker, not Peter," said one.

" Weddings make weddings," said another.

" One fool makes many," said Mark Upton.

" Flattering to you, Mr. Owlet," said St. Leger.

The early part of the morning passed in various light occupations ;
the ladies had cards to direct, garlands to weave, a thousand gay and
elegant nothings to attend to.   One o'clock was fixed for an archery
meeting, a favorite amusement at the Rosary.   Upton established
himself in Mr. Spread's study, and was soon immersed in his blue-
books, particularly his own Report on Metropolitan Sewerage.   Lord
John inflicted himself upon Laura Smyly, and gave her a detailed
account of his projected eremetical establishment, which, being also
called a Laura, led to a series of equivoques by no means pleasing to
the bachelor, who heard the words " my Laura" several times
repeated, while Owlet at the same moment was boring him to death
about the substitution of trial by ordeal for trial by jury.

Laura, however, was as eager to escape from the scion of the
house of Gonebye as Barker could have desired; she adroitly availed

herself of the first halt in his lordship's *fâde* discourse, and tripped out of the room, with a glance at the bachelor, as she flitted past him, in which there was wit and malice enough to demolish Oxford and all its works.

Barker then withdrew to a marquee upon the lawn, where he was soon joined by Spread, and they sat dreamily chatting in the sunny shade, upon the past, the present, and the future. The bachelor was harassed a little by the grasshoppers, and pronounced a sweeping anathema upon the entire insect kingdom. Presently, the warbling of silver voices was heard, and was soon succeeded by the tripping of light feet. Spread's eldest daughter and Laura Smyly passed close to the door of the marquee, on their way to the archery-ground.

" That is one of the cleverest and the best girls in England," said Spread, as the flounce of Laura's green silk dress brushed the bachelor's foot, which just projected an inch beyond the tent. Barker made no answer; but he bore the touch of the green silk frock better than he bore the grasshoppers' jumping.

" She is not quite so young as she looks," continued Spread, as if talking to himself: " Laura must be nearly thirty."

Barker still said nothing, yet he was inwardly pleased to hear that there was not so great a disparity of years between him and Laura as he had supposed.

" She is a singular girl, it can't be denied," Spread still went on. " If ever she falls in love, it will be with her understanding, not her heart; that won't do, Barker, that won't do."

" But it will do—it's the best way—there *is* an understanding, but a heart is a mere figure of speech," cried the bachelor, pugnaciously. He would have said more to the same effect, had he not observed a well-known twinkle in Spread's eye, which told him he had already said more than was quite discreet. In fact, his friend had laid a trap, and fairly caught him in it.

" Why, I confess," said Spread, " if *two* people should *agree* to love one another with their understandings, that might answer not so very badly."

A deputation now arrived to invite Mr. Barker to join the archers, who were making the greenwood ring with the gay clamors. He assented graciously, and was even prevailed on to bend a bow in his turn. Thrice, amid inextinguishable laughter, did the bachelor's shaft pierce the outer edge of the target, technically called the "*petticoat.*" Laura, with the vigor, grace, and dexterity of one of Spenser's sylvan heroines, or Diana herself, sent her feathered dart into the center of the gold. The bachelor was pressed to try his luck again. He consented, and his arrow was found lodged so close to Laura's, that they made but one wound in the burnished canvas.

" A certain aim he took," cried St. Leger,

> "And loosened his love-shaft smartly from his bow,
> As it should pierce a hundred thousand hearts."

" Ah," said Lord John, " I see pretty plainly that my Laura is not the Laura for Barker."

While this was going on, a servant came to acquaint Mr. Spread that a person desired to see him, on urgent business. Spread went into the house, and there found a man of humble rank, honest countenance, meanly clothed, with only one arm, much sun-burned, and covered with dust, as if he had traveled far upon foot. Spread was not a little surprised to learn that he had been directed to him by the Rev. Mr. Ramsay, of Cornwall, and that his object was to procure information respecting Miss Narrowsmith.

" Who are you ?" asked Mr. Spread.

His surprise was great to find that he was the domestic who had accompanied Grace Narrowsmith to England, and who was believed to have perished in the shipwreck. He had escaped, however, by attaching himself to some floating timber, which was flung upon the cliffs at the distance of several miles from the spot where the vessel struck; his arm and one of his legs were fractured, and he was picked up, almost lifeless, by the peasantry of an adjoining village. From thence, by some humane interposition, he was removed to an infirmary in a neighboring town, where his arm was amputated, and his other wounds cured; but he had not been discharged many days before he caught a fever (then raging in the wretched locality where his poverty had compelled him to seek refuge), and thus, owing to this series of disasters, several months elapsed before he was in a condition to make any research after the young female who had been intrusted to his care.

" You were a servant of the late Mr. Medlicott," said Mr. Spread, after the stranger had concluded the account of his misadventures.

The sun-burned man replied in the affirmative.

" Are you aware of his connection with a family named Narrowsmith, at Liverpool ?"

" My late master, sir, was brother to Mr. Isaac Narrowsmith, the rich merchant."

" How did it happen that he left no property ? His daughter, I have reason to believe, is totally destitute."

" Her mother's property (a large one) was settled upon her, but the title to it was disputed, and the courts of law at Bermudas decided against her claims."

" Did your master make a will ?"

" He did, although he had little or nothing to bequeath; but he thought that the appointment of executors and guardians might, in any event, be some advantage or protection to his child. He made a will, sir, deposited it in my hands, and charged me, immediately after his decease, to proceed to England with his daughter, to apply in the first instance to Mr. Narrowsmith of Liverpool (his brother, as I then learned for the first time); and in case he should not be living, or unwilling to recognize the relationship, I was then to have recourse to another gentleman—the other executor—"

" His name ?" demanded Spread, abruptly.

" Barker, sir—Mr. Peter Barker, the member of parliament."

" But what of the will demanded Spread; " is it forthcoming—or a copy ?"

" Here is the original, sir," said the man, producing from his pocket a little bundle of papers.

Spread glanced over the document, saw the appointment of Isaac Narrowsmith of Liverpool, and Peter Barker of the Albany, London, as joint executors and guardians to Grace Medlicott. the testator's only daughter; and the will seemed to have been duly witnessed and signed with the name, not of Medlicott, but Narrowsmith.

" What papers are these ?" he then asked, alluding to the other documents.

One was a colonial newspaper, containing a brief report of the trial and cause of Montserrat and Medlicott. Montserrat was the maiden name of the lady whom Grace's father had married.

Spread rung the bell, ordered the man to be well taken care of, and, taking the will and the newspaper, proceeded to look for Mr. Upton, whom he found in the library.

Upton rapidly perused the will, and pronounced it correct in form.

" Then Barker is executor," said Spread.

" And guardian of the minor," said Upton; " but is there any estate; has the lady any property ?"

" The contrary, I fear; she had large expectations from her mother, but an adverse decision of the local courts at Bermudas has left her a pauper."

" The decisions of those colonial courts are seldom worth a straw," said Upton, who had a large share of the colonial appeal business; "the judges are, in nine cases out of ten, the refuse of the bar in England and Ireland."

"Not of Ireland, certainly," said Mr. St. Leger, who happened to drop in at the moment; "the Irish bar have a very small share of colonial preferment, with one remarkable exception—Sierra Leone."

Upton laughed; but Spread was too full of matters of moment to suffer the conversation to be diverted into a new channel.

"Here," continued he, putting the newspaper into the solicitor's hands, "here is an abstract of the trial in the cause in question; I feel a deep interest in the fortunes of the young lady concerned; just cast your eye over the report."

Spread left the papers with Upton, who, having read them attentively, came to the conclusion (assuming the report to be substantially correct) that the decision was clearly against the law and the merits of the case.

"She has only to appeal to the Privy Council," he said; "the decree of the court at Bermudas will be reversed to a certainty; although the proceedings may be protracted if the defendants are wealthy."

"Wealthy!—the real defendant, I believe, will be Isaac Narrowsmith himself. The property in question went to his wife."

"Barker, then, must be the nominal appellant."

"Barker!—of all men!—my poor Barker!" exclaimed Spread, as he left the library to communicate all this interesting intelligence to his wife. "Only think of Barker being an executor, guardian of a minor, and plaintiff in a heavy appeal to the Privy Council—my poor Barker!"

And Spread pitied the bachelor with all his heart, for fortune seemed now to be actually pelting him with trusts and bombarding him with obligations.

Having communicated the news to Mrs. Spread, he went in search of his eccentric friend, whom he found at the archery-ground, receiving the congratulations of every body upon his brilliant achievement with the bow. He called the bachelor aside, and they went together into a sequestered walk, between two old and stately hedges of yew and laurel. Spread began by apologizing with humorous gravity for interrupting his friend's pastimes; he then proceeded to business, and informed Barker of the fair prospects which were beginning to dawn upon the young woman in whom they were both interested deeply, though for different reasons. The bachelor was exceedingly gratified.

"I sincerely rejoice," he said, "at the young lady's good fortune: luckily she has a rich uncle, whose duty it will be to see that she is righted; the responsibility will rest upon him."

"On the contrary," said Spread, not without some hesitation, "I apprehend it will rest upon you! The rich uncle is the very party wrongfully possessed of the orphan's property—it will rest entirely upon you."

"Upon me?" cried Barker, with surprise and anger. "Why, how upon me?"

"By the will of the poor girl's father—by the last will and testament of your old friend, you are—

"What am I?" demanded the bachelor, pettishly.

Spread paused a moment, looked fixedly at him, and replied—

"Last December, Barker, when I visited you in the Albany, you portrayed my situation in life, coloring the picture somewhat fancifully; permit me now to depict yours without exaggerating a single circumstance. In the first place, you are executor of the will of your late friend, Raymond Medlicott, or Narrowsmith; sole executor, I might say, because old Isaac has, by his heartless conduct, virtually renounced. Secondly, you are nominated, by the same testament, to the sacred trust of guardianship to your friend's daughter, who is still in her minority. Thirdly, as the legal protector of her rights against all the world, but especially against the Narrowsmiths, you are, or will be in a day or two, plaintiff in an appeal to the Privy Council to reverse the decision of the colonial tribunals. Ultimate success is probable; but, let me tell you, the Narrowsmiths will dispute every inch of ground; it will be a heavy suit, a very heavy one, depend upon it. Now, there is no shirking one of these serious obligations, and you must proceed with vigor upon my account as well as for the sake of the girl. I have already informed you of Philip's attachment: whether a pauper or an heiress, she is to be my daughter-in-law."

Barker kicked up the gravel of the walk with the toe of his boot; it was the only reply he made.

"Well, my friend," continued Spread, laying his hand kindly on his shoulder, "was I not right when I told you, that day in your chambers, that there is no living in society without taking one's fair share of its cares and its duties? What say you now? Be frank. Was I not right?"

"It would seem you were," said Barker, in a subdued tone, kicking up the gravel again, but not so waspishly as before.

"I told you at the same time another truth," continued Spread;

"and something prompts me just to whisper it again now.   If man wanted a helpmate in a lot of unmixed happiness and perfect repose, how much more does he require one in his actual state of certain toil and uncertain enjoyment?   You have lived in heresy long enough, out of the congregation of Love, contrary to all his canons. Come, you must do penance, and be reconciled to the church.   You see, I am reading you a homily.   'Woman,' says the wisest of profane writers, 'is the mistress of youth, the companion of middle age, and the nurse of our declining years.'   You are in the second predicament, Barker.   You want, and I recommend you, ' *a companion.*'"

"Come, Spread, there's no use in mincing the matter: you mean Miss Laura Smyly."

"I do, then—the girl with whom you exchanged watches at my house at Liverpool—who rescued your Madeira—who saved your life—the girl who carries her heart in her mind, and would love you after your own fashion, with a remarkably sound and well-regulated understanding."

CHAPTER XXVII.

I do much wonder that one man, seeing how much another man is a fool, when he dedicates his behaviors to love, will, after he hath laughed at such shallow follies in others, become the argument of his own scorn by falling in love. And such a man is Claudio.
Much Ado about Nothing.

The Bachelor's Proposal and Acceptance—How three Weddings were consolidated into one—State of the Rosary—What happened to Mr. Owlet—How he got a Living and how soon he lost it—Mistakes of the Morning—Personal Hazard of Mr. Barker—What kind of a Morning it was—How the Wedding affected Richmond—How Fulham felt it—How the Bachelor behaved at the Crisis—How the Dean looked, and how Mr. Mooney said Amen—The Breakfast—How Barker acted as Husband and Father—Mrs. Briscoe's last Attention—Conclusion.

To the speech of Spread, which concluded the preceding chapter, Barker made no reply, but *en revanche* he made that very evening a proposition of marriage to Laura Smyly. As the bachelor had long been agreeable to that young lady, who discerned the worth of his character through the distorting medium of his oddities, she accepted the offer of his hand and *understanding*, and graciously consented to become Mrs. Peter Barker. Nothing remained then but to fix the day for the ceremony, invite the excellent dean to perform it, and buy the license.

As Doctor Bedford had been already engaged to tie the Gordian knot for Elizabeth Spread and Mr. Owlet, it was determined, in a full session of the Spread parliament (which now comprised Mrs. Farquhar, and old Mrs. Briscoe), to consolidate the weddings, for the purpose of sparing the dean and Mr. Mooney as much professional trouble as possible. A not very distant day was agreed on, so as to reconcile, as far as practicable, the haste of lovers with the delays of dress-makers and the tardiness of tailors. The interval was filled up with a great deal of mirth and a great deal of business too. Barker had his parliamentary duties to attend to; and he also threw him-

K

self with a vigor that surprised every body into the affairs which the
guardianship of Grace Narrowsmith involved him in.   The Smyly
girls were at Far Niénte, but the Spreads insisted upon having
Grace Narrowsmith with themselves, and soon convinced her that
she would cause them only pain by continuing to hold out against
the addresses of their son.   Philip was very pressing to have his
marriage celebrated on the same day with his sister's and Mr. Barker's.   Many people thought he ought to have waited for the issue
of the cause in which Grace was deeply concerned.   But love is
rapid, and law is proverbially the contrary.   He loved Grace when
she had nothing either in possession or prospect; and as his resolution to marry her was independent of the issue of the suit instituted
on her behalf, there was no good reason why Hymen should be kept
dancing attendance upon Plutus.   His parents were of the same
opinion.   Their opposition to the union had long since yielded to the
undoubted sincerity of their son's affection; they had seen new and
decisive proofs of Grace Narrowsmith's sterling worth; she had
every mental quality that could make her a desirable member of such
a family; and the fact that she was the friend and protégée of Mr.
Barker, crowned all.   Accordingly, it was ultimately determined
that the three swains and the shepherdesses should pair off on the
same morning.

You may suppose the Rosary was a busy place for a few weeks.
What fun and what ferment; what a hubbub among the abigails and
mopsas: what running here, and running there, up and down, in
and out, helter-skelter, and pell-mell!   Night and day, there was
something comical continually occurring; or if it was not comedy, it
was just as good, for it set the whole house in a roar.   Owlet, was
a large contributor to the general fund of merriment.

We mentioned in the beginning of this history, that the minor canon was in expectation of a snug living of which a-tractarian peeress,
his friend and admirer, owned the advowson.   Three days before
the wedding he received the following note from his patroness:

"Oldham Hall, Feast of St. Lawrence.

"My dear Mr. Owlet—I have just seen in the newspapers the
death of old Mr. Fowler, incumbent of the parish in Suffolk, which
I have been so long anxious to bestow upon you.   The poor old gentleman, it seems, died at Brighton.   Write immediately to the
church-warden, Mr. Grubb, acquaint him with your nomination, and
inform him at what time it will be your convenience to go down to

take possession in the usual form.   Wishing you every joy in your approaching marriage, I remain,

"My dear Mr. Owlet,

"Yours, very sincerely,

"MATILDA OWLDENHAM.

"P.S.—You will find Mr. Grubb a good *Catholic*.   Give him particular directions about erecting the stone altar (which I have had executed), and the other alterations necessary to make the church fit for Christian worship.

"To the Rev. Bat Owlet,
  "The Rosary, Richmond."

A comfortable living was a very agreeable present for Owlet to receive on the eve of his marriage, and it may be supposed he lost no time in communicating with the Catholic church-warden.   In the space of forty-eight hours he received the following reply, which was read at breakfast to all the assembled company :

"Fatfield Rectory, "Chickenham.

"SIR—In the absence of Mr. Grubb, the church-warden, I beg to inform you that I have not departed this life, nor have I any present intention of doing so.   As you are curious about the income of my benefice, and the condition of my glebe-house, I am happy to tell you that the former is a well-paid seven hundred pounds, and the latter is the snuggest parsonage in the diocese.   That I may enjoy these good things as long as possible (by-the-by, my father lived to your favorite number, XC.), I take the best care of myself, and promise you I shall continue to do so, if on no other account, to prevent you, or any other Popish priest, from introducing your mummeries into this good old Protestant parish.   Excuse this short letter, as I am going out with my dogs ; and believe me

"Your obedient servant,

"TIMOTHY FOWLER."

This letter, read by Owlet himself, with all the simplicity of Parson Adams, caused infinite merriment to the company, in which Spread had his full share, notwithstanding his interest in the temporal prosperity of his son-in-law.   The living had not been reckoned on, and accordingly the disappointment made no change in the matrimonial arrangements.

On the very morning of the wedding one of those incidents took place which could only have happened in such a house as the Rosary, and among such a company as was there assembled.

At the point of day a question occurred to the mind of Mr. Owlet, as to the canonical propriety of the hour fixed for the nuptial ceremony, and he could not refrain going straight to Lord John Yore, to state the perplexity he was in. He rose, intended to put on his dressing-gown, but put on his surplice by mistake, and, thus spectrally arrayed, issued from his chamber, glided along the corridor, turned a corner, got into a strange lobby, and finally lost his reckoning altogether, and strayed about, unable even to retrace his steps to his own room. While he was wandering thus, it happened that Harriet, Mrs. Spread's maid, suddenly remembered some directions respecting part of her mistress's dress, which she feared she had neglected to attend to the evening before; and she instantly jumped up, and, in very nymph-like array, hurried to Mrs. Spread's dressing-room. In doing so, Owlet unfortunately crossed her path at about ten yards' distance. Harriet was near fainting— and, indeed, she was to be excused for taking him for a spirit, inasmuch as, between his white garment, his pale visage, and his tall, spare figure, nothing in the flesh could possibly have looked more ghostly. However, she only screamed, and ran into Mrs. Martin's room for safety. Mrs. Martin had no belief in apparitions—she was far too philosophical; she immediately concluded that Theodore was engaged in some new prank, at the expense of Owlet and Lord John Yore; and, armed with the fasces of authority, she hastened, with but slight attention to her toilet, in search of the delinquent. Mrs. Briscoe, meanwhile, fancying that she heard Pico, the Italian greyhound, wheezing in an adjoining room, and, thinking that a grain of nitre in his milk would do the little quadruped good, was bustling (with her wonted vivacity at unseasonable hours) about this benevolent office. Owlet saw her motions, and, fearful of alarming her as he had already alarmed Harriet, he redoubled his diligence to regain his chamber, and, in doing so, made repeated assaults upon the door of Barker's. The bachelor was at length roused, and rushed out in an excited state, to discover who the disturber of the peace was. It was still little more than darkness visible. At one point, however, there was a window; it was just at the head of a short stair-case, and a place where two lines of bed-rooms met at a right angle. In front of the window there happened to stand a large folding-screen. Mr. Barker peered down the stair-case, and saw the energetic Mrs. Martin, followed by the nervous Harriet, cautiously ascending it together, and, with instinctive propriety, withdrew behind the screen. Mrs. Martin advanced, until the bachelor, through a hole in the screen, saw her distinctly; and he puzzled himself thinking what could have brought the schoolmistress abroad at cock-crow. Mrs. Martin pursued her way, but in the direction of Barker's room, so that he could not leave his concealment. In a few moments Mrs. Briscoe came up, and, descrying Owlet, the same feeling of delicacy which prompted Barker to seclude himself operated upon the old lady, and she popped into the same hiding-place. The screen, however, was folded in such a manner that she did not perceive her companion in retirement. But the quick ear of Mrs. Martin caught the rustling of Mrs. Briscoe's night-gear; she was back to the spot in an instant, and, thrusting her left arm behind Barker's side of the screen, she pulled him out by his dressing-gown into the corridor. Mrs. Martin's movements were so brusque, that it was probably well for the bachelor there was now enough of light to distinguish faces and figures. The exclamations and amazement of all parties may easily be imagined. Mrs. Martin stared at the bachelor, and asked his pardon; the bachelor extricated his dressing-gown, stared at Mrs. Martin, and made his escape to his room.

"Bless me!" cried Harriet, "there is somebody else behind the screen: I protest it's Mrs. Briscoe!"

"Mrs. Briscoe!" cried the governess, drawing herself to her full height, and in her severest accents.

"Mr. Barker and Mrs. Briscoe!" cried Harriet.

"And Mr. Owlet, I declare, in full canonicals!" exclaimed Mrs. Martin, turning round, and seeing the unfortunate minor canon close beside her, lost in wonder at what he beheld.

The women soon reflected how apocalyptically they were arrayed, and the recollection soon dispersed them to their several rooms. There was inordinate laughing; it was as merry a beginning of a wedding-day as any in hymeneal history.

But every thing on this occasion was propitious. A lovelier, rosier, balmier morning never smiled upon a marriage, since that of Cupid and Psyche, in the parish church of Paphos, or the nuptials of the Rose and Nightingale in the gardens of Gulistan. The roses, indeed, seemed to have expressly reserved themselves for the triple wedding. Wherever nature had flung or art planted them, they were gushing into bloom with one accord, followed by the

other flowers of the floweriest of the months, blazoning the earth
with charming hues, and impregnating the air with delicious odors.
The fragrance of the garden mingled with the perfume of the
fields; the roses and pinks vied with the bean-flowers and the smell
of the new-mown hay for the prize of incense; the summer was
insolent with youth and beauty, and, intoxicated with the sun's flat-
tery, flung her smiles and graces round about her, over the silver
stream and along its enchanting borders, with the profusion of a
youthful queen on her coronation-day.

Nobody, however, thought of fields and flowers at a moment so
full of *moral* interest, not to speak of the extraordinary number of
fine women assembled on this festive morning, who gave the eye
enough to do. The spectacle of three lovely brides and fifteen
charming brides'-maids is not a phenomenon to be witnessed every
day. All Richmond went forth to see it, Fulham was wild with
excitement, and Putney went quite beside itself. How the bells
rung, how the horses pranced, how the handkerchiefs waved, how
the eyes sparkled, the tongues prattled, and the hearts throbbed.
But the observed of all observers were the Bachelor and his Bride
—Philip and Grace, Elizabeth and her Owlet, seemed mere acces-
sories to the principal figures in the scene. Barker bore himself
gallantly; he had pulled down the system of his past life with his
own hands, and he looked as proud as if he had demolished the fortress of an enemy. It was the pride of a wise inconsistency—the
glory of a seasonable retirement from a position no longer tenable
with advantage or ease.

The next most remarkable personage was the good Dean Bedford, so round and so reverend, so hearty, so courteous, so benevolent: you could not look at him and not be charitable to the church
he belonged to: he beautified a deformed system, and made one feel
kindly to sinecures and tender to pluralities. Supported by Mr.
Mooney, he moved from the church-door to the altar, showering
benedictory smiles upon all around him, and giving the English be-
holders of his voluminous person a magnificent conception of the
church in Ireland. He performed the nuptial service with a fervor
and an unction beyond all praise; and the "Amen" of his butler was
superb, without taking into consideration that it was, perhaps, the
first time he had ever pronounced the word, although a parish clerk
of twenty years' standing.

Altogether, there was never a matrimonial knot more handsomely,
as well as securely, tied; never was a bachelor metamorphosed into

a married man with more éclat, amid so much acclamation, or surrounded by so much to make the transition a triumph.

The breakfast at the Rosary was a banquet worthy of following
a sacred rite solemnized in so distinguished a manner. It was in-
tellectually and gastronomically perfect. Barker and Mrs. Harry
Farquhar were reconciled to one another upon that occasion;
Spread suggested a libation of champagne to hallow it, but Barker
(with a pleasantry which Mrs. Harry perfectly understood) proposed madeira.

The events that followed are to be related in a few words. Barker prosecuted the appeal to the Privy Council with almost malignant perseverance, and eventually wrung the fortune of Mrs.
Philip Spread from the tenacious gripe of the Harpagon of Liverpool.

In process of time crept little Spreads, young Owlets, and small
Barkers into the world. Barker made a nervous husband, and
rather a fidgety father; but, on the whole, he supported marvelously well the multiplicity of cares and duties in which he was involved before he reached his fiftieth year. The last responsibility
was imposed upon him by Mrs. Briscoe, who, never forgetting his
gallantry at the rail-way station, left him a legacy of fifty pounds, and
appointed him trustee for the fat Letty, to whom she bequeathed
an annuity of a hundred a-year.

· THE END.